Fake

A
WEST
HOLLYWOOD
NOVEL

D0870159

KYLIE SCOTT

NEW YORK TIMES BESTSELLING AUTHOR

ISBN: 978-0-6484573-3-6

Fake

Chapter One

H E SLUNK INTO THE RESTAURANT MID-AFTERNOON wearing his usual scowl. Ignoring the closed sign, he took a booth near the back. No one else was allowed to do this. Just him. Today's wardrobe consisted of black jeans, Converse, and a button-down shirt. Doubtless designer. And the way those sleeves hugged his biceps . . . why, they should have been ashamed of themselves. I was this close to yelling "get a room."

Instead, I asked, "The usual?"

Slumped down in the corner of the booth, he tipped his chin in reply. For such a tall guy, he sure went out of his way to try to hide.

I said no more. Words were neither welcomed nor wanted. Which was fine since (A) I was tired and (B) he tipped well for the peace and quiet.

Out back, Vinnie the cook was busy prepping for tonight, his knife making quick work of an onion.

"He's here," I said.

A smile split Vinnie's face. He was a huge fan of the man's action films. The ones he'd made before hitting it big time and taking on more serious dramatic roles. Him choosing to visit the restaurant every month or so made Vinnie's life complete.

Especially since the restaurant, Little Italy, was the very defini-
tion of a hole in the wall. Not somewhere generally frequented
by the Hollywood elite. Meanwhile, I was less of a fan, but still
a fan. You know.

"Get him his beer," Vinnie ordered.

Like I didn't know my job. Sheesh.

He was busy with his cell by the time I placed the Peroni in
front of him. No glass. He drank straight from the bottle like an
animal. Just then, a woman in a red sweater dress and tan five-
inch-heel booties strode in through the front door.

"I'm sorry, we're closed," I said.

"I'm with him." She headed straight for his booth and slid
into the other side, giving the man a dour look. "You can't just
walk out, Patrick. You're going to have to choose one of them."

"Nope." He took a pull from his beer. "They all sucked."

"There had to be at least one that would do."

"Not even a little."

She sighed. "Keep this up and you'll be obsolete by next
week. Beyond help. Forgotten."

"Go away, Angie."

"Just another talented but trash male in Hollywood. That's
what they're saying on social media."

"I don't give a shit."

"Liar," she drawled.

I wasn't quite sure what to do. Obviously they knew each
other, but he did not seem to want her here. And she really wasn't
supposed to be here. Vinnie had okayed after-hours entry to only
one person. On the other hand, if I asked her to leave, she'd probably sic her lawyers on me. She looked the type.

The woman spied me hovering. "Get me a glass of red."

"She's not staying," countermanded Patrick.

Angie didn't move an inch. "They were all viable options. Pliant. Young. Pretty. Discreet. Nothing weird or kinky in their backgrounds."

"That might have made them more interesting."

"Interesting women is what got you into this mess." The woman frowned, taking me in. Still hovering. One perfectly shaped brow rose in question. "Yes? Is there a problem?"

Now it was Patrick's turn to sigh and give me a nod. He was so dreamy with his jaw and cheekbones and his everything. Real classic Hollywood handsome. Especially with his short light brown hair in artful disarray and a hint of stubble. Sometimes it was hard not to stare. Which is probably why his personality tended to scream "leave me alone."

I headed for the small bar area at the back of the restaurant to fetch the wine like a good little waitress.

"We shouldn't be discussing this here," said Angie, giving the room a disdainful sniff. Talk about judgy. I thought the raw brick walls and chunky wood tables were cool. Give or take Vinnie's collection of old black-and-white photos of Los Angeles freeways. Who knew what that was about?

Patrick slumped down even further. "I'm not going back there. I'm done with it."

"This isn't safe." Angie looked around nervously. "Let's—"

"We're fine. I've been coming here for years."

"You just got dropped from a big-budget film, Patrick," she said, exasperation in her tone. "The industry may not find you bankable right now, but I'm sure gossip about you is still selling just fine. This week at least."

A grunt from the man.

"The plan will work if you let it. Everything is organized and ready to go. It's the perfect opportunity to start rewriting the narrative in your favor." She jabbed a finger in his direction to accentuate the word "your." The woman clearly meant business, and then some.

I set the glass of wine down in front of her and returned to my place at the back of the room, polishing the silverware and restocking the salt and pepper and so on—all the jobs best performed when things were slow. And while it was nosy and wrong to listen in on other people's conversations, it wasn't my fault the room was so quiet that I could hear everything they said.

"None of them felt authentic," he said, stopping to down some more beer.

The woman snorted. "That's because none of them are."

"You know what I mean."

"When you first came to me you said you wanted to become a star, make quality films, and win an Oscar. In that order," she said. "As things are at present, you may be able to resurrect your career to some degree through the indie market. Pick up roles here and there and slowly build yourself back up. But that's going to take years and you'll likely never be in the running for the golden statuette. You can kiss that dream goodbye."

Patrick ran an agitated hand through his hair.

"You worked your ass off to get this far," she said. "Are you really going to give up now?"

"Fuck," he muttered.

"Liv is busy saving her own ass and you're unwilling to set the record straight. Not that anyone would even necessarily believe you at this point. So our options are limited." She picked up her wine, taking a delicate sip before wrinkling her nose in distaste. Since it came out of a box, that wasn't much of a surprise. She'd only asked for a glass of red; she hadn't specified quality. "I know you were hoping it would all die down, but people are still talking. And with social media how it is, this was the worst possible time to get caught up in a scandal. However, there is hope. We can still salvage things if you'd just work with us. But we need to act now."

Patrick declined to respond.

It had been all over the internet a month ago. Photos of him leaving Liv Anders's Malibu residence at the crack of dawn. And it was clearly a morning-after picture. Totally a walk of shame. He'd been all disheveled and wearing a crumpled tux. Liv being half of Hollywood's current darling couple was part of the problem. Along with Patrick and Liv's husband, Grant, having just done a movie together and supposedly being best buds. That Patrick had spent his earlier years dating a string of models and partying hard didn't help matters either. His reputation was well established. Headlines such as "Patrick the Player," "Walsh Destroys Wedded Bliss," "Friendship Failure," and "Not So Heroic Homewrecker" were everywhere. Maybe it had been a slow news week, but the amount of hate leveled at him was surprising.

Of course, there had to be more to the story. There always was. But Liv was seen weeping in a disturbingly photogenic fashion as she and her husband walked into a marriage counselor's office the next day. And the pair had been hanging off each other on the red carpet ever since. Meanwhile, Patrick's name was mud. Worse than mud. It was toxic shit.

It could all be true. He could indeed be a trash male who thought with his dick and behaved in a duplicitous and manipulative manner. I'd dated my fair share of dubious men, so it wouldn't exactly surprise me. And plenty of assholes had been publicly outed recently. Men who used their fame and power for evil.

But this all just felt more like gossip.

First up, there'd been no actual evidence that this wasn't two consenting adults doing what they wanted behind closed doors. Patrick hadn't taken any wedding vows and Liv hadn't made any accusations of mistreatment. In fact, Liv hadn't said anything at all. Patrick and Grant being best buddies, though . . . that was a hell of a betrayal. If it was true.

"Fine. I'll do it," he said, his voice rising. "But not with any of them."

"Patrick, we've been interviewing for weeks to find those three alternatives for you," she said. "One of them must be tolerable if not perfect."

"She doesn't need to be perfect. She needs to be real."

"Real?" asked Angie with some small amount of spluttering. "Give me strength. That's the last fucking thing we need right now."

The bell pinged out back. Vinnie gave me a wink and nodded to the waiting dish, Penne Ragu and Meatballs with Parmesan. It smelled divine. As the size of my ass could attest, I loved carbs and they loved me. And what was more important, jeans size or general happiness?

Vinnie took pride in his food. Pride in his restaurant. It was one of the reasons I liked working for him.

"They're all waiting. Come back to the office," said Angie as I reentered the room.

"No."

"Patrick, how the hell else are you going to find someone? If word of what we were doing got out . . ."

"That's not going to happen."

The woman looked to heaven, but no help was forthcoming. "If you won't choose one of them, then who?"

"I don't know," he growled.

As stealthily as possible, I set the meal down in front of him. Invisibility was an art form. One I didn't always excel at when he was around. It's not my fault. Attractive men make me nervous. So of course my fingers fumbled over the silverware and the fork clattered loudly to the table.

"Her," he said, staring right at me. Possibly the only time we'd made direct eye contact. It was like looking into the sun. I was all but blinded. The man was just too much.

"What?!" Angie shrieked.

I froze. He couldn't be referring to me. Not unless it was in the context of a "you are totally clumsy and not getting a tip today" sort of thing.

"You cannot be serious," Angie all but spluttered, looking me over, her eyes wide as twin moons. "She's so . . . average."

"Yeah," he agreed with enthusiasm.

Wow, harsh. I was pretty in my own way. Beige skin and long, wavy blond hair. A freckle or two on my face. As for my body, not everyone in this city had to be stick thin. But whatever. The important thing was, I was a nice person. Most of the time. And I was kind. Or at least, I tried to be. Personal growth can be tricky.

"Enjoy your meal," I said with a frown on my face.

"Sit down a minute." Patrick gestured to the space beside him in the booth. "Please."

Instead, I crossed my arms.

"I want to talk to you about a job opportunity."

Angie made a strangled noise.

"I have a job," I said. "Actually, I have two."

"What's your name?" he asked.

"You've got to be joking," hissed Angie. "They'll never believe it."

"Norah," I said.

"Hey, Norah. I'm Patrick."

"I know," I deadpanned.

He almost smiled. There was a definite twitch of the lips. For someone whose charm-laden devil-may-care grin had graced billboards all over the country, he sure knew how to keep that sucker under wraps. "How'd you like to make some serious money?"

"Don't say another word until she's signed an NDA." With a hand clutched to her chest, Angie appeared to be either hyperventilating or having a heart attack. "I mean it!"

Patrick just sighed. "Angie, relax. I've been coming in here for years and she's never once put anything on social media or taken a creeper shot. I bet you haven't told a soul about me, have you, Norah?"

So I respected his privacy. So sue me. I also kind of liked hearing him say my name. Him just knowing it was a thrill. Definite weakness of the knees. "You seem to enjoy the anonymity."

"Even stopped that girl from asking me for an autograph."

"The owner's daughter," I said. "She's still not talking to me."

Another almost-smile. There was definite amusement in his pretty blue eyes.

Angie downed the last of her boxed wine in one large gulp.

Patrick and I stared at each other like it was a contest. Who would dare look away first? Me, apparently.

"What's the job?" I asked.

"I'd need you full time for a couple of months," he said.

"A year, and live-in," corrected Angie.

Patrick cringed. "Six months and live-in. No more."

With a wave of her fingers, Angie relented.

I cleared my throat. "Um, doing what, exactly? Being your gofer or an assistant or something? Or do you need like a housekeeper or a cleaner?"

"No," he said, calm as can be. "I want you to be my fake girlfriend."

Chapter Two

PATRICK WALSH LIVED IN THE BIRD STREETS IN WEST Hollywood—which was about as exclusive and expensive as can be. The car dropped me at the end of a quiet cul-de-sac up in the hills above the Sunset Strip. I peered in through the bars of the gate at a private driveway disappearing around a bend. Lots of greenery, mostly succulents and olive trees. The only landscaping around my previous apartment building had been the parking lot with overflowing trash bins.

I took a deep breath and tried to summon some courage. Any would do. Because without a doubt, this was a bad idea. Just an awful, terrible idea. Yet here I was, contract signed and cash in hand. A great deal of it. And there'd be more to come. I'd already been able to move Gran into her own room at a much nicer nursing home with better care and facilities. I'd also quit my jobs and given up my apartment. Talk about standing on the edge of a precipice.

All of a sudden, the gate started opening, and I stepped back in surprise. Guess someone was watching the security cameras. The wheels on my battered suitcase rattled along the asphalt behind me. I'd brought along only a few of my favorite things and left the bulk of my belongings in storage. They'd be providing the necessary Hollywood girlfriend wardrobe. Whatever that entailed.

And this was fine. Everything would be great. I was a grown-ass woman who could totally do this. This was an adventure to be both embraced and enjoyed.

Heck yes.

I believed this right up until I saw him standing in the door-way of a white, sprawling single-story building that was either modern or mid-century, or a bit of both. The house was cool, but it didn't compare to yet again seeing Patrick Walsh in the flesh. He was like a work of art, more than deserving of the pedestal he sat upon. You can't grow up in LA without seeing celebrities, but this was different. How his presence hit me in the heart and loins. Maybe I'd never get used to him. Annoying and embarrassing, given that he was now my boss.

I didn't expect to be greeted by the man himself. I figured he'd be too busy and important for something like this. For someone like me. I hadn't seen him since the other day at the restaurant. Everything had been handled by his "people," as in, his lawyers. I doubted I could sneeze without express written permission for the next six months.

I'd done my fair share of wondering *why me?* As Angie stated so succinctly, I was average. But I guess my lack of glamour worked for the whole reformed-and-no-longer-shallow-player persona they were attempting. I don't know. But he'd paid me a lot to put my life on hold and resurrect his reputation. So that's what I'll try my best to do.

"Norah," he said with a frown, which seemed to be his face's go-to setting. "Let me take that."

"Okay."

"Thanks for, ah . . . for doing this."

"Sure," I said.

With my suitcase trailing behind him, he headed inside. As wrong as it was to objectify people, the man had an amazing ass and his jeans really showcased it. I'd never considered myself a connoisseur of asses, but his was something else. Don't even get me started on the breadth of his shoulders.

The interior of the house wasn't bad either. Open plan with polished concrete floors and pristine white walls. A chunky cream couch and a shaggy gray rug, along with a fireplace and various pieces of art. One side of the building seemed to be constructed entirely of glass walls or fold-back glass doors. We were perched on the side of a hill, overlooking the entire city. Talk about, wow. It almost distracted from the shaking of my hands.

Two people were waiting for us in the living room. One was Angie the publicist. AKA the Dragon Lady—which is mean and insensitive to dragons, but, oh well.

"You must be Norah," said an Asian woman with a beautiful smile and shoulder-length dark hair. "I'm Paddy's assistant, Mei."

"Nice to meet you."

She beamed. "Don't you two look great together? The press are just going to eat you up!"

Patrick gave me side-eye. Like incorporating me into this grand plan hadn't been his bright idea. Idiot.

"Thanks," I mumbled.

"I've got stuff to do." He took several steps, then stopped and turned back to me and frowned some more. "Later, baby. Babe."

My stomach did not perform somersaults. It was just gas or something. "Later."

"That doesn't feel right."

I froze. "It doesn't?"

"No. Wrong terms of endearment." His gaze narrowed. "We'll work on it."

"Okay."

Mei appeared charmed by our weirdness. It had been decided by Angie that she would be our first audience. A trial audience to test out our characters, if you will. To see if we were in the least bit believable as a real couple. I didn't like our chances of fooling her.

"Do you need anything?" he asked.

"I'm fine. Thanks."

He nodded and took a small and somewhat cautious step my way. As if he might kiss me on the cheek, or pat me on the head, or something that could be perceived as being semi-affectionate. Only, he changed his mind at the last minute.

Huh.

Not to be mean, but this was definitely not his finest acting performance. (I much preferred his work in *Zombie Run*, where he'd been part of a brave group of people about to finish a marathon when an outbreak occurs. A cool, if somewhat gruesome, film.) He about-faced and headed for the other end of the house. Guess that's where the bedrooms were, et cetera. This area consisted of the living room, dining room, and kitchen. A pale blue kidney-shaped pool sat outside at the far end of the house, sparkling beneath the morning sun.

So this was how the other half lived. Nice.

Mei leaned in close. "Don't mind him. Patrick isn't exactly used to being in a relationship. Having someone in his space. You know."

"I do know," I lied.

"Of course you do. It's huge that he asked you to live here with him."

"Yeah. My, um, lease was up and he said, why not?"

"That's fantastic. Might be the first spontaneous thing the man has ever done. Guess when it's the right person, you just know," she continued. "I always told him he needed to find a civilian. Someone outside of the industry. I can't wait to hear how you met and everything. Whirlwind romances are so . . . romantic."

I'd been in training for the last week for just this moment. Mostly in front of the bathroom mirror. Oh how my cheeks had hurt after one particular session of fake smiling. I'd iced them internally with a vodka, soda, and lime. Since I'd passed on drama club back in high school, I had a lot of catching up to do.

I smiled. It was my happy-with-a-hint-of-whimsical smile. Not the easiest one in my arsenal, but I felt it projected a sort of young-and-in-love vibe—which seemed appropriate for the situation. And with Patrick paying me top dollar, it was important that I gave this my all. "We met at my work, at a restaurant. He, uh, kept coming in and eventually we started talking and—"

"The rest is history," finished Angie.

Mei kept right on smiling at me with nary a hint of doubt on her face. "That's so sweet."

Whew. I'd done it. Someone actually believed that I and a Hollywood heartthrob were an item. How extraordinary. The rush of victory rolled through me from head to toe. Not that lying to people was a good thing. And Mei seemed like a lovely person. Though it was just a small white lie. Sort of. Okay. So the truth was, the morals in this situation were murky as fuck. But at the end of the day, I needed the money and no one would get hurt. That's what mattered.

An audience of one certainly scared me far less than facing the inevitable red-carpet events lurking in my future. I kind of wanted to puke at the idea. The last formal thing I'd attended was my prom, over a decade ago. My date ended the evening by stumbling drunkenly into one of Gran's rosebushes and getting scratched to shit. Sadly, my taste in men hadn't necessarily improved since then. No wonder I hadn't dated in the past year or so.

Angie's cell pinged. "That'll be the aesthetician team and so on arriving."

"The what?" I asked.

"Think of them as your fixers," said Mei.

"I need a whole team to fix how I look?" I laughed, because, awkward. "Things are really that dire?"

Angie's smile was all teeth. "Yes."

"This is bullshit," I grouched.

"There, there." Mei patted my hand. "The French manicure looks great and your hair is so soft and shiny."

Angie's gaze remained fixed on her cell. "What's your problem?"

"Let's just say that was an extreme amount of waxing," I said. "And I really should have had a say in some of it."

"Au naturel was not acceptable. What if we decide to do a bikini shoot as part of the 'relaxing at home' article we're planning?" asked Angie. "You can't have all that going on down there. Even Photoshop has its limits."

"It wasn't that bad. And a bikini shoot?" I asked with horror. "No one mentioned that."

"The things we do for love," said Mei.

Angie ignored me.

But I was not done, dammit. "A woman's bush is sacred and the state of it should be no one else's business but her own."

Mei laughed, then quickly cleared her throat. "Yes. Totally. Very true."

"Well." Angie's brows rose. "I had no idea either of you felt so passionately about it."

Patrick wandered in. "About what?"

All day, he'd been in hiding down at the far end of the house while people marched in and out of his home. The nail technician, hairstylist, facialist, and an aesthetician to handle the body treatments and waxing. A clothes stylist to explain my new wardrobe to me while I stood there like an idiot in my underwear. Along with a makeup artist to give me lessons in shading and so on. And this is when he decides to show up?

"Pubic hair," says Mei.

Patrick blanched. "Forget I asked."

"Don't be so delicate," chided Angie, rising to her feet and heading for the door. "We've all seen you in a merkin. At any rate, we're done here for the day."

"Bye." Mei waved, while straightening the cushions on the big, plush modern sofa. "Okay, Paddy, it's time for your daily update. I sent your mom flowers and received a full refund for the New York trip. The new personal trainer is booked for tomorrow and there's some clothing from that designer I told you about hanging in your wardrobe. And Mary cancelled tomorrow night's meeting."

"She did?" he asked, tone aggrieved.

"Yes. Sorry. No reason given."

He scowled.

"Do either of you need anything else?" Mei asked us.

"Just a printout of the Freisen script," he said, leaning against the wall all cool and hot and disgruntled. Of course, his breathing and general existence was cool and hot.

"It's on the office desk."

"Thanks."

"And I'm done. See you tomorrow!"

For the very first time ever, we were alone. Somewhat nerve-wracking. Patrick's gaze skipped over me, taking in the day's work. The team had done a good job. I still looked like me, just a slightly shinier version. His expression, however, remained a perfect blank. Completely unreadable. I might as well have tattooed a pony on my forehead for all he cared. Next, he crossed his arms over his chest, turning his attention to the view. It didn't seem like he was able to relax fully even in his own home. Though that might have more to do with me being here.

While I knew he preferred me silent and submissive, I couldn't possibly keep my mouth shut for six months. "What's a merkin?"

"A pubic wig. They use them in sex scenes sometimes to cover your junk."

"Huh."

He said nothing more. The silence wasn't wildly uncomfortable at all.

"We need to discuss the home situation," I say, taking a seat on the couch. "The contract didn't really cover that side of things apart from me not inviting anyone to the house or giving out the address, et cetera. Which is totally understandable. Your privacy needs to be protected and all."

His brows drew in, but not a single word was uttered.

"If you'd prefer that I spent the evenings out or in my room—"

"You're going to be living here for half a year, Norah. I don't expect you to be in hiding the entire time. We'll get used to each other." The man did not sound convinced. Which was fine. It's not like I'd been kidding myself. This was strictly a business arrangement. We weren't going to be best friends or something.

"Okay," I said.

His frown amped up to eleven. How could someone so handsome be so cranky? Living in a place like this, having everything laid out at his feet. Give or take the recent scandal fucking with his career and resulting in him having to turn his world upside down to incorporate me and this subterfuge. I believe I just answered my own question.

He sighed. And it was quite possibly the greatest and heaviest sigh of all time. No man had ever been so put upon. So misunderstood. "I'm messing this up. Let's start again. Are you hungry?"

"You don't have to—"

"I know I don't. But we need to get to know each other sufficiently well to sell this. So we might as well spend some time together and get that out of the way," he said. "And I don't know about you, but I'm starving."

I got up and followed him to the kitchen. It was nice, with a long white stone island/breakfast bar and a huge six-burner gas stove. A fridge full of vitamin drinks, fruit, and pre-prepared meals. He stared in at the contents, his brow a wrinkled mess. Still handsome.

"Chicken, beef, or vegetarian?" he asked. "Mostly it comes with a sweet potato mash and steamed broccoli, but the vegetarian has cauliflower and tofu in it too."

I opened my mouth, shut it, and pondered the right words. And yay, me, for not blurting out my first thought regarding his food choices. "Guess you have to eat really clean for the whole perfect body and everything."

His expression relaxed just a little. "Sounds pretty bland, huh?"

"Well . . . yeah."

"Now you know why I like to hit up Little Italy. I just can't do it too often."

"You must be very disciplined."

One muscled shoulder lifted in a shrug.

"I'm disciplined enough to stop at six Pop-Tarts, but that's about as good as it gets."

The corner of his mouth twitched. "Right."

"I'll take a chicken," I said. "Thank you."

He nodded and put two meals into the oven to heat. Being that close, it was impossible not to breathe him in. He had an ever-so-slightly salty, but fresh, scent. There was a hint of wood or sage in there too. Like he just stepped out of the ocean and frolicked in a forest before hitting up the kitchen. I'd bet any money it's some big-brand cologne. And sniffing him was creepy, so I'll just stop that.

Next he produced a jug of cold water and two glasses and set them on the dining room table. A round wooden mid-century-looking thing with four chairs. Guess he's not prone to throwing large dinner parties. I wondered if he selected the furnishings or had a decorator help him. But then, I was curious about everything when it came to this man.

"So we met at the restaurant where you worked and I asked you out," he said, taking a seat and pouring the two glasses of water. The deft way he handled the task was familiar.

"You've done some waiting," I said.

"Doubt there's an actor who didn't start out working in restaurants or tending bar." He settled back in his chair. "Angie talked about running with the whole super-fan-getting-to-date-her-hero fantasy."

"Okay." I shrugged. "We can do that."

His gaze narrowed. "But you're not a fan?"

"I didn't say that."

"You didn't say you were, either."

"Do I need to be a fan?" I asked.

"No." Again, with the almost-smile. "Just curious."

"I like some of your movies. But it's not as if you're the screensaver on my cell or anything." My mind scrambled for the right words. "I think you're a good actor. And obviously you're a handsome specimen of manhood."

He sat perfectly still, watching me. Despite the blank face, I could have sworn he was amused.

"It's not like you need me fawning over you. Your online following must be in the millions."

He tipped his chin in acknowledgment. "You seem like a pretty honest, straightforward person. Are you going to have a problem misleading people about us?"

"I wouldn't have taken the job if I did. Though Mei seems nice. I don't like lying to her."

He nodded. "Yeah. I doubt she believes it."

"Really?"

"Mei is one of the smartest people I know."

I'm not sure if that made me feel better or worse.

"You said you had two jobs—what was the other?"

"Ah, updating accounts and pricing inventory at a boutique a friend owns. Just a couple of mornings a week when needed." I took a sip of water to soothe my dry throat. "I also sometimes delivered for another restaurant when Little Italy was closed. Until my car died a few months back."

"So three jobs, then. You're hardworking."

I shrugged. It wasn't a big deal. Like everyone else, I have bills to pay.

"College?" he asked.

I pushed back my shoulders, sat up straighter. Not that I was defensive about the topic or anything. "I dropped out during my second year. You?"

"Acting at USC."

"But you're from Phoenix originally, right?"

He cocked his head. "You Googled me? Checked me out on Wikipedia?"

"Um . . ."

"It's fine, Norah," he said. "Research for the job, right?"

"Right."

"What'd you find out?" All relaxed, he sat back in his chair. With his legs spread and an arm lying on the table. The most at ease I'd ever seen him. Still, there remained a tension to him, a dissatisfaction of sorts.

"Well, you're thirty-six years old. Born and raised in Arizona, but you've been a resident of LA since you were eighteen."

"Mm-hmm."

"You have two younger sisters. You've appeared in twenty-eight films and a few television shows," I recite from memory. "A supporter of the World Wildlife Foundation and a Dodgers fan. And you were declared Sexiest Man of the Year a while back. Congratulations."

"Thanks," he said drily. "It was good PR. I'll give it that."

Outside, a scattering of lights lay spread out across the nighttime city. And far off in the distance, the ocean did its majestic thing.

"That's pretty much it," I said.

"No rumors or innuendo to add to the list?"

I took a deep breath. "I'm sure you're aware of what they say about you. There's no need for me to repeat any of it."

His fingers tapped out a soft beat against the table. "You must be curious about Liv and that whole fucking mess."

"It's none of my business."

"Yeah, but you're bound to get asked about it, eventually."

"At which point I'll tell whoever is asking that everyone has a history," I said. "Whoever you were involved with in the past has nothing to do with us here and now. They couldn't possibly compete with how pure and true our love is. Why we make Cinderella and Prince Charming looks like a pair of losers."

He snorted, and it was a sort of vaguely happy sound. Score one for me.

"Or something along those lines." I shrugged. "Whatever you and Angie want me to say."

"Got any acting experience?"

"Not even a little."

Another almost-smile. "I'm sure you'll be fine. Just be yourself."

Glad one of us was a believer.

"Tell me about you."

"Oh come on," I said. "I know you had a private detective do what was no doubt an extensive background search. The lawyers mentioned it a time or twelve."

He just looked at me. "Yeah, Norah, I did. Then I asked Angie to read the report and tell me if anything in particular stuck out as being a problem. It didn't, so that was that."

"You didn't read it?"

"No."

I wasn't sure if I was insulted or relieved. A bit of both, maybe.

"Tell me about yourself," he prodded again.

"Thirty years old. You already know about the year and a half of college," I said. "Born and raised locally."

"What did you want to study?"

"Business, maybe. I hadn't really decided."

"Why'd you leave?"

"Life happened." I rubbed my hands along the sides of my wide-leg jeans. Pale blue and very nice. Because Patrick Walsh's live-in girlfriend didn't hang out at home in saggy old yoga pants, thank you very much. "You know. Things just . . . don't turn out the way you expect."

He nodded and let it go.

Who'd have guessed that one day I'd be sitting across from Patrick Walsh discussing my life and its various failures? It was tempting to keep pinching myself just to check that I was awake. The whole situation was bizarre. Crazy. A Hollywood heartthrob and a house in the hills. It was all I could do not to stare about me in wonder. And there was small chance I'd fooled him about not being bedazzled. He had to be well used to peasants like me staring at him in abject wonder. Which was really just a nice way of saying I was objectifying him. An awful but damn hard thing not to do. I mean, the man was basically proof of God and I now lived with him. Lucky I'd packed my vibrator.

Which made me think of something else I'd been wondering. "Why didn't you just get a girlfriend?"

He chin jerked up. "Hmm?"

"You're rich and handsome. It can't be hard for you to find company. You weren't tempted to get a real girlfriend to see you through this?"

"No," was all he said.

Fair enough. I shut my mouth.

"I've had enough drama," he said after a minute. There was

a hardness to his gaze now. Like a wall had been erected keeping me firmly out. As if he wasn't intimidating enough already. The very idea of touching him, of acting familiar enough to sell this whole girlfriend charade, was absurd. He obviously neither invited it nor wanted it. "Are you seeing anyone?"

"Me?" I asked. "No. Just as well. Your contract requires me to go without. It wouldn't be a good idea to get caught in any compromising situations."

A nod.

"How are we tackling PDA?"

"Public displays of affection?" he asked. A deep line appeared between his dark brows. "Wasn't that covered in the contract too?"

"I thought it might be best if we went over it to make sure there are no mistakes."

"Okay," he said. "Holding hands, hugging, light kisses. Touching is restricted to my arms, or my chest and back above the waist."

"That's what you're comfortable with?"

"Yes," he said, looking as uncomfortable as humanly possible. "What about you?"

"I'm the same."

He paused and cocked his head. "You're comfortable with me touching your chest?"

"Ha. On second thought, maybe not. Might be best if we leave the boobs out of it. I think Angie wanted things kept to a PG-13 rating." I popped up out of the chair. "I'll check on the meals."

Nothing from him.

"They look about right," I reported. "Where are your oven mitts?"

"Cupboard on your left."

"Would you like me to plate it or do you prefer to eat out of the container?"

"The container's fine." He too got to his feet, his frown having returned. "Let me. You don't have to—"

"It's not a big deal. You're paying me a lot of money. The least I can do is help serve dinner," I said with a smile. "Where do you keep the dishes and silverware?"

Without another word, he fetched the items. And all the while, the edges of his mouth drew downward while his brows drew in. I don't know what I'd done, exactly. But the man was definitely unhappy. Maybe I'd stepped on his toes, doing stuff in his kitchen, making myself at home. Sort of. Having people invade your space was never fun. And it's not like he'd ever been a fan of the whole fake girlfriend thing. Guess we both had some adapting to do if this was going to work.

"It was, ah, it was good to talk to you. I'm going to eat in my office," he said. "I've got to start on that script."

"Okay."

"You're all right with everything?"

"I'm fine. Thank you for dinner."

"Sure," he said. "Norah?"

"Yeah?"

For a long moment, he just stared at me. And I'd have given back every cent he'd given me to know what he was thinking. "Nothing. Never mind."

And he was gone.

Chapter Three

"THAT PRESSED JUICE IS TWENTY DOLLARS," I SAID, pointing to the concoction in question.

Patrick didn't even look. "Hmm."

I just shook my head. Celebrities didn't grocery shop like normal people. Pop-Tarts were right the hell out, for starters.

We were on our first ever outing as a couple at an upscale super-cool organic market. Angie decided this was as soft a launch as possible. A sneak attack on the celebrity life, if you will. Patrick wore basketball shorts, Converse, and a hoodie. While I had my minimal makeup face on (forty-five minutes application time), a messy bun, skinny cuffed jeans, a Helmut Lang 1950s-style white polo shirt, and plastic slides. They were ugly but comfortable. And I guess very cool, or the stylist wouldn't have chosen them.

"Not only does this grocery store of yours have a café. But you can buy a latte for the bargain price of fifteen dollars." My mouth hung open. "That is wild."

"You want one?"

"No. Just getting used to how expensive and exclusive your world is."

He said nothing and kept on pushing our shopping cart into the fruit and vegetable aisle.

Then it happened.

Someone had their cell pointed our way over by the display of pomegranates. Patrick obviously realized it too, because he paused, slipped an arm around my shoulders, and drew me in close. It was like he'd flipped a switch. All of a sudden touching was fine; cuddling was happening, apparently. He was no longer the large, intimidating, dispassionate fake boyfriend of a moment ago. Showing I too could improvise, I slid my arms around his waist and stepped into his body. Heaven. Just heaven. Hugging this man was indeed a not-to-be-missed opportunity. He was hot and hard and all-around swoon-worthy. And my hands were definitely within the agreed upon touching zones, despite the allure of his ass. One of his big hands rubbed up and down my back. Very comforting. Much romantic. The man had some smooth moves. If I hadn't been so nervous about everything, I'd have enjoyed it immensely.

Then the moment was over.

Cool as can be, I took a step back, grabbed a package of something, and placed it in the cart. Because we were totally a normal couple restocking their pantry and nothing more. Despite the weirdness of having people now staring at us. Which I could totally ignore.

"You like dandelion greens?" he asked.

"No clue. I just grabbed the closest thing."

Nothing from him.

"Do you think they have boxed mac and cheese here?"

Again that twitch of the lips. "Probably not."

"I feel sad for the way you eat, Patrick. Your relationship with food is . . . not yummy."

He just gave me a look.

"But then you're the one with millions of dollars and a legion of fans, so you're obviously doing something right with your life."

"Thanks, Norah. That means a lot."

He definitely had a dry sense of humor. And he was talking to me again. After last night's attempt at bonding, there'd been nothing but awkward silence. Maybe he'd been thinking big thoughts. Large, unwieldy ideas that filled his head to the point where he couldn't possibly make conversation. Or maybe he was just as uncomfortable with me as I was with him.

"There's not much in the cart," I said, hiding my shaking hands by shoving them in my jeans pockets. "What do you normally buy?"

"I don't normally do my own shopping."

"You just have those meals delivered?"

He shrugged. "Basically. Sometimes Mei's mom sends over fried rice and egg rolls."

"What if I grabbed the ingredients for grilled salmon with a salad on the side and then we bulk up on those waters you like to drink?"

"You can cook?"

"You can't?"

"Not really," he admitted.

"Okay," I said, my mind going a mile a minute. "Well, I can cook and I am willing to cook for you. I actually enjoy letting loose in the kitchen now and then. When I have time. Though my boss at Little Italy was always sending me home with leftovers, so there hasn't been much cooking recently."

Nothing from him.

"And you can't just exist on reheatable meals all the time," I continued. "That's sad. I mean, they're not horrible. I thought the sweet mash potatoes in particular were quite nice. And not to be a picky bitch, but I bet you're paying top dollar for them.

Which is crazy since the greens were flaccid and the meat dried out in the oven. You must have noticed?"

Still nothing.

"I get that you have to be careful with your diet, but I'm sure we can do better than that. Some grilled meats and fresh low-fat sides or steamed vegetables. Something along those lines." I smiled. "You have that beautiful chef's kitchen. Seems a pity not to use it. I'll need to know if you have any allergies or whatever. Do you?"

The man just stared at me. Guess that was a no.

"This is a great idea and it'll give me something to do in the evening. I'm not really used to having so much spare time on my hands. I don't know what to do with myself. Guess I should think about getting myself a hobby for the next six months. So I'll cook unless we've got an event or a party to attend or whatever," I said, finishing up. "Does that sound good to you? Plus it will seem weird to our audience if we go grocery shopping and only buy dandelion greens and bottled water."

He kept right on staring with a mix of dismay and awe. Like he didn't realize I had quite that much talking in me. If there wasn't a subsection of the contract detailing a hard limit to my daily allowed word count, there would be soon. Maybe he was one of those celebrities who had a rider stating no one could look at him on set, let alone attempt conversation. And there I'd gone getting all up in his face. Worst fake girlfriend ever.

"Sure," he said eventually. "That would be great. Thanks."

"You're welcome."

We walked on a few more steps. The Weeknd played over the shop's sound system.

"I tend to babble sometimes when I'm nervous."

"Right."

Sweet baby Jesus, strike me down. Just kill me now and save me from further embarrassment. This was a disaster.

"That's not a problem," he finally added, though he didn't really sound convinced.

A lady with a stroller and cell pointed our way lurked at the end of the aisle. Patrick reached out and rubbed the back of my neck. Damn, he was good. Strong fingers dug into all of my tense muscles and wooed them into submission.

"Relax," he muttered. "You're doing fine."

Oh those fingers of his. All I could do was close my eyes and moan in wanton bliss. Which was when he leaned in and pressed a kiss to the top of my head. Like a real boyfriend would. A good one. I'd swoon under any circumstances, but it's entirely possible I was also a little touch starved.

I pulled myself together and opened my eyes. "Thanks."

The tops of his lips curved up like a solid two hairsbreadths at least. We were making progress. Then he stopped and studied me for a moment. "Hon. Honey?"

"You want me to find some honey?"

"No," he said. "I was trying out another nickname."

"That's important to you?"

"Couples always have stupid cutesy pet names for each other, right?"

"I dated this guy once who insisted on calling me 'dude' all of the time. That was not good."

"Tell me you dumped him."

I winced. "Eh."

His frown increased.

"How does 'honey' feel?" I asked.

"Still not quite right."

"Never mind," I said. "Am I supposed to be coming up with a name for you?"

For a moment, he thought it over. "No. It's okay."

"Okay. Let's get this shopping done."

Angie warned us not to take too long, and yet not to rush things either. It was a delicate balance. We didn't want to look like we were hanging out waiting to be noticed. On the other hand, it wouldn't look good if we walked out with practically nothing. That would be dubious as fuck. We were a normal couple doing our weekly grocery shopping. Nothing more, nothing less.

With Patrick trailing behind me pushing the cart, I got busy grabbing everything I'd need. Along with the world's most expensive rotisserie chicken, green beans, and potatoes. Because a life devoid of carbs was no life at all.

People definitely kept on paying attention to us. At first, they'd stop and stare at Patrick. Then, sure enough, their interest would wander over to me. The woman at his side. Or leading him around the grocery store. It was weird enough having people gape at me from a distance. But when we got outside, it really happened. Four paparazzi were waiting, cameras at the ready. I hid behind a pair of sunglasses to maintain a little mystery. Angie didn't want to give them too good a look at my face until we were ready for the big reveal. Whatever that meant.

They followed us, coming close to getting in the way several times, as we walked to Patrick's Range Rover. And they shouted questions the whole way. Who was I? Were we dating? What would Liv say? Was Grant talking to him? Had Patrick been dropped from more movies? Was his career over? On and on it went. Talk about intrusive. Not unexpected given the situation, but not exactly welcome either.

I frowned and ducked my head, not enjoying it at all. Patrick tried to put himself between me and them, but it didn't really work. We were surrounded. At least for me it was temporary, and I was getting paid well. Strange to think that this was a normal, accepted part of his life. Though I suppose he was well paid for it too. This was the cost of fame. You'd really have to love acting, money, or attention in general to put up with this shit on a regular basis.

I don't think I took a breath until Patrick closed the car door for me and we were on our way.

"You okay?" he asked, tone subdued.

"That was . . . I don't know what that was."

"It can be confronting."

"Yeah," I agreed. "But I knew what I was getting into. I mean, I basically knew what I was getting into. That was just . . ."

"A lot," he finished for me.

"Mm."

His frown seemed particularly heavy. "I'm sorry."

"What?" I asked, surprised. "No, don't be. It's fine. I'm fine."

He sighed. "Media interest is the one real downside to this. To acting."

"The fame aspect doesn't ring your bell?" I asked.

"It was kind of fun at first. To be validated that way. But these days . . . I could live without it," he confessed. "Are you sure you're okay?"

"Absolutely." I pasted a smile on my face. "We survived our first public outing. Yay."

The worry in his gaze was replaced by mild amusement. Which I much preferred.

And I'd done it. I'd run my first gauntlet. Passed my first test. Sure, there'd been moments of what the heck and general discomfort, but I'd made it. I could totally do this.

I could not do this. Not even a little.

At first, it wasn't so bad. The photos were okay, apart from a few taken at awful angles. Double-chin nightmare. No one had any idea who I was. Headlines ranged from "Patrick Walsh Spotted with New Mystery Woman" to "Liv's Heartbreak as Patrick Moves On." Like she hadn't been playing happily-in-love-with-her-husband for the past month. I doubt she even cared. The way they made shit up was amazing and clickbait should be a crime.

But a couple of hours later my cell started to buzz with incoming texts. Followed fast by an avalanche of calls. Mostly from numbers I didn't recognize. Seemed everyone was curious. And I did not answer a single one of them.

"Someone's identified you," said Angie, sitting on the sofa with a glass of wine in her hand. "It won't be long until your name is all over the internet. I hope you're ready."

Deep, even breaths were key. A panic attack would help nothing. I'd agreed to this. Time to suck it up and get on with the show. My fifteen minutes of fame were about to begin.

"Just don't react. Don't do a damn thing."

"You can't control what they say anyway," said Mei with a sympathetic smile. "Best to just not answer. Ever. If it wasn't for this job, I'd have mine on silent until the end of time."

Seemed like solid life advice.

"We'll release a statement soon," continued Angie. "First let them work themselves into a frenzy trying to track down information about you and the relationship. It all suits our cause."

"There's paps at the gate," said Mei. "They started gathering just after you guys got back from shopping."

Angie nodded. "To be expected. There isn't a viable angle for a long-range lens to see anything from up there. It's one of the reasons Patrick purchased this place."

"He does like his space." Mei smiled. "Guess you've noticed that, what with you two sleeping in different bedrooms."

"I snore," I lied. "Yeah . . . it's really bad. I even wake myself up sometimes."

Her brows rose. "Oh."

Patrick retreated to his home gym with a personal trainer as soon as he carried the groceries in and helped to unpack them. How he felt about all of this was hard to say. His stoic and stony demeanor never seemed to falter. Even though he'd agreed to this, it still had to suck for him. Having a veritable stranger in his house. Generating all of this extra interest in his life.

My cell vibrated its heart out on the coffee table and a name flashed across the screen I could most definitely not ignore. "Shit."

"Trouble?" asked Mei.

"No," I said. "Well, probably not."

"Explain," demanded Angie.

Instead, I picked up the cell and answered the call. "Hi, Gran."

She cleared her throat, making me wait. Because the woman still knew how to own me just fine. Age hadn't softened her in the least. "Norah, is there something you'd like to tell me?"

"Ah, yes. Um . . ."

"There's a nice young man here from a newspaper asking me for a quote with regards to my darling grandchild's exciting new relationship with a superstar."

"Shit," I muttered again.

"That was almost exactly my reaction."

This was all my fault. Avoidance is a bitch. Life and consequences can rarely be contained and controlled in neat little parcels. "I'm so sorry, Gran. I had no idea they'd track you down. Let alone this fast."

"What's her address?" asked Angie. "I'll get security over there now."

"It's in the file." Mei rose and headed for the office.

"I just moved her to a new place," I said.

"We know."

Of course they did. They and their private investigators. I took a deep breath and let it out slowly. "Gran, they're going to send someone over to make sure you're not disturbed again. I'm very sorry that happened."

"Norah. Stop. Explain what's happening."

"Ah, I met someone. Isn't that great?"

"You said you were done with men. That you were taking a break."

"Yeah," I said. "What's that saying about how plans are what you make while life is happening?"

"And he's an actor," she prompted.

"Yes. Patrick Walsh. He's nice. Kind of quiet . . . you know, the strong silent type. I think you'd like him."

"When did you meet him?"

"We started getting serious about a week ago, but he'd been coming into the restaurant for a while." While it wasn't the whole truth, it wasn't actually a lie.

"That's not long."

"It's not," I agreed. "But, um, we're taking our time and getting to know each other like mature and responsible adults. Though I moved in with him a couple of days ago. He has this nice house in the hills. It has a pool and everything. Great artwork and—"

"You've moved in with him?" she snapped. "Already?"

"Y-yes."

"Some people might call that rushing to the point of stupidity."

"And those people would be harsh despite having a point, I guess."

"Hmm," said Gran. "I thought you learned your lesson about moving too fast with Mason."

"Well, he's not Mason. He's a completely different person who hasn't once asked to borrow my credit card for a special surprise thing he doesn't want to tell me about just yet. But yeah, I see what you're saying." I frowned at the memory. "Though of course if Patrick were stringing along another two girlfriends and a fiancée, then it's safe to say the press would have found out about it by now. They are all over him night and day."

"Norah," she said chidingly. "Don't make light of it. How can you be sure about this boy?"

"The 'boy' is a thirty-six-year-old man. And I myself might be considered an adult at thirty. Some might even think me able to make decisions for myself."

She clicked her tongue. "Answer the question."

"Please don't make your mind up about him so fast. He's a nice person. Really."

"They all seem nice at first." She sighed. "I don't want you getting hurt."

"And I appreciate that."

"I don't want you getting led around by your pussy, either."

"Your language shocks and stuns me," I said. "I thought you were supposed to be a nice old lady."

She snorted.

"I have to go. Can I call you later?"

"No doubt you'll be too busy staring love-struck into his pretty blue eyes and forget all about me."

"Probably." It's important to note that I came by my sarcasm honestly. "You looked him up, huh?"

"I never did trust the handsome ones. And he's . . . goodness gracious."

"I know, right?" I smiled. "I love you, Gran."

"I love you too. Goodbye. And watch your back." She hung up first. Gran was so punk.

Angie and Mei were watching me intensely. But if they had the file on me, they probably already knew about my disastrous history with men.

"He asked to borrow your credit card for a special secret surprise?" asked Mei, voice dripping with condemnation.

"Yes."

"Did you give it to him?"

"No," I said. "It was overdrawn because I'd been running late with a few bills. Luckily. He dumped me soon after. Guess I wasn't affluent enough for his tastes. Can't con someone out of money they don't have. Then a woman contacted me online asking some questions. That's when it came out about all of his different lady friends."

Mei groaned. "There's always that one bastard in a woman's background that just makes you want to sew yourself shut."

This was true. My problem was that I wanted to be loved and accepted so badly that I'd put up with things I shouldn't have. Guess it was thanks to my lack of parents. My father was unknown and my mother died when I was young. Numerous online articles, quizzes, and self-help books guided me toward this conclusion. They'd also helped me make the decision to take a break from dating. To stop and think a while.

Perhaps Patrick and I had a few things in common, after all.

Trust issues and a tendency toward isolating ourselves. Neither of these was necessarily beneficial.

"Was the sex that good?" asked Angie, sounding only mildly interested.

"No," I answered without hesitation. "That's the thing. That's why I needed to learn to make better choices."

Mei sighed. "Don't be too hard on yourself."

"Love makes idiots of us all," said Angie, pausing to take a sip of wine. "And there are some rabid assholes out there."

Mei held up her cell. "You've already been given a couple name! You're Natrick!"

"Natrick?" I asked in a dubious tone.

"It could be worse," said Angie.

"You were such a cute teenager," continued Mei, looking at her cell. "Look at you rocking those Daisy Dukes. Though I don't suppose you gave them access to your photos or permission to share them, which is gross."

"Probably got them off an old school friend's social media account," said Angie. "Bound to happen. We all have a history floating around out there on the internet these days."

"And there's you out with your friends." Mei smiled. "You look so happy and relaxed."

Angie made a noise. "What she looks is intoxicated."

Meanwhile, my eyebrows climbed ever higher. I'd known there would be difficult moments. Times when I'd rue my decision to play this part. I just hadn't thought it would happen so fast. "Holy shit. They're really going to get all up in my business, aren't they?"

"Yep," said Mei, with a shrug. "But Paddy's worth it, right?"

"Right." I forced a smile. "This is fine. I'm fine. Patrick and I are very happy together."

Mei just blinked.

"All they're going to find is how perfectly average you are. The girl next door who got to date a superstar," said Angie. "We've got coverage on all of the main gossip sites. Keep your shit together, Norah. This is only the beginning."

Chapter Four

CERTAIN ELEMENTS MAKE UP THE CLASSIC Hollywood love story. Such as being spotted on a date at an exclusive, opulent, and expensive restaurant. Chandeliers, crystal wineglasses, candlelight, and linen tablecloths. Patrick even asked Mei to book the tables closest to our velvet circular corner booth so we'd have the illusion of privacy. All while being visible to the paparazzo cunningly hiding in the garden outside the restaurant. Someone must have received a hell of a bribe to stash him amongst the foliage. If you didn't know to look for him, you'd never know he was there. Patrick had again done his best to put himself between me and the paparazzi outside. There'd been all the usual shouting of questions and the blinding light of their flashes. With an arm around me, Patrick had steered me into the restaurant. Hard to tell if he was just playing the part or being protective. Though the former was most likely.

"So . . . how was your day?" I asked.

Patrick sat opposite me in a slick black suit, over a pristine white shirt unbuttoned at the neck. He had a nice neck. Muscular and thick. Biteable. Ugh. Me and my lust.

"Good," was all he said.

"Great. What did you do?"

A flicker of a frown crossed his face before he smoothed it

away. Like how dare I interrogate him, i.e. make conversation. Eventually he said, "Finishing up PR duties for the latest movie. They had us do a bunch of interviews."

"You and your co-stars?"

"Yeah." He fussed with the silverware. "Grant and me."

I nodded in encouragement. If he didn't offer any further information about spending quality time with Liv's husband, then I wasn't going to ask. Though it had to have been uncomfortable as all hell for him. For them both.

"Also had a meeting with my agent."

"Sounds like a busy day."

"It was."

One of us had to be brave and start the touching. So I reached across the table, offering my hand. And after a moment, he took it. His big hand dwarfed mine, his skin warm, with slight calluses. From all of the working out, I guess. Okay. Now we looked more couple-like and romantic. Angie would be pleased.

"Got asked a lot about you," he said. He had a nice voice, low and a little rough.

"What did you say?"

"I don't answer questions about my private life."

"That makes sense."

"If I started answering now, it would look off."

The candle flickered between us while some moody hypnotic music filled the room along with the quiet hum of conversation. I could feel the curious gazes of the other diners. People in general enjoyed looking at Patrick. They wanted to do things for him. Being an accessory to someone like that was interesting, to say the least. People don't look at waitresses. Not really. You're disposable. There to fulfil a function, then be forgotten. Of course, there's always the exception. The drunk asshole out to cause trouble or the moron who thinks he's charming. But to be plucked from relative obscurity and thrust beneath the spotlight like this was a whole lot of whoa.

With my free hand, I picked up my glass and took a sip of the lime and basil gimlet. When I licked my lips, his eyes tracked the movement before he returned to frowning. Interesting. He hadn't seemed to register me as an actual female of the species in a sexual manner before. But it probably meant nothing. Who was I kidding?

"Did you want a taste?" I asked, offering the drink. "Gimlets are a great cocktail. Excellent for helping to stave off scurvy."

"No. Thanks."

"Okay."

"What did you do today?" he asked, frowning some more.

I leaned in and smiled. "I worked with the stylist to pick an outfit for tonight and read a book and called my friend Zena and stayed out of the way of your house cleaner. That's about it. I'm not used to having so much free time. It's been interesting to slow down. I might even look into doing some online courses since I've got the time and money."

"It's a lovely dress."

"Thank you."

It was a short black puff-sleeved, V-neck midi dress, with a cinched waist. Elegant without being showy. Just right for the supposed everywoman/girl-next-door part I was playing. And along with the Louboutin black suede block heels, my outfit had cost him a bomb. My highlighted hair was styled into beach waves and my lipstick was red. All in all, I felt . . . capable of the job. No, that's not right. I felt fucking awesome. If he had any sense, the man would worship at my feet.

Alas, he did not. Instead, he grimaced as if either paying

me a compliment or just having to communicate actually hurt. "I mean, all of you looks nice. Not just the dress."

"Thank you. You look nice too. Very handsome."

For a moment, he just stared at me, then he gave my fingers a gentle squeeze in lieu of a response. At least it was something.

"I can't actually remember the last time I held hands with someone," I said.

"No?"

I shook my head. "I've taken a break from dating for the past year after about a decade's worth of questionable choices. I feel like online dating has sucked the soul out of the experience. But how else are you supposed to meet people?"

Nothing from him.

"Though I guess that's not an issue for someone like you."

"Not usually."

I smiled and waited for him to say more. Anything would do. But nada. And this was the problem with our fake relationship. Well, one of the problems. His reluctance to engage on any sort of personal level about himself and his life and pretty much everything. Getting to know the man was next to impossible. If I ever actually got interviewed about him, I'd just have to say something along the lines of "He seems nice enough. Very good-looking. Has a great house." And that's about all.

The waitress placed our meals in front of us with a great deal of ceremony. And she definitely eyeballed my date. Patrick thanked her and let go of my hand, neatly spreading the linen napkin out on his lap before taking a sip of his red wine.

"How does yours look?" I asked, peering over the candle and the floral centerpiece. "Wow, are those kale chips?"

He popped one into his mouth and chewed. "Yes."

"Huh."

The side of his mouth twitched. "How's yours?"

"I'm being a food bully, aren't I? Constantly picking on your healthy choices. I should be ashamed of myself." I tried to think of one nice thing to say. It wasn't easy. "Your chicken does appear to be nicely seasoned."

He just looked at me.

"I got steak with broccolini and fancy artisan fries. Hand-carved potato perfection." I picked one up to show him. "Look at this gorgeous bastard, Patrick. It's probably the most expensive fry in town."

"Give it here."

"Since you asked so nicely."

All hesitation aside, I just up and did it. The romantic cutesy thing. I reached out, offering him the fry from my fingers. An expression of surprise slipped across his face. Then, after a brief pause, he leaned in and took it with his mouth. Something low in my stomach stirred in a thrilling fashion. I couldn't believe he actually met me halfway. Why, an explorer teaching a wild animal to take food from their hand couldn't have been more exhilarated. I had somewhat tamed a paranoid, emotionally closed-off heartthrob.

A little, at least. Not that we were even really dating.

"Is that who I think it is? To my left, a few tables back?" I asked, carving into my steak.

Patrick glanced up and nodded. "Yeah."

"My grandmother loves his films."

"He's one of the greats. I used to watch his stuff all the time when I was in high school. One of the people that inspired me to get into acting." He looked around the room, taking it all in with sudden interest. "The other guy at the table with him is an

Academy Award-winning director. Then down the front of the room, there's a couple of big-name producers and a pop star."

"Wow. I spy a big-time social media influencer and a world-famous guitarist and his partner also. This place is pretty popular."

"Hmm," said Patrick.

"We're surrounded by greatness."

Amusement once again showed in his eyes. "We're surrounded by egos."

"That too. Do you think people come here for the food or to be seen?"

"A bit of both," he said. "Just like us."

I popped a fry in my mouth, chewed and swallowed, all the while thinking deep thoughts. Because I'm a multitasker like that. "You know, it occurs to me that if we were really in the throes of a passionate whirlwind romance, we wouldn't be sitting on opposite sides of this booth."

He froze mid-sip of wine.

"We wouldn't tolerate being so cruelly and unnecessarily separated from each other."

He set down his drink.

"Just a thought."

With all due care, Patrick collected his silverware and plate, moving them over to my side of the booth. His wineglass and napkin soon followed. Then the man carefully shuffled around to sit beside me.

"How's that?" he asked.

I stared at him lovingly. Because that was my job.

"You're better at this than I am."

"You'll get the hang of it," I said, reaching for another fry. "I *might* be the kind of person who overthinks things. Especially when it comes to the opposite sex, dating, and relationships. Which, as it turns out, might be quite helpful in this instance."

"Yes, it is."

"Now if I could just monetize my knowledge of old song lyrics and ability to quote *Mean Girls*, I'd be set for life." I pointed a fry at him to emphasize my next point. "Something else occurred to me, by the way."

"What's that?"

"At least one of those plants our photographer is standing amongst is a cycad. Spiky as all hell. He cannot be comfortable."

This time, I definitely witnessed him hold back a smile. "You know what, Norah? I'm actually okay with that."

"I'm going to respect your choices and not tempt you to sin. But you'll tell me if you're interested, right?" I asked, fork hovering over the blueberry galette with vanilla bean ice cream.

Slumped back, an arm lying across the top of the seat behind me, Patrick appeared to be the epitome of at ease. Our knees were less than an inch apart. For some reason this seemed wildly important. It amazed me how relaxed he was in these environs. Billionaires, business types, and other assorted babes were in the room and he couldn't care less. Or rather, the man was one of them. He sat amongst his own kind.

"I don't believe you," he said at last, swirling the last of his red wine around in the glass.

"What don't you believe?"

"That you would willingly share that dessert."

I laughed.

"Look at you, hunched over the plate, holding the fork like you might stab me at any moment if I make a move."

"First of all, it is really good and I don't actually want to give any away. I was just being polite. And second of all, you made a joke." I smiled. "It was about me, which is kind of harsh, but I'm willing to let that slide."

He sipped his wine.

"You don't even get scared when I talk at you anymore. At least, you haven't tonight."

He looked away for a moment. "I may be a bit wary of having new people around after what happened."

"The Liv thing."

"Yeah."

I nodded and ate some more of my heaven-sent pastry. So good.

"You're still not going to push me for details?" he asked. "I know everyone's dying of curiosity about it."

I just looked at him.

"What?"

I put my fork down and pushed the plate away. "Patrick, you keep expecting me to do that, and honestly it's kind of insulting. I'm sure that as charmed a life you lead, a person in your position can get used and abused in all sorts of ways. People wanting to feed off your fame or talk you out of your money or use your connections and so on. Now, you don't know me that well, but I'd appreciate it if you could give me the benefit of the doubt. At least until I do something to prove otherwise."

His frown returned tenfold. Unhappy as heck.

"I mean, I'd like us to be friends. But of course that's up to you."

He sighed. "Norah . . ."

"Yes, Patrick?"

"You always just speak your mind like that?"

"It's one of my more charming qualities."

His Adam's apple bobbed. Weirdly attractive. "Right."

"Though my Gran says that I was in fact born with a perfectly functioning filter, I just forget to use it most of the time," I said. "Guess I'd rather be honest and get things out there and dealt with, you know?"

For a moment, he said nothing. Then came, "Yeah."

"I'm not amazing at making friends," I confessed, because my mouth just wouldn't stop. "I tend to say too much or say the wrong things."

Nothing from him.

Right. I'd overshared and made it awkward. Nothing new there. It was possible I had a slight crush on my fake boyfriend, which made me even more anxious and likely to overshare than normal. But who could blame me? Given how long I'd been alone, I was probably primed to fall. Didn't mean I couldn't ignore and deny.

Time to finish my dessert. Because, priorities. The man would say, do, and think whatever he liked. All in all, there wasn't a hell of a lot I could do about that. When I finally finished all but licking the plate, I pushed it away and relaxed back with my hands on my tummy and a happy sigh. Good pastry was its own reward.

Then I remembered, I was here to do a job. And I was not acting like the lovelorn fool I'd promised to be. Dammit. Getting to wear shiny clothes and eat in high-end restaurants like this blew my mind. Sitting next to a man whose face had graced countless billboards and magazine covers amazed me. This really was the adventure of a lifetime. But I needed to deliver on the girlfriend front.

So I turned to Patrick with a beatific smile. One that said you are my whole world, and then some. "How are you doing?"

"Good."

"You liked the wine?"

"Yes."

"And the food?"

"Sure," he said.

Excellent. We were back to monosyllables.

Just when I thought he might be getting comfortable with me being around. Considering he'd been missing in action all of last night and today, it wasn't like he should be reaching saturation levels now. We spent plenty of time apart. It was a pity that the time we spent together couldn't be pleasant. Or pleasanter. Because all in all, this wasn't a bad night or anything. Despite me getting overly honest and making things weird.

"You know," I said. "You can always tell me if I'm talking too much."

A little line appeared between his brows. "You're not."

"Are you sure about that?"

His gaze was as serious as serious could be. "Yes. Look, Norah . . . I don't know how to say this."

"Just tell me what's on your mind."

"Honestly?"

"Trust me, Patrick. I have no interest in hearing lies."

He took a breath. "Alright then. The truth is, I'm embarrassed I have to pay you to do this. To pretend to be with me to clean up this mess. In all honesty, I fucking hate it."

"Oh, my God." My mouth fell open. "That's why you've been so grumpy?"

"I wouldn't say *grumpy* exactly."

"I would. And not to tell you how to feel, but you don't need to be embarrassed about that," I said. "I have no idea what went down with you and Liv and Grant. But guess what? It's actually none of my business. I'm sure as hell not judging you according to what some internet gossip site said."

"You're not, huh?"

"No. I'm judging you by how you treat me."

His expression turned thoughtful. "Okay. I can live with that."

A strange sort of silence fell between us after that little revelation.

"Not to brag," I said, "but I totally got through dinner without spilling any food on myself."

Then he sat up and took hold of my chin. His gaze seemed oddly intense all of a sudden. "Not quite. You have sugar on your lips."

"I do?"

"Yeah," he said, his thumb rubbing over my offending body part. Then he stuck said thumb in his mouth and sucked the sugar free. Just like that. How brazen.

We were incredibly close now. Bare inches separated our faces. I'm not quite sure how or when that happened, but he didn't retreat or move away. Having his entire focus on me was . . . unsettling. Like the way my sex lit up like a stadium. It should know better. This was a work thing. Nothing more. Of all the times to get turned on. Anything involving Patrick Walsh was bad and wrong and all of my body parts should have been fully aware of this fact.

"Sweet," he muttered.

"Sugar usually is," I whispered back at him. Because I'm an idiot.

Happily, I'm an idiot who entertained him. Because he actually gave me a half smile. Good God. It was beautiful. The whole world fell away and it was just me and him. And the photographer in the bushes, because, business as usual.

"That's very true," he said.

Then, to compound the situation, I opened my mouth and said exactly what I was thinking. "You haven't kissed me yet. You should probably do that. For the photographer and all . . . you know."

What a wonderful terrible idea. I was the best worst.

Easily proving he was light-years smoother and cooler than me, the man said nothing. He simply angled his head and pressed his mouth against mine in a chaste, sweet, and not short closed-mouth kiss. Warm breath played against my lips and his body heat was overwhelming. The force of him up close and personal could not be denied. He was magnetic. My fingers twisted in my lap, dying to grab hold of him, but not daring to move.

And then it was over. He sat back, taking all of his hotness with him. Meanwhile, I trembled from head to toe. My brain officially blanked. I was shooketh. Which was odd. Kisses were nice and all, but they weren't usually quite so devastating.

By the way, I'd been wrong. Patrick Walsh could act up a storm when it was warranted. The current state of me proved that just fine.

"Maybe you should try that as the next term of endearment," I blathered. "Sugar."

"Sugar?" he asked, thinking it over. He did this by studying my face intently—a level of scrutiny I was in no way prepared for. Not after that kiss. Then, at long last, he shook his head. "No."

"Um. Okay." I sat up straight and pulled my shit together. "Time to go?"

"Yeah." He turned away. "Let's go."

Chapter Five

WHEN I WOKE, IT ALWAYS TOOK ME A MOMENT TO remember where I was. I lay spread-eagled in the middle of a big white plush bed in a room out of some interior design magazine. Like the rest of the house, the décor was a mix of mid-century and modern, expensive but minimal, with lots of cool art. And then there was the view out over the city through the French doors. A moderately smoggy day. Not too bad.

Dinner last night had been . . . interesting. I still didn't know if I should high-five myself or smack myself in the forehead for asking for that kiss. As per usual, Patrick disappeared as soon as we arrived home. I mean, as *soon* as we arrived. So I got ready for bed and started another book, *Act Like It* by Lucy Parker. My dreams were a mix of smutty and strange.

Taking the last year off sex hadn't been as much of a struggle as I imagined it would be. It wasn't like I didn't know how to use toys, and I was ready to take a break from men's bullshit. But getting up close and personal with Patrick made things trickier. My thirst for the man was real, despite all of our lies. Not that I couldn't control myself. Of course I could. I just hadn't had to in a long time.

Turning thirty might be a downer for some. The whole idea

of leaving your twenties and your supposed youth behind you can be tough. But for me, it resulted in a shedding of fucks. Both figurative and actual. And you wouldn't believe how much lighter everything felt after I deleted the dating apps from my phone. I just gave up on the ideal of a steady relationship and a dynamic career, and focused on learning how to be happy with me in the here and now. I was a work in progress, but that was okay.

Anyway.

The collection of texts, emails, and messages on my cell had grown overnight. Social media was an unrelenting bitch. Gran never much minded what other people thought of her and I tried to follow her example, but it wasn't always easy. The DMs included vile comments about me, occasional threats from crazy fans, naked pictures from women who were sure they could make him happier, and so on. What with being female, I'd become used to the occasional unsolicited dick pic. This barrage of pussy and boobs, however, was both new and unusual. Not sure what they hoped to achieve. To so shake my confidence that I'd pass their photos and phone numbers on to Patrick, perhaps? Give up and go home?

The messages from my fans were nice, though. Of course, just having fans felt bizarre. I'd done nothing of note beyond date someone famous. Guess they enjoyed seeing my normal alongside the spectacular. How sad was our society that a girl with curves and the occasional bad hair day could still be deemed a novelty? But I knew being lifted from minimum-wage drudgery into a life of luxury was a dream. And they might like me for that reason. Or who they perceived me to be.

There were requests for interviews and an offer to write a relationship advice column. No thank you. I barely knew what I was doing on a good day. And Patrick's new partner preferred keeping a low profile according to Angie. Apart from the strategic public appearances we were making about town, of course.

Fakery sure could be a complicated endeavor.

So I ignored everything on my cell except the messages labeled "urgent" and "sorry" from Mei. And that's when everything went to shit.

Patrick's bedroom door was still shut, so I knocked. Nothing happened. Maybe because I'd knocked so softly it would take a person with super-enhanced ears to have heard my gentle tapping. My stomach curdled, my shoulders slumped. And the way shame and anger fought it out inside of me pissed me off.

I knocked again. This time with meaning.

A moment later, Patrick, wearing nothing but a towel around his waist, skin still damp from his shower, appeared before me. Given the situation, I couldn't even enjoy the view.

"Norah," he said, frown in place. "What's wrong?"

"You haven't talked to Angie or looked at your cell?"

"No. Not yet. Why?"

I'd taken the time to put on old jeans and a faded black tank—not the kind of clothes Patrick's partner should be seen in, but who knew how much longer this role would last? And I needed the comfort of the familiar. Soft cotton and good memories. Also, this definitely wasn't a pajamas moment.

My hands balled into tight fists. "A photo has leaked. It was taken of me about five years ago. Me and a guy I was seeing at the time."

He just blinked.

"There's not that much on display . . . I mean, there's some nipple that the sheet isn't quite covering. But mostly it's just cleavage, you know?" I turned away. "It was a personal thing for me and him. Just a happy snap taken in the bedroom. It was never meant to be seen by other people."

His frown turned into a scowl.

"I realize this will interfere with your plans to rehabilitate your reputation and all. The damn internet trolls are loving the drama," I said. "*Patrick's New Girl's Raunchy Past*. Assholes. Like they've never taken a nude. Or partially nude."

Still nothing from him.

"At any rate, I, um, I've spent some of the money—"

"Stop," he growled. "Some asshole either stole or released a photo of you without your consent. That's either revenge porn or theft."

"Yeah."

"You must be furious."

"I would really like to burn shit down right now."

His gaze was full of empathy. The worst possible response, because I did not want to cry. As he'd said, this was a time for righteous fury. Not hopeless, stupid, useless tears.

"Let me get dressed and we'll sort it out," he said.

"Okay."

That was a lie. We didn't sort it out. Mostly because he fled as soon as he got dressed and got off the phone from Angie. Bastard. Men sucked.

"It was supposed to be private," I said, for not the first time. It was nobody's damn business that that photo had been taken. None.

I'd been sitting on the sofa, nursing a coffee and feeling sorry for myself, when Mei arrived. Then Angie called and asked to be put on speaker, and here we were.

"How do you want to handle it?" asked Mei.

"I don't know."

"Do you want me to call Patrick's investigator to see if they can find out under what circumstances the photo came to be released?" asked Angie.

"It's been years since I even talked to this guy," I answered. "We were dating for like a couple of months at most. I don't have a clue if he sold it or posted it for a laugh or what the hell happened."

"Okay," said Angie.

I hid my face in my hands. "I don't want to make any moves that involve spending someone else's money on investigators or lawyers until we know what he wants."

He being Patrick. The man missing in action.

"Well, Patrick is out and not answering his cell. What we do is up to you for the time being," said Angie, which was rather magnanimous given the contract.

My fake boyfriend had deserted me. A bare five minutes after he heard about the situation, he was dressed and out the door. Gone. That had hurt almost more than having my right breast publicly exposed to a not-so-adoring public. I'd texted Gran and told her the situation was under control. A bald-faced lie if ever there was one.

It wasn't even eleven o'clock yet and my world had officially gone to shit.

"It is my nipple," I grumbled. "It should be my decision."

Mei nodded. "And that's all that's in the shot. As leaked nudes and sex tapes go, it's pretty tame."

"It's mostly just cleavage and bed head," agreed Angie. "We

can run with outrage over the invasion of your privacy. Or you could simply ignore it or make a joke. You have options."

"Some celebrities have counteracted by releasing their own tastefully shot nude photo to bring the situation sort of back under their control," said Mei. "At least it means they have the final word on the situation."

"I don't think so."

"It was just an idea." Mei shrugged. "What you need to remember is, this happens all the time in this town. You are in neither a new nor unique situation. While it completely sucks that this has happened, this crap does not get to define you."

"Thank you," I mumbled.

"That's true," said Angie. "And at least we have everyone's attention."

"Great. Doesn't mean Patrick's going to want anything to do with me after this." I leaned my head on the back of the white couch and stared at the ceiling. Never had I been in such a rotten and irate mood. Or at least, not in a really long time. I'd been reduced to a pair of tits and a punch line. A gossipy scandal and a sex crime. People's online ugliness was the worst.

"I don't know about that." Mei shook her head. "Paddy really likes you."

I wrinkled my nose. "How can you tell?"

"Trust me. I've worked with him for years. He rarely lasts past the second date, let alone actually allowing someone into his house." Mei patted me on the shoulder. "Whatever your situation with him is, Norah, he's choosing to allow it to continue. He wants you here. Don't underestimate the importance of that salient little fact."

"Hmm."

"Do you want some liquor in your coffee?"

"No." I sighed. "Thanks."

Mei smiled. "Basically everyone under eighty with a cell has taken nudes at one time or another. Any puritanical assholes feigning outrage can go jump."

It was nice having Mei at my side through this. Even if she was being paid to be there. I'd lost touch with my friends from college a long time ago. And work friends tended to drift off into the ether once you or they moved on to a new job. We were all like ships passing in the night on social media. Though it seemed we were communicating and keeping in contact, our relationships were pretty shallow, to be honest.

"I sent my first husband a shot of me doing a handstand in the nude," said Angie. "It was for our anniversary. He said it was the best present he ever got."

"That's fantastic," said Mei.

Heavy feet striding through the doorway announced Patrick's return. I almost jumped up, ready to apologize again, when I stopped myself. Because hell no. This was not my fault and I'd done nothing wrong. Truth was, the fuckery had been done to me. Whatever the reason he'd run out of the house earlier, I would not say sorry. If he wanted me to leave, then I'd do so. And I'd try to repay the money somehow, some way.

God. What a mess.

If possible, he was even more beautiful than normal in all of his glowering brilliance. Hair in disarray as if his fingers had gone through it a hundred times or more. His gaze as somber as I'd ever seen it. It would hurt to get banished from his presence. For reasons far beyond the money.

"Talked to my lawyer. They're doing their best to get the picture taken down, but . . ." He didn't bother to finish.

"The internet is hard to fight," said Angie. "Especially once something goes viral."

"Thank you for trying," I said.

"They'll make a statement. Get the word out that if any more magazines or sites think of sharing it, then we'll be taking legal action." The set of his jaw was magnificent. "I trust that's acceptable?"

I nodded.

"You shouldn't have to put up with this shit. No one should."

"We're going with outrage?" asked Angie via the cell.

Patrick turned to me.

I took a deep breath. "I guess we are."

"Yes," hissed Mei.

"There's something else." He shoved a hand into his jeans pocket and pulled out a small box. He opened it to reveal dark blue velvet padding and a shining diamond ring. And the diamond was not small. "Norah, this is for you."

"What the fuck?" I wheezed. My throat had closed up. Who even needed to breathe?

"That's so shiny," said Mei in obvious awe.

"What is it?" asked Angie. "What's happening?"

"Norah and I are getting engaged," announced Patrick. Like it was nothing. Like him getting down on one knee beside me was a simple everyday occurrence worthy of no more excitement or attention than taking out the trash.

"Patrick," said Angie, "tell me you're not serious!"

"This morning on the phone you said it was a good idea."

"I was joking."

He shrugged. "Well, I thought about it and decided it was the right thing to do."

"But it's so soon."

Mei just smiled. "Well yeah, but I think it's a great plot twist. They won't have seen that one coming. I mean, everyone's going to know why you proposed, given the timing. But it sends a wonderful standing-by-my-woman message."

All I could do was shake my head. And try to breathe. Breathing remained an ongoing concern.

"Oh, good Lord," said Angie.

"Say yes," urged Patrick.

I had nothing.

"Fine. Whatever. Let's do a close-up shot of you two holding hands with Norah wearing the ring. Just your hands," said Angie. "We'll post it on his Instagram. Something simple for the wording like *she said yes*. We'll let the suits handle the leaked nude while we focus on this. Sound good, Mei?"

"On it," she answered, picking up her cell.

"How does it look on her?"

Mei got up in my face with concern in her eyes. "Ah. She's kind of busy hyperventilating. Hasn't tried it on yet."

"Is it over two carats?" asked Angie. "I never trust anyone who proposes with under two. It sends the wrong message."

"It's five. An emerald-cut ethically sourced diamond on a platinum band from Harry Winston. I got them to open early for me." Patrick gently lifted my hand and slid on the ring. "Norah. Norah?"

"I haven't said yes yet." I stared at the beast of a stone in wonder. "This is crazy."

"No," said Patrick. "This is me having your back."

"Well, congratulations and all that. I have things to do," said Angie, and she finished the call.

Eyes wide open, I stared in . . . something at the ring. Wonder.

Horror. Shock. One of those. Or maybe a bit of each. "We can't get engaged."

"Sure we can," said Patrick.

"You don't want to get engaged to me," I said, finally taking in his face. His determined expression and tranquil gaze. How could he be calm?

"Sure I do."

"But Angie was right—it's too soon."

He lifted one thick shoulder in a half shrug.

"And everyone's seen my nipple," I said.

"I haven't." He kept right on holding my hand, tilting it this way and that so the diamond caught the light. The thing was fucking huge.

"You haven't?" For some reason, my heart lightened. Guess common decency comes as a pleasant surprise sometimes. "You didn't look at the photo?"

"Of course not."

"You haven't seen her nipple?" asked Mei, snapping pictures of our hands. "Or perhaps both of them?"

"We've been waiting for marriage," answered Patrick with a straight face. "That's why we're in separate bedrooms."

"Right," she drawled. "Though Norah said it was because she snored."

"That too."

Mei didn't appear convinced in the least, and fair enough. This was all beyond farcical.

In and out. That's all my lungs had to do. It was fine. Well, it wasn't fine, but it would be. I just had to find the words to express myself. "Patrick. It's a beautiful ring. And you wanting to send this message of solidarity means everything. Thank you."

He just watched me. As if he was maybe mildly curious about what might come out of my mouth next.

"The thing is, I had always thought getting engaged would be . . . different. I mean, like, it would be a big thing that would happen after I'd spent a while in a *real* serious relationship." I gave him my best fake smile. "Know what I mean?"

"This is your choice, of course. But I'd really like it if you'd let me protect you."

"You already are with the lawyers and everything."

"Yeah, but . . ." He sighed. "This wouldn't have happened if it wasn't for me being in your life."

"It's not your fault."

"Eh," said Mei. "It sort of is."

"I'd be proud to have you as my fiancée," he said, killing me inside with his sweetness. For a man who didn't say much, he sure packed a punch when he chose to open his mouth. "Say yes."

Ugh. I didn't know what to say next. A rare thing for me. "I . . ."

"Was that a yes?" he asked, only mildly curious. "I think it was."

"When was the last time someone said no to you, just out of interest?"

He scratched at this chin. "It's actually happening much more than I'd like lately. Please don't join the trend."

I sighed.

"I think you should just wear it for a while and see how it feels," announced Mei. Out of nowhere. "It's not necessarily a big deal."

We both looked at her. Both of us wearing frowns.

"People get engaged and call off their engagements all the time."

"Do they?" asked Patrick.

"Absolutely," said Mei with a grin. "If you paid more attention to real life and less to fictional film characters, you'd know these things. It's like a hobby in Beverly Hills and Bel Air."

"I don't know," I said.

"If it works out, then great," Mei continued. "If not, Norah gets an ah-mazing ring and Patrick gets some great press. Because they definitely won't be dwelling on that hiccup with Liv once news of you and your number-one fan here getting engaged is out. People are going to fall over themselves with swooning. It's a modern-day love story."

My forehead furrowed. "That's true. About the press, I mean. I'm not keeping this ring; it must have cost a fortune."

"Oh no, go ahead and keep it." Mei grinned. "It looks great on you. Or you could sell it and put a down payment on a house. Your choice."

Patrick gave his assistant a bemused look.

"What?" asked Mei. "You want her to keep it, right?"

"Of course she can keep it." He turned back to me, his blue eyes earnest. "Whatever she decides. It's the least I can do."

"You're getting great at this romance stuff, Paddy. I'm so proud of you." Mei socked him in the shoulder before returning to whatever she was doing with the cell. "Okay, you two crazy kids, enough with the dallying. Am I posting this beautiful picture and engagement announcement to Instagram or not?"

I squeezed my eyelids shut and took the leap. "What the hell. Do it."

Chapter Six

I N THE EYES OF THE WORLD, I WAS NOW OFFICIALLY engaged. To Patrick Walsh. It still didn't feel real, which was fair enough since it wasn't. Though it did make for a hell of a distraction from the horrible nipple thing. I'd discovered that being a bottomless pit of rage got old after a while. Random strangers on the internet did not get to ruin my life. And yet, fuck every last person who'd looked at the photo. I hope they got crabs.

In an effort to shift my mood, I got busy grilling salmon and making a salad. Having a clear-cut achievable goal was a good thing. It got my brain to stop freaking out and focus on the here and now. Washing the vegetables. Heating up the pan. All of those things.

"You're not wearing the ring?" asked Patrick, appearing at the end of the kitchen island.

"It's in my pocket. I didn't want it to get damaged."

"It's a diamond. One of the hardest known substances on the planet. You should be safe."

I put some extra oomph into chopping up the cucumber. There was something soothing about slicing and dicing a phal-lic-shaped object today.

"Can I help with anything?" he asked in a slightly more subdued tone.

"No. Nearly finished."

He pulled up a stool and sat his fine behind down. Not that I was in a mood to appreciate it right now. Or him as a whole. "Just talked to Angie. The legal threats worked. We've managed to get it down off all of the bigger websites."

"Good."

"Apparently the guy is claiming he didn't release the picture of you."

"Is that so?"

"He was approached by a journalist in New York where he lives now," said Patrick. "Said he lost his cell on the subway a few days ago. He definitely reported it to the authorities. That much has been confirmed."

"Oh."

"Doesn't mean we still can't look into things and double-check his story."

A few days ago, Patrick and I had barely been a whisper on the internet. The likelihood of someone planning this in advance seemed low. And what was the chance of hunting down some random asshole who'd found or stolen the cell and decided to make some money off of me? It didn't seem likely. But mostly, it was fucked that people felt entitled to look at any part of my naked body without my consent.

"Whatever you want to do," he said. "It's up to you."

I shook my head. "No. I'm done."

He waited for me to say more, to explain, before eventually coming out with, "Alright. If you change your mind, just let me know."

Truth is, I never wanted to think about it again. This shit didn't deserve my time, energy, or emotion. The price of fame was being the subject of this sort of prurient interest. This bullshit.

And it sucked. I set aside the cucumber and started in on a to-mato. It was, however, a little too delicate to truly satisfy my need for violence. Chopping up the feta cheese worked much better.

"Norah, talk to me. Please."

I looked up, startled.

"Usually you've got plenty to say," he continued in a gentler voice. "I'm not used to you going all quiet."

I had nothing.

"Tell me what's on your mind," he said, quoting me to me. Elbows resting on the island, he waited me out with all due patience.

"I think I'm having a bit of a bitter and twisted moment."

"That's understandable." His expression was calm, composed. But his gaze never strayed from my face. When it came to Patrick, you got the sense that there was a lot going on beneath the sur-face. He was just better at hiding his thoughts and feelings than most. "You know, there's a fire pit outside. If you still want to burn things, we can do that."

I softly laughed. "Really?"

"Sure. Whatever you want to do."

I took a couple of deep breaths and shook off the detritus of the day. For the time being, at least. "Let's just move on . . . I, um, I called Gran to give her the news about the engagement."

"How'd it go?"

"Fine. Good. I mean, she was surprised and had some con-cerns. But that's to be expected." And while lying to Gran sucked, no way in hell would she be okay with me doing all of this to get the money for her new place. Though to be honest, I was doing this for both of us. We would both be better off in the long run. At least, that was the plan.

"You should introduce me to her some time," he said.

"You want to meet her?"

He shrugged. "If you want me to. I mean, she's your family. If she doesn't at least meet me once, it's going to look pretty strange."

"That's true." I plated up the food and carried it to the table. "Can you grab the silverware and napkins?"

He did as asked and we took seats opposite each other at the round table. After precisely two mouthfuls he said, "You're right. This is much better than the reheatable meals."

I just nodded. Because duh.

"You still got concerns about the engagement?" he asked. "I mean, of course you do. Should we talk about that?"

"I'm not going to suddenly change my mind on you or something," I said. "I think it just kind of surprised me coming so soon and everything. There was the possibility of it mentioned in the contract, but . . ."

"It was a shock."

"It was."

"I get that it's the kind of thing a lot of people dream about," he continued. "Having the right person make a big romantic statement. I'm sorry I'm not that person."

I tried to smile, but it didn't quite work. It was easy to dismiss him as just a pretty face. But the man could also be damn smart. Then there was the whole feeling of how the power dynamic between us had shifted. Up until now, it had been me coaxing him along a lot of the time. Now, however, we felt almost like partners. Or something along those lines.

What we weren't was a real couple with real emotions, and that was for the best. I'd have to be crazy to want this level of scrutiny from the media and general population all the damn time. Today had been shit. Patrick was a nice guy and all once you got to know him. Once he decided to let you in a little. But whoever his actual future missus might be, the woman would be made of sterner stuff than me. Maybe someone who came from his world and had learned how to deal with it.

"You could think of it as a friendship ring if you prefer," he said.

"Are we friends, Patrick?"

"I'd like to think so."

Out of my pocket came the ring and back on my finger it went. "It is beautiful. Stupidly large, but beautiful."

"The sales rep called it a ring fit for Hollywood royalty." He studied me for a moment. "I know. You could be Princess."

"Princess?" I wrinkled my nose. "Me? Really?"

"I'll take that as a no," he said. "How about Duchess?"

I raised my brows in question, waiting on his decision.

Eventually, he shook his head. "Still not quite right. I'll figure it out eventually."

"I have every faith in you." I ate some more. It was quality salmon, that's for sure. And how nice that for once the silence between us wasn't horrible and awkward. Tonight things were more comradely in nature. "What did you tell your family about all this?"

"I've got it covered," he said, and not a word more.

"Okay. What do you normally do at night?"

"It varies."

"I'd have thought you'd be out taking part in LA's glamorous nightlife with a supermodel on your arm."

"It's been a long time since I had a girlfriend, real or otherwise. Usually I'm busy with work." He looked around the room with a . . . I don't know what the expression was. The man certainly didn't seem enthused with his luxury surrounds. "This is probably the most time I've spent here. Most often I'm on sets working. And those sets can be anywhere."

"Lots of travel, huh?"

He nodded. "I prefer to keep busy. If I hadn't been fired from that movie, I'd currently be training with swords and perfecting my horse-riding skills over in England. Working with an acting coach I'd heard a lot about. I was looking forward to it."

"Wow."

For a long moment, he just stared at his plate.

"Not to be an unfeeling asshole, Patrick, but maybe this is a chance to take a break. To relax a little."

He grunted. Fair enough.

"Is acting your passion?" I asked. "Was it your first choice of jobs, or did you want to be something else?"

He paused. "If I tell you, you have to promise not to laugh."

"I solemnly swear."

"I wanted to be a dog trainer."

My brows rose. "That's so cool."

"We had this little mixed breed called Murphy when I was a kid," he said. "I'd spend hours teaching him to play dead and roll over and all sorts of stuff. We were the neighborhood stars."

"How old were you?"

"About eight."

"When did you start acting?"

"When I was a junior. I broke my arm playing football and had to wear a cast for six weeks. Really messed it up," he said. "Instead of just sitting on the sidelines during PE, I let the drama teacher drag me into her class. Think she felt bad for me sitting there all sad and bored."

"And a star was born."

"Something like that." He gives me that small smile. I had to hand it to him, the man had coaxed me out of my bad mood. It was hard to hate on everything when he was sitting right there. "What about you? What did you want to be when you were a kid?"

"I was going to be a fashion designer. Right up until I realized I hated sewing. Just didn't have the patience for it," I said. "It's not like my style is exactly cutting-edge either. My idea of high fashion is jeans and a tee. There are many reasons why it wouldn't have worked. Then I fell in love with reading and that became my main thing. Waitressing, hospitality, whatever you want to call it . . . it's just a job. It helps to pay the bills."

"You didn't want a job that involved reading?"

I sighed. "Reading or clothing would have been great. But they're not necessarily easy to get into. I've kind of just been getting by. Maybe now I can catch my breath and find something that's a better fit."

"And what do you normally do on your nights off?"

"Most recently, I would take myself on a date."

"How does that work exactly, dating yourself?"

"Well, I'd often start the night by getting tacos from this great little place close to my apartment. Next, I'd make up a pitcher of margaritas and take the whole meal with me into the bath along with a good book or two."

"I see."

"Light some candles. Put on a little music. Set the mood."

"Very romantic."

"The bath was the main reason I chose that apartment. It was small, but sublime," I said. "So my version of dating yourself is all about doing fun and or indulgent activities while getting to know yourself and working on your shit."

He blinked. "Okay. I'm going to need a bit more information."

"Of course you do, you're a man." I set down my silverware. "You see, this activity and others similar taught me to be comfortable on my own. It reinforced the idea that I can have a great time with just me."

"You were uncomfortable being alone?"

"Not exactly." I sighed. "It was more that I had bought into the idea that I needed to be with someone to be whole. Then there's the thousands of years of programming urging us to find a mate and reproduce. Media, hormones, social expectations . . . they can all be a mighty pain in the ass that warp our view of ourselves and our accomplishments."

"Right."

"And that led to me tolerating behavior that I shouldn't have," I explained. "Lowering my expectations and boundaries to fit in with some jackass who added nothing of joy to my life."

He just watched me all thoughtful like. "Maybe you should write a self-help book."

I laughed. "Nah. I think there's enough unqualified woke white women out there giving advice. If I was ever going to write a book, that's not what it would be about."

"No? What, then?"

I just shook my head.

He opened his mouth as if to say something, but his cell vibrated and the frown returned. "Sorry about this."

"It's okay."

"Hi . . . You are? Okay." Then he stood and walked over to the security panel on the wall. A little screen lit up and he pushed a button. Curiouser and curiouser.

"Everything alright?" I asked.

"No."

"No?"

He sighed. "My parents are here."

"Your parents?"

"It's a surprise visit. They, ah . . . they didn't tell me they were coming."

"Huh. I thought you said you had it covered?"

"I was going to call them. I just wasn't sure what to say. Then they heard the news, got all excited, and wanted to meet you."

My eyes were wide as twin moons. "They did? Wow."

"Yeah."

"And I take it they're not aware that all of this is fake?"

"No," he said. And that's all he said.

"Holy shit, Patrick. What are we going to do?"

Renee Walsh was a vibrant, beautiful statuesque woman. While her husband, Tom, was a handsome older gentleman with a beard. You could see where Patrick got his good looks from. They were both rocking jeans, sneakers, and sweaters. Nothing ostentatious. And they both hugged me.

"She's adorable," gushed Renee with tears in her eyes. "Oh my God. I'm so happy to meet you, Norah."

"Sweetie," said Tom to his wife with an indulgent smile.

"You could have called." Patrick started unloading the luggage from their rental car. "That would have been nice."

"Well . . ." began his father, giving his mother a definite I-told-you-so look.

His mother just flipped her mane of silver hair. "We did, when we got to the gate."

"A little sooner maybe next time," said Patrick. "Say, before you leave home."

"Shut up and come here. It's only a brief visit. You'll survive."

His mom grabbed hold of his face and smacked a kiss on his cheek. "We're just so proud of you."

"Thanks, Mom."

Tom thumped him on the back in a manly fashion. "It's wonderful to be here and to get to spend time with you both."

Patrick gave him a hesitant smile. Like the universe would come crashing down if he actually admitted to being happy about something. "It's good to see you too."

"What did you think was going to happen when you announced your engagement on social media without us ever having met your fiancée?" asked Renee. "Seriously?"

Patrick scratched his head. "I was going to call."

I gave him a look that hopefully said "this is so all your fault."

The man just sighed.

"We've barely heard from you lately," she said.

And all of this made me wonder, when was the last time he'd seen his parents? Really talked to them? I'd like to think since the whole Liv thing happened, but something told me not so much. Maybe his mom had known perfectly well what she was doing by not calling first. Don't give him an option.

Renee grabbed hold of my hand this time. "Come and sit with me. I want to hear everything about you and how you two met."

Patrick and I exchanged glances. Nervous ones.

"Okay," I said with a new smile in place. This one projected an aura of "please don't hurt me, I'm a nice person really." It had been a while since I'd met a significant other's parents. Fake or otherwise. And this was sounding more and more like a pleasantly voiced interrogation.

After dumping his parents' luggage in the other spare bedroom, Patrick headed straight for the liquor cabinet. And he did not delay. I was ensconced on the couch with Renee on one side and Tom on the other while Patrick got busy tending bar. Gin and tonics for his mom and me. Scotch on the rocks for him and his dad. Without waiting for anyone to make a toast, Patrick downed a good half of his liquor. I took my cue from him and also drank heartily. Hooray for liquid courage.

"So, how did you meet?" asked Renee.

I sat up so straight a ruler would be jealous. "At a lovely little Italian restaurant not too far away from here, actually. I was working there, and Patrick liked to sneak in between lunch and dinner when things were quiet."

"Because he wanted to see you," she supplied.

I smiled, which wasn't technically a lie.

"And this had been going on for a while?" she asked.

"He'd been coming in for a few years, actually."

"Paddy always did take his time." Tom laughed. "Not one to rush in, are you, son?"

Let the record show, my fake smile was once again way better than Patrick's. And he called himself an actor. Ha. What a loser.

"We'd almost given up hope he'd ever meet the right person." Renee happy sighed. "And as for that unfortunate affair with that Anders woman . . ."

"Sweetie," said Tom with a mild edge to his voice.

"I know, I know." Renee straightened her shoulders. "We're not going to talk about that. But you can't imagine the awful comments and judgmental nonsense we heard from some people. Everyone makes mistakes, but whoo . . . that one was a doozy."

Patrick kept a white-knuckled grip on his drink.

"When are you thinking of having the wedding?" she asked.

"There's no rush," said Patrick in a rush.

"We're still deciding," I added diplomatically.

"How about Christmas?" Renee clapped her hands all excited like. "Wouldn't that be divine? We could go to the snow!"

"Um," I said in a rare flash of brilliance.

"Of course that would make it hard for some of the family in Phoenix to attend," Renee continued. "But just imagine the photos. Or you could have a winter wedding back home while the weather's nice and cool. There are so many beautiful gardens to choose from."

"Norah and I are still deciding," said Patrick in a deceptively calm tone.

"Of course you are." Tom gave me his best supportive dad face. Damn, it was good. "Your mom and I have been married for nearly forty years. It's a marathon, not a sprint. Take your time and enjoy yourselves. Enjoy this period in your lives and getting to be together, just the two of you."

I downed some more of my drink.

"Renee has enough grandbabies to keep her busy for now," said Tom. "Don't you, sweetie?"

It was at this point that I choked and spluttered. Never a good look.

"Don't go there, you guys," said Patrick. "I mean it."

Renee's expression fell just a little as she patted me on the back. *Babies. Holy shit.* I wiped my mouth with the back of my hand, because I'm classy like that.

And everyone's eyes were on me.

"What he means to say is, that's, um . . . that's a ways off still." My heart hammered inside my chest. Cardiac arrest wasn't out of the question. "We haven't really . . . I mean, we've talked about it. Of course we have. It would be foolish to get engaged without making sure we agreed on important matters such as having children."

His mother nodded encouragingly.

"And so we discussed it at great length," I continued. "Mostly we came to the conclusion that it was a one-day-in-the-future thing for us. Not a let's-get-started-on-this-right-away kind of situation. Because like Tom said, we want to enjoy this time together, just the two of us. That's, ah, that's the main reason and our current plan. So yeah. Great."

Patrick downed the last of his drink and got up to fetch another. I was fast getting the impression that surprise family reunions really weren't his thing.

"That's good that you've talked about it," said Tom, crossing his legs. "There are a number of important topics a couple should discuss before looking at making a long-term commitment. Take finances, for example."

"There'll be a prenuptial, of course?" asked Renee, no-nonsense all the way.

My brows felt halfway up my forehead. "A prenuptial?"

Patrick returned to the couch with his fresh drink. His face appeared to be turning a distinct shade of red. Which was odd. I'd never seen him do that before. "Did you two actually cross state lines for the sole purpose of asking as many intrusive questions as possible?"

"Don't be like that, darling," said Renee, with the best disappointed expression I've ever seen. Wow, did she have the mom thing down. "We're happy for you."

"Very happy," seconded Tom.

"So happy." Disappointment had morphed back into a loving gaze. "We just want to make sure you're protected. You've worked hard to get where you are."

But Patrick would not be appeased. "Norah's a hard worker too."

Three sets of eyes turned my way. No pressure at all.

"Thank you," I said. "That's kind of you to say. But your parents have a point. In fact, I insist upon it. Patrick, if you think you've a chance of making off with half my collections of concert T-shirts, romance books, and hair ties, just because all you can bring to the table is a beautiful house and one or two fancy cars, you've got another thing coming."

Tom snorted with laughter.

"Concert T-shirts, romance books, and hair ties?" asked Patrick, smiling despite himself.

"Don't think I haven't seen you eyeing them."

Renee and Tom were both smiling now. I was going to chalk that one up as a win.

"The pre-nup question is settled. My people will talk to your people. So what else shall we talk about?" I asked. Because I was a glutton for punishment, apparently.

"Are you close to your family?" asked Renee.

"I'm very close to my grandmother, yes."

"That's nice." Her smile faltered. "And definitely no husband?"

Tom cleared his throat, loudly.

"Just checking," exclaimed Renee. "Sorry. I won't say another word about it. I promise."

Patrick rubbed at his face with one hand.

"I can understand why you'd have reservations," I said. "Your son getting engaged all of a sudden to a woman you've never even met."

"It has been a little nerve-wracking," agreed Renee in a quiet voice.

"I made her dinner on our first date," said Patrick, in a valiant effort to distract them. His boot tap, tap, tapped against the floor. Talk about stressed.

"You made me dinner?" I asked, ignoring his parents for the moment. "You?"

"Don't you remember?"

"I do, I do. It's just . . . is *made* really the right word?" I gave him a teasing smile. "I mean, you put reheatable meals in the oven."

Amusement filled his gaze. "I said what I said."

"Your intentions were pure, I'll give you that."

"Thanks, cupcake," he said in his usual dry tone. His shoulders had eased down some and the lines of tension on his face relaxed just a little.

"Cupcake? Oh, no. There's no way I'm answering to that."

"No?" A small smile graced his mouth. And just for a moment there was him and me and some breathing room. Thank God for that. "But you're sweet as a cupcake. Pretty as one."

I laughed. "It's awful. But thank you for the compliments."

"Hmm. I guess we'll see."

It was me and Patrick Walsh against the world. Or at least presenting as a united front against his parents. Which was nice. Very nice.

"I tried to get him interested in cooking, Norah," said Renee, taking charge of the conversation once more. "It never worked. Unlike Abby, our middle child. She is a baker and a half, that girl. Her cinnamon scrolls are second to none."

Tom nodded in placid agreement.

"Abby is the veterinarian," said Patrick. "Remember I told you all about her and my other sister? About our whole family history, really. And I showed you all of those pictures, too."

"Oh, yes," I lied. Way for the man to throw me in the deep end. If we'd been sitting at a table I'd have stomped his foot. Honestly. "I remember now. Of course I do. We've talked about so many deep and personal things. I just kind of forgot there for a minute."

"That's okay," said the jerk with a smirk. At least he was enjoying himself.

"Lord only knows what Patrick has told you. I'll just take it from the top. Our youngest is Emily. She's married to Guadalupe and they have one-year-old twins. Would you like to see pictures?" In no time at all, Renee retrieved her cell from her handbag and shoved said pictures under my nose.

"Those are some very cute babies."

"Aren't they just?" She smiled. "Look at those little faces. Don't they make you want—"

"Stop," barked Patrick. "Mother. We talked about this."

"Sorry. Sorry. I solemnly swear to not raise the topic of you two having babies again." Renee put the cell away. "This visit."

Patrick just sighed.

But her husband bit back a smile. "Nice save, sweetie. You just can't help yourself, can you?"

Holy hell. My uterus had never been under so much pressure to perform. Also, I found it interesting that Tom always seemed to refer to his wife as sweetie. Guess that's where Patrick came by his penchant for pet names.

"What line of work are you in, Norah?" asked Tom.

"She's a waitress," said Renee. "I read those news articles to you, remember?"

"Yes, I am. Or I was." I forced a smile on my face. "I, ah . . ."

"She's taking some time off right now to be with me," said Patrick. "But she's been thinking about doing some online college courses."

"Great idea," enthused Renee.

"I'm still looking into it." I nodded. "It wouldn't have worked, me being at the restaurant with all of the media interest in your son and me."

"No, of course not," said Tom. "They're damn vultures, aren't they?"

Renee shook her head. "We even had some outside our house after all of that nonsense that we're not talking about happened. It was awful."

"I'm sorry, Mom." Patrick's frown was back in place. Dammit.

"Yes, well ... we all survived." Renee crossed her arms. "The media are a necessary evil, unfortunately. They're not going to go away for as long as Paddy's in the business of making movies. Will you be able to handle that?"

"Yes," I said.

They both waited for more. Sheesh. Even Patrick just watched me.

"I'm not saying I like or enjoy it." I shrugged. "And I'm sure you're both aware of the picture of me that was released without my consent today."

For once, Renee had nothing to say. Perhaps that was best.

"That's been awful. In so many ways."

"You are not to blame," said Tom, face serious.

"I know." My smile felt brittle as fuck. "But it's all part of the attention that's put on me and Patrick. It's no more his fault than it is mine that the picture is out there. But I'd be stupid to ignore that these things are going to happen if I continue to be involved with him."

Patrick's lips were a flat unhappy line.

"No one has ever listened to me like your son does. No male at least. Not in a long time," I confessed. "And he never dismisses or diminishes my opinions, whether he agrees with them or not. He cares about my feelings and he has my back. These things may seem ... small in a way. Trivial, almost. Like, everyone should be kind and thoughtful and respect other human beings. The thing is, not everyone does."

The edges of his mouth curled up just a little.

I grinned. "And when I make him smile, even the tiniest bit, I feel like a fucking champion."

Renee promptly burst into happy tears.

Tom's eyes were also suspiciously bright. "Sweetie."

"I think you won them over," mumbled Patrick.

Chapter Seven

"I DON'T KNOW THAT WHAT I SAID WAS ESPECIALLY romantic or anything." I lay on the bed, staring at the ceiling, thinking deep thoughts. So much better than being freaked out over this new and even more anxiety-ridden situation.

"No," agreed Patrick, emerging from the bathroom on a cloud of steam. While his sleep pants were on, his shirt was most definitely off. Made for a hell of a view. All of the dips and planes of his sculpted chest. All of it leading down to a faint line of hair from his navel. And now that I looked, there was a definite dick imprint in the soft cotton of those pants. It was a struggle to not be a pervert and keep my eyes on his face. "But what you said came across as genuine. That's more important to some."

If my brain had been functioning, I definitely would have responded.

He started fussing with the cushions on the couch. Unlike my room, his had a fireplace and a sitting area with two armchairs and a couch. A small couch. One he was never going to fit on lying down. This was an issue because his parents believed we were a real normal couple who shared the same room. And inside that room, there was only one bed. What were the odds I'd make it through the night without drooling or farting?

"C'mon. You can't sleep on there." I rose up on one elbow. "You'll wake up with a whole-body cramp. If you manage to get to sleep at all."

"Then I'll just stretch out on the floor."

"I can take the couch."

"No," he said.

Ugh. "Am I really that frightening or are you being overly polite?"

He just looked at me.

"Patrick, this bed is huge. We can share it no problem. Please."

"Are you sure?"

"Yes." I let my head fall back against the pillow. So soft. "Your virtue is safe with me."

"Oh, good," he drawled. "That's exactly what I was worried about."

"I can still wait a while, then slip back into my room if you'd prefer."

He sighed. "I'd rather not risk it if that's okay?"

"No problem."

The mattress dipped slightly beneath his big body as he settled on the other side. I was in bed with Patrick Walsh. How thrilling. Or it would be if I wasn't so tired. Today's bullshit followed by tonight's performance had exhausted me. Then, because I'm a genius, I knocked myself in the forehead.

"Ow," I grumbled, rubbing at my skull.

"What?"

"Hit myself with the ring."

His brows rose, but he apparently decided not to comment. On that subject at least. "Listen, I'm sorry my folks were such a handful, carrying on about babies and all that."

"I thought the prenuptial question was fair enough, honestly. If a random stranger suddenly appeared attached to my well-to-do son, I'd want to know what the hell was going on."

"Even if that child is almost forty?"

"Even then," I said. "I can't imagine you ever stop wanting to watch out for your children."

He did not look convinced.

"It's a good thing they care. You're lucky to have them."

"Hmm."

"As for the push for us to reproduce . . . yeah. Your mom needs to calm down. The usage of my uterus is not up for public debate."

"Agreed."

"She's a force of nature," I said. "I notice your dad just kind of shuts up and lets her lead."

"She's definitely the one in charge there," he said, his voice a low rumble. "When we were growing up, she was always involved in everything. Which was both good and bad. My friends all loved her, the way she took an interest in everything, but having to live with her getting all up in your business all the time was a lot."

"Do you think maybe that's part of why you're so quiet? So reluctant to share your thoughts? Because she wasn't great at giving you space?"

"Are you suggesting I have mommy issues?"

"One way or the other, everyone probably has mommy issues."

"Maybe you're right." He sighed. "I have no idea."

"Though having the general public sticking their nose into your life all the time would also do it."

Only silence came from the other side of the bed.

The house was so still late at night. No city noises, muffled conversation, or the occasional slamming of doors, like at my old apartment. God only knew the thread count of the sheets I was lying on. I barely recognized my life these days.

"The real question here is, how good is the soundproofing in this room?" I asked.

He turned his head on the pillow in my direction.

I pulled the blankets up to under my chin. Despite wearing one of his big tees and my underpants, this whole situation felt revealing in a weird way. Me being in his bed. Him lying next to me. Us being together in an intimate setting. So of course I got nervous and couldn't shut up. "I mean, do your parents expect us to be having sexual relations? Is that the next obvious step in our intricate portrayal of a crazy-in-love couple? Should I shout out 'yes daddy yes' or attempt some loud, vaguely orgasmic-sounding screeches or something?"

"No," was all he said.

"Okay. Just checking."

He reached out and clicked off the bedside lamp. The room went dark. And he was quiet for approximately half a minute. "These screeches ... were you thinking pterodactyl?"

"Are you asking if I make dinosaur sounds when I have sex? Because that's just plain rude. Seriously."

"You're the one who brought it up."

I giggled in a somewhat maniacal fashion. "It would certainly make for strained conversation over the breakfast table tomorrow. God knows what your parents would think."

He laughed quietly. It was a beautiful sound, all low and rough and thrilling.

"You can laugh," I said. "It's a Christmas miracle!"

"It's April."

"Eh. Whatever."

Fake

"You did great tonight, Norah," he said.

"Why, thank you."

It was alarming the way my insides went all warm and fuzzy at his words. Maybe I should see a doctor. Or a therapist. The thing is, I'd finally met a man who not only liked me, but he supported me and said he was proud of me. He actually listened when I got verbal diarrhea. Too bad we were fake.

"Night, Patrick. Sweet dreams."

Nobody would define me as being big on cuddling. As much I enjoyed kissing, hugging, and sexing, when it came time to sleep, I liked my space. Which was why it was a surprise to wake up with Patrick all over me. The man had not stuck to his side of the bed. Not even a little. One of his legs was thrown over mine, his arm lay curled around my middle, and his face was shoved into the back of my head. I knew this due to the soft in-and-out of his breath against my hair. And he was heavy. I wouldn't be going anywhere without waking him up.

I had no idea the man even liked me this much. And he really did if the erect penis prodding my butt cheek was any indication. Just joking. Morning wood isn't always caused by things sexual in nature. I looked it up once. But still, knowing it was there had me overheating in an instant. My nipples hardened and my sex ached. Every inch of me was suddenly wide the fuck awake.

Of course, he could have just stumbled across me in his sleep. This was the most likely explanation. There he'd been, dreaming of winning an Oscar or whatever, when he'd encountered another body in his bed. All perfectly innocent. Didn't make it any less awkward, though.

It would therefore be best if I made my escape before he woke. Yes. Good plan.

I wriggled forward. Nice slow, gentle movements. Nothing that would wake him. But I'd no sooner managed a whole two inches of separation than the muscles in his arm flexed and he pulled me back against him. Heck. There wasn't a breath of space between us from head to toe. Dammit.

"Patrick," I said, giving his arm a little shake.

A groan from him.

"Patrick, wake up."

He yawned and stretched and settled full body against me once more. And promptly went back to sleep.

There was nothing else to be done. I pushed at his leg and twisted out from beneath his hand and pulled down my shirt all at the same time. Hooray for multitasking. However, the whole twisting out from under his hand hadn't worked out so well since his palm now lay warm across my thigh. His fingers even gave the flesh a little squeeze. This guy. I swear. While he might be a gentleman when he was awake, he was damn grabby in his sleep.

Big blue eyes blinked up at me all mildly perturbed. "Norah, what are you doing?"

And he was so cute all sleep rumpled. I really couldn't help myself. Fucking with him was both a privilege and an honor. "Morning, big boy."

"Morning," he mumbled.

"Thought I'd make you breakfast. You must have worked up quite an appetite after last night. I love it when someone else does all the work," I said. "Would you like waffles or pancakes?"

"Pancakes," he said, closing his eyes once more.

"I'm so glad we gave in to our rampant lust and just went for it, you know?"

He frowned.

"You were amazing," I purred.

Both eyes opened and he gazed up at me all confused. Then he snorted. "Very funny."

"Thanks."

"You could just say good morning like a normal person."

"Indeed I could. But look where your hand is, my friend."

He blinked some more and looked down our two bodies to where his hand remained curled around my thigh, all proprietary like. I'd never seen a man move so fast to unhand me without the aid of my knee in his groin. It was impressive.

"Shit. Sorry, Norah."

"It's okay."

"I just ... shit."

"You already said that."

"I didn't mean to maul you in your sleep."

"I know. Relax," I said. "We were both out of it. And there are worse things in life than being your cuddle bunny for a night."

He frowned some more. Then he grabbed at the blankets we'd kicked off and covered the middle section of his body. The poor man with his hard-on. This was why having a vagina was so superior in every way.

"You know," I said. "Normally I toss and turn and wake up a few times and can't always get back to sleep. My brain gets busy, you know? But you seem to have done the work of a weighted blanket. Because I slept remarkably well."

"Great."

"How did you sleep?"

For a moment, he thought this over. "Good, actually."

"There you go. Apparently, we're a winning sleeping combination."

He grunted. The man was not a morning person.

"Do you think us having slept together will change things?" I asked.

He just looked at me.

"I still respect you. Just in case you were wondering."

"You're getting way too much mileage from this," he grumped.

"You still want pancakes?"

At this, his crankiness eased. Truly the way to a man's heart remained through his stomach. "Yes, please."

Renee and Tom had left early this morning, having ascertained that I was not out to hoodwink their son or break his heart. As much as I liked them, it was kind of a relief to have them gone. Since I was like ninety percent certain that Mei knew Patrick and I weren't a couple (my acting skills really weren't that great), the house was the one place I didn't have to pretend. Or pretend hard, at least.

Our next appearance was at the launch party for a new brand of vodka. The owner was a big-name actor Patrick was friends with and had been in a film with a few years back. If you haven't heard of Cole Landry, I don't know where you've been. Having made movies for almost thirty years, the man was the gray-haired fox of action adventure films. And he kissed my hand. Talk about swoon.

Patrick reclaimed my limb with his usual frown. "Leave her alone, Cole. She doesn't even like you."

"I do like you," I countered.

Cole grinned and said in his sexy husky voice, "Of course you do. I'm very likable."

My knees went weak.

Patrick just looked to heaven.

We all paused and pasted brilliant smiles on our faces as the event photographer appeared. Patrick slid an arm around my waist. As per Angie's instructions, I made sure the engagement ring was visible. And then we were done and could relax once again. Mostly.

Lots of shiny people were in attendance. Quite a few familiar famous faces. And both males and females watched my date with lust and avarice in their eyes. The party was being held in an exclusive nightclub in East Hollywood all done in '70s décor. I lived in fear of the heels on my Saint Laurent black leather mules getting caught in the shag pile carpet. For this event, the stylist dressed me in jeans and a black silk tie-neck blouse with my hair in a slick ponytail. The Loewe leather clutch and diamond solitaire earrings were rather splendid. Lord knows what it all cost.

"Let me guess," said Patrick. "You're a fan of his?"

I had the good grace to look ashamed. Just a little.

"She's not a fan of yours?" asked Cole.

Patrick sighed. "Not as much as she is of you, apparently."

Cole laughed his ass off. He even did that attractively. Then he grabbed a drink off the tray of a passing waiter. "Nor, drink this. Tell me what you think."

"She didn't say you could call her that." More frowning from Patrick. "*I* don't even call her that."

I took a sip. "It's very good quality."

"How can you tell?" asked Cole, one brow raised.

"Because in a vodka, soda, and lime, there's nothing to hide the liquor. If it's crap, you can taste it," I said. "But this is smooth, with just a hint of flavor. I like it."

Patrick stole my drink and took a sip. Apparently we were the kind of couple who shared.

"Did I pass your test?" I asked.

"You did," allowed Cole. "Why don't you dump this fool and we'll blow this joint. I'm not one for marriage, but I think we could have a lot of fun."

"Tempting." I pretended to think it over. "But I only just won over his parents. It would be a shame to undo all of my hard work so soon."

"Isn't Renee terrifying?"

"Yes."

He mock shivered. "Gorgeous, but terrifying. I'll never forget the day she visited the set. Being so afraid and yet turned on at the same time was a complete revelation."

I tried not to laugh at the expression on Patrick's face. It didn't work.

"Stop talking about my mother," said Patrick, his brow furrowed. "And stop fucking hitting on my fiancée."

Cole clapped him on the back. "Glad you could make it, Paddy. It's damn good to see you. And Nor, I'll have my assistant give you my number. Just in case you change your mind."

I gave him a finger wave. "Thanks."

Cole strode off to socialize with his other guests. There had to be a couple of hundred people in attendance. Though most seemed too busy checking out everyone else to actually have a good time. I don't know. There was just a cool-table mean-girl vibe to the room that I hadn't encountered since high school. It can't be easy enjoying a conversation when you're constantly on the lookout for someone more important to talk to. Talk about a daunting level of fakery. And while many people watched us, few approached. No wonder Patrick didn't have many friends, if these were the people he had to choose from.

"Really?" he asked, handing back the drink.

"What?" I took a sip and looked about the room. In one corner a DJ spun some grooves at a volume that still allowed for conversation. The vodka fountain was a neat if somewhat liver-destroying idea. Lord knows how much this had all cost. "This is a very fancy party."

"Yes, it is. He's put a lot of money behind this enterprise. Been working on it for years. Cole's got a good head for business." He gazed down at me. "You let him call you Nor."

"I actually prefer the full Norah."

The frown eased. "Oh. Okay."

"Gran's sister was Nor," I said. "She used to visit when I was little. They'd drink a bottle of wine and complain about men. My mom used to join in before she got sick."

"The men in their lives were that bad?"

"The men in their lives were that gone. Poof! Disappeared," I corrected. Which was incorrect. "So they weren't actually in their lives. I'm confusing the issue. It all goes back to the family curse."

His brows rose. "Hold up. There's a family curse?"

"Yeah."

"How have I not heard about this?"

"I'm telling you now." I took another sip. "So certain members of my family believed they were doomed when it came to love. This belief was based on the following facts. My great-grandfather ran off with an erotic dancer. His brother choked on an appetizer at his own wedding reception. My grandfather died in a car crash not long after my mom was born. Nor got left at the altar. And my own father disappeared as soon as he found out about me. If you wanted to get dramatic, you could also say my mom died of a broken heart. But I think it was mostly the breast cancer."

His gaze softened.

"Hence their belief in a family curse," I concluded.

"But you're not a believer?"

I shook my head. "No. I made bad choices. We've discussed this already."

"Are you really interested in getting Cole's number? I know he was just winding me up in part, but he really seemed to like you."

I said nothing.

"I mean, it's none of my business what you do after—"

"No."

"No? Okay." He gave me side-eye while he waved to a passing waiter to get another drink. This one was much fancier, being a shade of purple with flowers floating on the surface. "What do you think this is?"

I took it and sniffed and sipped. Because I'm classy like that. "I think it's a Prince. Vodka, lemon, sugar, and crème de violette. I worked at a bar a few years back," I explained, in response to his raised eyebrows. "It was popular right after he passed."

"*Purple Rain* was a great album." He downed a mouthful. "A bit more floral than I usually like."

Two women approached. Both beautiful and thin, as per the usual in this town. And their two sets of beady little eyes were most definitely all over my fake better half.

Before they could open their mouths, Patrick slid an arm around my shoulders and said, "This is my fiancée, Norah."

The women exchanged glances, gave us lame smiles, and hastily backed away.

"I've never been used as a dating defense system before," I said.

Patrick took another sip of the drink. "Where were we? Oh, yeah. You were going to explain why you're passing on getting Cole's number."

"No, I wasn't."

"Had your fill of Hollywood types?" he asked, persevering.

"You're not going to let this go, are you?"

He did a one-shoulder shrug. A dismissive sort of gesture. "Just curious."

"Patrick, I'm here with you. It would be rude as hell to get another man's number. My grandmother would be appalled."

His smile was small, but it was there. What a win. "I think I'm going to like your Gran."

"We'll see how you feel when you meet her," I said. "How did your audition go today?"

The smile disappeared and he paused for a moment, choosing his words with care. "I think it went well. It can be hard to tell. The director seemed enthusiastic about the idea of working with me."

"Good."

"The online hate seems to have died down," he said. "Ticket sales are back up. It's not good that I got dropped from that other movie. Once one producer thinks you're tainted goods, they can all just follow suit. But hopefully these new people don't see me as such a risk anymore."

"What's the next step with the audition?"

"I wait to hear if it's a yes or a call-back or a no."

"I'll keep my fingers crossed for the first one," I said.

"Yeah. Me too."

"Guess we better see to our schmoozing duties." I looked about the room. "Who else would you like to talk to?"

The frown returned. "Honestly? No one. We're here entirely as a favor to Cole. I suppose there's probably a couple of people I should talk to, but . . ."

Which was when it happened. Liv Anders swept in on the

arm of her husband. Holy shit. She was everything she seemed in the movies and more. Tall and slender and perfect in every way. Her red body-con dress and towering stiletto heels were amazing and the silken curtain of her long hair was breathtaking. Grant wasn't bad either—all tall, dark, and handsome. No wonder they were *the* power couple.

And this was not good. Lots of sets of eyes seemed to suddenly be on us. Way more than those who'd taken an interest before. Dammit.

I took a step closer to Patrick, sliding my hand up his chest. The man's eyebrows bunched up as he gazed down at me. Like he wasn't quite sure what I was up to. Then he slid an arm around my waist, drew me in closer against his body, and asked in a low voice, "Is it a photographer?"

"No," I whispered. "Don't look, but Liv and Grant just walked in. We've got a lot of attention on us right now."

"Fuck."

"It's alright."

His muscles tensed beneath the palm of my hand. His whole body was strung out and solid. So many different emotions seemed to pass through his eyes. Hurt, anger, and regret. Guess this was the first time he'd been in the same room as her since it all happened. Without a doubt, whatever happened between him and Liv mattered. What a mess. What would be in his eyes if he looked at her? I don't think I really wanted to know. My position by his side might be temporary, but on some level it would hurt. Silly me.

"They were supposed to be in New York," he said. "Angie checked."

"Guess we were bound to run into them at some point," I said. "How do you want to handle this?"

"Whatever we do, people are going to talk."

"Yeah."

"Less chance of a scene if we leave now, though."

"Okay. Should we say good night to Cole?"

"No. He'll understand." Patrick leaned down, getting close. Close enough that the rest of the world kind of blurred. It was a magic trick of his, to making everything but him disappear. And I don't doubt it looked intimate and romantic to those watching. "Let's get the hell out of here."

Chapter Eight

Out in the cool night air, the flashes of the paparazzi's cameras were blinding as Patrick helped me into his Porsche 911. Good thing I'd worn pants. The low-slung beast of a sports car was something else. We drove in silence. No music or anything. Just the faint hum of the road and the wind and the world we were passing by. It was only when we were heading back into the hills that he started to speak. "They'd been separated for months."

"Liv and Grant?" I asked, tone cautious.

A brief nod from him.

"You don't have to tell me if you don't want to."

"I know." He cleared his throat. "I want to tell you. I feel like I should explain."

"Okay."

"They hadn't made an announcement or anything, but they'd been living apart for a while, were planning on getting divorced. They'd still appear at things together now and then, but . . ."

I shifted in my seat so I could watch him better. "You thought they were over."

"Yeah. She said she was ready to move on and I believed her."

I just waited.

"Grant and I were friends. We'd known each other for years.

Worked together a couple of times," he said. "But we'd hung out together off set as well. He has a place in Kauai I'd visited."

"Right."

"I talked to him and he agreed that they were over, but he obviously felt differently about things later. The truth is, I shouldn't have gone near her. No excuses. I knew I shouldn't and I did it anyway. Even if you do break up with someone, the last damn person you want to see them with is a friend. Someone you're supposed to be able to trust." He angrily thumped the steering wheel with the palm of his hand. "Sorry. Sorry. I just . . ."

"Should I drive?"

"No. It's okay." He sighed. "You're safe with me, I promise."

I nodded, trying to relax.

"Liv and I had always had chemistry, but I should have known better."

"Did you have feelings for her?" I asked.

His brows rose. "I thought I did. Now I'm not so sure. It's all been buried by what came after."

"Consequences suck."

"This is true."

"On the other hand, you do seem to have saved their relationship."

His laughter was wholly devoid of any happiness. "And caused my own career to tank."

"That's temporary."

"I wish she'd have picked up the phone and told me what the hell was really going on. Having to find out they were back together through the fucking media . . ."

"That must have hurt."

"I deserved what happened," he said.

I relaxed my cheek against the cool leather of the car seat, watching him. The unhappy furrows in his brow and tense line of his lips. He was one pissed off male with a whole lot of emotional baggage. Guess sort of breaking the bro code would do that to you.

"It's not like there haven't always been plenty of women around, you know?" he asked, his fingers tightening on the wheel. "I've never had to work too hard for sex."

"No, I'd imagine not."

"I wanted her and I could finally have her and I didn't stop and think beyond that. It was stupid and selfish and I shouldn't have done it."

I said nothing.

"Well?" he asked, darting me a glance.

"Well, what?"

"Aren't you going to say something? Pass judgment?"

"What would be the point?" I asked. "You already know you made a mistake. Next time, if a situation like this ever comes up again, you'll handle things differently. Wait longer or not go there or something."

Another glance from him.

"So forgive yourself, move on, and do better."

He grunted. Men were so emotionally awkward. Honestly.

He flipped on the indicator as we turned into the home stretch. One brave paparazzo stood waiting by the fence as the front gate started to open, along with a woman standing back in the shadows. A fan, I guess. And we definitely also had one photographer who'd followed us from the party on the motorcycle behind. What a crazy job, being a professional stalker. As we slowed down, waiting for the gate to fully open, a camera was shoved up against the window. We both stared straight ahead. Weird how fast you could get used to something. It wasn't like it mattered what we did, though. The shots would run with the usual bullshit headlines. The car moved forward and we headed toward the house, leaving the paparazzi behind. Thank God.

We pulled into the garage beside the house and the engine went quiet. The whole world went quiet, actually. One lone light shone by the front doors. Everything was shadows and darkness.

"You feel like doing something?" he asked.

"Like what?"

"I don't know. Watch a movie or something?" He hesitated, his jaw working. "You don't have to. I mean . . . it's not part of your job description to keep me company when we're not at functions."

"Do I get to choose the movie?"

There was a teasing light in his eyes "Are you any good at choosing movies?"

"Guess you're about to find out."

"Not funny," he grouched.

"I didn't put this on. It was just there when I turned on the TV."

We'd settled into the home theater with a couple bottles of beer and good intentions. So of course, Patrick's naked body appeared on screen the minute I managed to turn it on. And it was not a small screen, either.

"Oh, that's right," he said. "They sent a new director's cut over for me to check out a while back. I watched a bit in fast forward before giving up on it."

"You don't normally watch your own movies?"

"No." He shook his head. "I had a huge pimple on my left butt cheek. You can just make it out."

I tilted my head. "I see."

"Those lights were hot as hell. I kept sweating off the makeup and they kept having to touch it up."

"They have butt makeup?" I asked.

"Body makeup," he corrected with a small smile. They were definitely happening more often. It was a beautiful thing to see.

The room had graphite-colored walls and six matching comfy chairs. Some black-and-white photography hung on the walls and a red popcorn machine took pride of place over by a bar fridge full of booze. I loved this house. Honestly. The place was just so cool. It had everything you could need without tipping over into sprawling mansion territory. It still felt like a home. Even if Patrick didn't spend much time here usually.

"What's it like filming a sex scene?" I asked, helping myself to the bowl of popcorn on the little table between us.

On screen, he and a beauty rolled around on an endless bed. Music swelled and lighting dimmed and it was all quite horny, honestly.

"Horrible." He held his hand out for the remote and I passed it over, since I couldn't figure out how to work the stupid thing anyway. A moment later, an array of movie titles appeared on screen. "They have a closed set and limit the number of people there, but it's still pretty fucking mortifying. Being naked apart from a cock sock in front of a bunch of people."

"I saw tongue," I said. "That's actual French kissing. I thought you stage kissed like you did to me the other night at the restaurant."

"Depends."

"On what?"

"What the actors have agreed to. What the director wants. What the story needs," he said. "Pick a film."

I turned back to the screen. "How about *When Harry Met Sally?*"

He ignored me and said, "Hey, there's *Taxi Driver*. Have you ever watched that?"

I wrinkled my nose. "Ooh, *Lord of the Rings?*"

"*Apocalypse Now* is great. A real classic."

"*Casablanca?*" I counter offered. "It's a classic too."

"Sure."

Phew. Look at us compromising. He could save his angry man films for another time. We both watched in silence for a while, just chilling after the stressful event earlier.

"I wish I were as cool as Rick," I said.

"No one will ever be as cool as Rick. Bogie was something else." He stared at the screen, tossing popcorn into his mouth every now and then. And he almost always caught it. The big show-off. "Would you abandon me for the leader of the Resistance and leave me waiting like a loser on a train platform in Paris?"

"If we were really involved and somehow able to time travel and insert ourselves into movies?"

"Right," he said.

I thought it over. "I'd be on the train platform."

"You're a romantic."

"Not necessarily. I mean, Bogie would be better in bed than the other guy. And he genuinely loves her."

"You don't think the other guy loves her?"

"Not in the same way. Not with the same passion."

He sighed. "But the other guy's richer."

"That's not why Ilsa goes to him. She owes it to him, or thinks she does. Anyway, that's got to be such a stressful situation, marrying for money."

"How so?"

"Well, you have an amazing wardrobe and a fancy car and everything," I said. "Live in a mansion and fly all over the world doing whatever you want whenever you want. It's fun for a while, right? But eventually you're going to get bored. Your chosen partner isn't your soul mate and your sex life is probably shit. Let's be honest. So you're bound to go looking for more. And cheating has got to be stressful as all hell."

He just blinked. "Please explain."

"Think about it: having to sneak around, lying all the time, remembering who you told what lie to." I winced. "So stressful. The next thing you know, you're having to up your Botox appointments because your life of duplicity is running you ragged and you're getting worry lines."

"I still think you're a romantic."

"Or I could just be lazy, disorganized, and scared of needles."

"Most of the people in this town would go with the rich guy."

"Not necessarily," I said. "Good dick attached to a decent man is its own reward."

He laughed.

"The other problem with that guy is that he has this calling. This big important mission," I said. "She will never get to come first with him. She will never be his priority."

"And that's important?"

"It's everything." I took a deep breath and put my thoughts in order. "As nice as he is, who wants to be with someone who treats you like an afterthought? If they're not your best friend, if you can't imagine having crap to say to them every day for the rest of your life, if you're not willing to work your ass off to stay together, then what the heck are you doing?"

Nothing from him.

"You don't have to be in a relationship. Being alone is a totally viable decision. And even if you are in a relationship, you both need to have your own life and interests. But don't you get the feeling with him that his heart has already been given?"

"You have a point," he said. "Rick would never let anyone put Ilsa in a corner."

"You're mixing your movie metaphors, but I'll allow it this once."

He smiled. And I could have sworn it was slightly bigger again than the ones previous. Amazing. "Thanks for not leaving me waiting on a train platform like a loser."

"You're welcome, Patrick."

In terms of relationship milestones, we were certainly hitting them quickly. The next day we very bravely visited my Gran. Brave, at least, on my part. I learned a long time ago not to take a boyfriend anywhere near the woman. Patrick, however, was clueless. And he wanted to meet her, so he only had himself to blame.

"My granddaughter tells me you're famous."

Patrick sat on the chair beside me with a small polite smile on his face. He really was trying, bless him. But Gran refused to be charmed. She sat in her wheelchair, short silver hair immaculate and wearing a new white blouse. Even her mother's pearls had made a rare appearance. We'd found a spot out in the garden since it was such a nice day. However, the scent of jasmine on the cool late spring breeze failed to improve her mood.

"It's part of the job," he said.

She studied his handsome face over the top of her glasses. "And you've been quite the playboy apparently."

My mouth fell open. "Just going straight for the throat, huh?"

Gran barely spared me a glance. "This is between Patrick and me. Why don't you go for a walk, Norah?"

"It's fine." He lay a comforting hand on my knee. "Of course your grandmother has questions. Why don't you go grab a coffee or something?"

"Oh, I'm not going anywhere," I said.

Gran clicked her tongue. "Fine. But be quiet."

Before I could make a smart-ass reply, something super mature along the lines of "you're not the boss of me," Patrick squeezed my knee. Then he rubbed his thumb in small, soothing circles. Fine. Whatever. I could keep my mouth shut. For now.

"You two haven't known each other for very long," she said.

Patrick nodded. "That's true, ma'am. But your granddaughter is the best thing in my life right now. I'd be a fool to let her go."

"Hmm." She studied him over the top of her glasses. "According to the internet, you're an accomplished actor, have a net worth of ninety million, and an unfortunate habit of sleeping with other men's wives."

My mouth opened and his hand squeezed again. For fuck's sake.

"That was a mistake," he said calmly. "It happened once. It will not happen again."

"How can you be sure?"

"Because I would never hurt or embarrass Norah that way."

Gran raised her chin. "Pretty words, Patrick. You might mean them now, the early days of love are always passionate and exciting, but it's the long term I'm interested in."

"Ma'am?"

"Do you actually know the kind of person my granddaughter is?" she asked, drawing herself up tall. "When I had my accident and damaged my back, she dropped out of college and came home to look after me. All without being asked. There was no hesitation, no recriminations. Most of my money had gone toward paying off her mother's medical bills. So Norah found a job. When that wasn't enough, she found a second job. It soon became obvious that I'd need an assisted living situation. After all, she couldn't work two jobs and look after me. The sale of my house covered some of the costs and Norah has been paying the rest ever since. That is the sort of person my granddaughter is. Giving and kind and selfless . . . even if she does have a smart mouth."

Patrick looked at me with something close to awe. Which was both crazy and unnecessary.

"Are you done?" I asked.

"I knew your granddaughter was special," said Patrick, completely ignoring me. "Now I know how special."

I looked to heaven. This wasn't wildly uncomfortable at all. "You looked after me when Mom died. It was my turn to look after you. That's all."

Gran looked at me.

"Can we please play a game of Scrabble and call it a day?" I asked. "I'll even let you win this time."

Gran sniffed. "As if you've ever managed to beat me."

His hand continued to curve around my knee in an oddly proprietary manner.

"Patrick, you will treat her like the priceless jewel she is," ordered Gran. "Am I understood?"

"Yes, ma'am."

And I didn't like this. I didn't like that one day she would feel let down by Patrick because we would inevitably be staging a breakup. But there wasn't a hell of a lot I could do about it right there and then. Not without breaking my contractual obligations. The same ones that funded her new nursing home.

"You're setting his expectations way too high." I pushed my sunglasses up on top of my head and discreetly wiped away a tear. Probably just allergies.

Gran barked out a laugh. "Please. He knew enough to grope your leg every time you were about to open your mouth and say something unfortunate."

Patrick bit back a smile.

"Yeah, well, I don't require a pedestal," I said. "Mostly my hobbies include enjoying having one drink too many and dancing in the living room in my underwear."

"I wouldn't mind seeing that," said Patrick.

"You always did like doing that." Gran smiled, easing up for the first time since she started grilling Patrick. "The only difference being that when you were little, the drink was a bottle of milk and you were wearing a diaper. Toni Braxton was a particular favorite. Every time she came on the radio you'd get all excited. I'll show you some photos sometime if you like, Patrick."

"Yes, please," he said.

I grabbed the arms of my chair. "Not a chance. He does not need to see my baby photos."

"I absolutely need to see them. The sooner the better."

"What was this story today about you two having a fight on your way home from a party last night?" asked Gran all casual like.

I wrinkled my nose. "Huh?"

"Exactly that, ma'am," said Patrick. "A story. Something they made up to go with the photos they took of us. Nothing more."

Gran's brows rose in surprise. Guess it's one thing to know the gossip sites were in the habit of telling lies and another to see it in action. To have it confirmed.

"So when can I see these photos?" asked Patrick.

Seldom did I manage to rise above petty taunting and keep my mouth shut. This was one of those rare times. So instead, I turned to look out at the garden. A tall Black gentleman was completing yet another lap of the garden. What was interesting was how his gaze was so frequently turned our way. "Who's the old guy who keeps shuffling past giving you heated looks?"

"My new boyfriend, Harold." Gran preened. "I rather like this nursing home. Made a small fortune the first week pretending I was bad at cards."

"You shark."

"Hustler, thank you," she said primly. "It's more ladylike."

Patrick snorted.

More people than just Harold were watching us. As always, going anywhere with Patrick was an adventure. Everyone made eyes at him. From the receptionist who wanted to bang him to the janitor who wanted to be him. I couldn't imagine what it would be like to walk through the world getting all this attention all of the time. Mostly he seemed not to notice.

"You told him about the family curse?" asked Gran.

"There is no family curse," I said.

Patrick patted my knee. "I'm willing to take my chances, ma'am."

"Hmm. Give me strength," she said. "Mildred and Katherine are hiding behind that tree over there staring at us."

"Really?" I frowned.

"They're fans of his." She poked a finger at Patrick. "You should have heard them at the ice cream social yesterday. Wouldn't shut up about him."

"Huh. You appeal to all ages."

"My demographics are good," he confirmed.

"Katherine's got her damn camera out." Gran cursed beneath

her breath. "Patrick, give me a roguish smile and then laugh like I just said something hilarious."

It was amazing. As directed, he snapped straight into character. A devil-may-care grin stretched his mouth wide, white teeth flashing, then a booming laugh echoed up from deep in his belly. He smacked a hand against his muscular thigh and everything. But that smile . . . holy shit. My heart basically gave up and just handed itself over. Same went for my sex. Patrick Walsh up close letting loose the full force of his good looks and charisma was nothing short of dazzling.

All I could do was stare. Here I'd been working for ages on trying to coax anything so much as a grin and Gran just got the whole show. It was fake, of course, but then that was a running theme in my life right now.

"Well done," said Gran, side-eyeing our spies. "Right. I have quilting circle shortly, so you'll have to go. It's been a nice visit. Very constructive. Let's do it again soon."

"You give your blessing, then?" asked Patrick, now back to his normal subdued setting.

Gran gave him a long look. "You know, young man, I believe I do. But don't let it go to your head. I'll be watching you."

"Yes, ma'am."

"And there will be no elopement. I expect to be at the wedding."

"Yes, ma'am."

"Good boy," she said with a smile.

When I tried to help push her chair, she brushed me off and made her own way along the path. Leaving behind my slightly stunned fake fiancé.

"She likes you," I said. "Thank you for being kind to her and performing when requested."

"My pleasure."

Truth was, he'd been in full fake boyfriend mode. Amusing and adoring and everything you could want. His hand was even back on my knee. Even though we probably no longer needed to be in character. I should remove it, boundaries being both good and wise, but I didn't. Let's not question why.

"We never talked about knees, did we?" he said, now also looking at where his hand lay.

"Guess it's good that we're used to each other now. Makes the touching a bit less weird."

He nodded and sat back in his chair, taking his hand with him. Which was sad, but for the best. "I'm not ashamed to admit I'm slightly afraid of your grandma. She's a hell of a woman."

"I thought you did quite well."

"She and my mom would either get on like a house on fire or actually set the house on fire."

"In all likelihood."

"You'll have to dump me, you know," he said.

"What?"

"When our time is up, it'll have to be you ending it. Publicly, too. It can't be me that's to blame. I can't let down your Gran—I couldn't live with myself."

I thought it over. "Not so sure about that. I'm the one who has to be with Gran for the rest of her life. I think I should get to be in her good graces."

"I don't think you could do anything and not be the light of her life." He turned in his chair to better face me. His gaze was curious. "Were you ever going to tell me about her accident being the reason for you dropping out of college and working all those jobs?"

"I don't know. It's not really something I tend to talk about."

For a moment, he said nothing. Then he held out his hand, little finger extended. "Pinky swear."

"To what?"

"Total honesty," he said. "With the caveat that if we don't want to talk about something, fair enough. But what we do say we mean."

I wrapped my pinky finger around his with a smile. "I can agree to that. But it's not like I lied."

"Never said you lied. But I think it's a good rule just the same."

"Okay."

While his smile wasn't the blindingly brilliant one he'd performed for Gran, it was real and warm and all for me. It was way better.

Chapter Nine

"WE MET AT THE RESTAURANT AND OUR FIRST date was here at my house," said Patrick. "We've been friends for a while and just got serious recently."

I fake smiled my little heart out. "It's been an exciting time and I couldn't be happier."

We sat gathered on the couch, preparing for an interview. Our first ever. God help us. While Patrick was known for keeping his private life private, it had been agreed that his public persona would benefit from an exclusive chat with the reigning queen of daytime TV. And if she surprised us with any trick questions we were officially screwed. While the interview would take place to-morrow, today was prep and a photo shoot for their online mag-azine. Busy as all heck.

Yesterday had been wonderful. Gran had been charmed and Patrick and I felt like a team. Like we were friends working to-gether as a cohesive unit. Today, however, not so much. The first hint was when he took the seat farthest from me, at the opposite end of the couch. Like I had cooties or girl germs or something. Next, he'd grunted at me when I said good morning. Always a delightful way to be greeted. I kind of wanted to throw some-thing at him.

"Making her dinner should score well with women," reported Angie, tapping a stylus against her leg. "What was your first impression of Norah?"

Patrick licked his lips. "She seemed nice."

I snorted.

"Jesus Christ, Paddy," moaned Mei.

"That's the best you've got?" Angie frowned. "Really?"

"She was pretty, too," he added, earning a C for effort.

I crossed my legs, settling in for the long haul. "You couldn't even throw a *very* in there?"

He ignored my comment and rubbed at his temples like he had a headache. Poor baby.

God only knows what he was doing last night. He'd stumbled in sometime after four in the morning, making enough noise to wake me. And I did not leave my room to help him, because I'd dealt with enough drunken idiots while working in bars.

"Work on it," ordered Angie.

Patrick just grunted. Again.

"Norah, what was your first impression of Patrick?" asked Angie in a brisk tone.

"I thought he was ridiculously handsome," I said, staring deeply into his eyes because that's what it said to do in the lover's body language article I read. No way was I going to screw this up and have Gran thrown out of her new digs. "Of course I did. But the more we got to talking, the more I fell for that beautiful deep voice and the way he has of speaking. How he picks his words with care. I could listen to him all day."

If anything, Patrick appeared to be mildly perturbed at both my adoring stare and my speech. But Angie nodded in approval.

"I like it," said Mei. "Shows that you care about who he is as a person and you're not just in it to bang him like a drum."

"Right?" I asked with a grin. "I think it makes me sound deep."

Mei gave me a thumbs-up. "Totally."

This was the great thing about Mei. She made even stressful work things fun. And holy hell, did I need the support of a friend. The thought of setting myself up for another possible public flaying was not fun. We had to get this interview right. The world must believe we were in love. True love.

"Ask me again," said Patrick. "I'm ready now."

"What was your first impression of Norah?" repeated Angie.

It was like he changed before my eyes. One moment he was his usual slightly disgruntled self. And the next he was the romantic hero out of a movie. His gaze warmed and his lips curled upward in a small, secretive smile that seemed to suggest a lot. Most of those suggestions were dirty sex stuff. But there was just the right amount of undying love and devotion thrown in for good measure. My stomach did some weird swooping thing. I couldn't have looked away if I tried. Then he opened his mouth and said, "The minute I saw Norah I just knew."

Angie clapped. "Bravo."

"That was great," said Mei.

"Then why were you sleeping with other women?" I asked, completely raining on their parade.

All eyes turned to me.

"I just mean . . . wouldn't it be safer to say that one day in the not-so-recent past you looked at me and you suddenly knew that I was the one," I said, "as opposed to saying you always knew but kept playing the field because why not?"

"Valid point," said Mei. "Why'd you keep her waiting, Paddy?"

Patrick shifted in his seat, his expression beleaguered. "It wasn't like that."

"Rework the line," ordered Angie, making a note on her tablet.

"Next up. When did you meet each other's families and how did that go?"

"It was actually just recently and I was so nervous," I said, ad-libbing my little heart out. "But his parents are wonderful people. So kind and giving. They really welcomed me to the family."

"Good," said Angie. "The trick here is to answer the question without really giving them any personal information. Or at least, nothing you're not willing to own up to and possibly have thrown back in your face during every slow news cycle forever."

Patrick cleared his throat and said, "Norah's grandmother is a wonderful woman."

We all waited a moment, but he was done. What a champ.

"Would an espresso help with your hangover?" asked Mei.

"No," he said. "Thanks."

"The question is, how much of your background are you willing to discuss, Norah?" asked Angie. "The details of your mother's death and your grandmother having custody are all pretty much a matter of public record. So far, articles about you have concentrated on the waitress-and-the-heartthrob angle. There's been some digging into your past, as expected, but only the basic facts have been presented. Beyond the episode involving the nude photo, of course. Do you want to give them more? It would—"

"No," said Patrick, tone adamant.

"I was asking *her*." Angie pointed a shiny red fingernail in my direction. "Norah's a big girl. She can make her own decisions."

"What did you have in mind?" I asked.

"Let's see . . . there's the trauma of losing your mom at a young age," said Angie.

I winced. "I don't know."

"How growing up in an all-female household, first with a single mother, then with your grandmother, helped to make you a strong, independent woman fit to tame a superstar. We could also touch on your previous bad dating experiences," continued Angie. "How that asshole tried to rip you off, in particular. Those would all help you come across as both sympathetic and relatable."

Patrick's frown amped up to a scowl. "Norah, please say no. This isn't necessary."

"You want to save her from the scrutiny of fans and the media," said Angie. "It's laudable, really. But she's already in the public eye, Patrick. You're too late."

Something shifted in his jaw.

"Just over a month ago you were caught up in a sex scandal with one woman," she said. "Now you're engaged to another. Both of you need to work hard if we're going to sell this. We need to keep our eye on the prize . . . and that is fixing your reputation, Patrick."

"Along with you two having a long and loving committed relationship, right?" Mei raised her chin. "I mean, that goes without saying."

"Right," said Patrick, his voice lacking all credibility.

My fingers twisted in my lap. "Let's just concentrate on getting the facts right for our whirlwind romance first. We can think about the rest later."

My cell buzzed and I picked it up without thinking.

Angie sighed. And while she had a point regarding cell phones distracting people during important meetings, I kind of needed a minute's break. A barrage of new emails and messages had arrived. Nothing new in that. I opened the text and ignored the rest.

"You sent Gran flowers?" I asked, turning to Patrick.

Two small spots of pink blossomed on his cheeks. "Figured I better keep Harold on his toes."

"Thank you."

"Sure," he said, without meeting my eyes.

"I suggested he send some to you as well," said Mei. "But he said you had allergies."

"Allergies?" It wasn't as if I needed flowers, but still. "Right."

"Such a bummer." Mei smiled. "I love getting flowers."

Patrick, meanwhile, seemed mostly miserable, all huddled up down his end of the couch. This was right and just, since he'd vetoed all flowers for me forever. Just joking. Business arrangement. No flowers required. An unnecessary expense.

"Have you done the sensible thing and taken some Advil?" I asked. "Rehydrated with water?"

"I'm fine," he told the ground.

"Oh, really? Because you look like shit."

Patrick's laugh was rough. "Thanks, sunshine."

I just shook my head.

"She's right," said Mei. "And the photographer and his crew will be here soon."

"That's today?" asked Patrick, doing a very convincing portrayal of a deer caught in headlights. A sickly deer who needed a nap and some Hydralyte.

"Yep. What exactly did you do last night, Paddy?" asked Mei with interest. "I'm sensing some tension here."

"I know what you were doing," said Angie. "And you're damn lucky no paparazzi were following you."

Which was when the door to the spare room opened and the tall, lanky man wearing jeans and not a hell of a lot else wandered down the hallway scratching at his flat belly. Lots of tattoos. Longish straight blond hair. I'd been unaware we'd gained another house guest. Let alone one who looked like he'd just stepped out of the pages of Lady Boner Weekly. Which wasn't actually a thing, but probably should be. I mean, he was no Patrick Walsh, but still . . .

"Holy hell," was all he said, voice rough.

"Hi, Jack." Mei waved. "Happy divorce. What is this, the second one?"

"Who's keeping count?" The dude yawned loud and proud. "Coffee?"

"In the kitchen. Help yourself."

"Oh, shit," he said, catching sight of me on the couch. Immediately he came toward me with a hand outstretched. "You must be Norah. Damn good to meet you. Patrick wouldn't shut up about you last night. Cole either, for that matter."

"Is that so?" I asked, bemused.

He took both of my hands, studying the rock on my wedding finger. "I would have bought you a bigger one."

"Fuck off," grumbled Patrick, slumping farther down in his seat.

"Aren't you going to introduce me?" asked Jack, still holding my hands. Which was odd.

Patrick ignored him.

I smiled and slipped my hands out of his hold. "I take it you're Jack?"

"The son of rock legend Angus Gilmour," said Angie, looking down her nose. "Jack is best known for playing lead guitar in his father's band before they had a very public falling out. After which he moved on to working with some of the biggest and best acts in the industry. His hobbies include trashing hotel rooms—"

"That only happened one time," he groaned.

"Riding a motorcycle through the house."

"I was twelve and Dad thought it was funny."

"Right up until he found out you'd ruined his Persian rug."

Jack slumped onto the couch beside me. "Tell me all about yourself, Norah."

"Aren't you even going to say a proper hello?" asked Angie.

"You always were my favorite stepmom, Angie," said Jack. "You know that."

"Mm." Angie blew out a slow breath. "Dating your father was the second worst mistake I ever made. But it was the nineties. Things happened. You, however . . . what the hell did you think you were doing pouring liquor down Patrick's throat and dragging him around strip joints until the small hours of the morning?"

Jack groaned. "It was a burlesque club Cole's thinking of buying. Quite a cool place, actually."

"Huh." And I didn't mean to say that in a judgy tone; it just came out that way. Oops.

"While I'm prepared to admit that the drinking may have gotten ever so slightly out of hand," said Jack, "nothing of interest really happened, I swear."

I opened my mouth. Then I shut it. Because that was the smart thing to do. Also, Patrick was watching me.

Angie, however, did not look impressed. I got to my feet and heading for the kitchen. I grabbed the Advil and a bottle of water and took them to my fake fiancé still slumped on the couch. "Take these. You need them."

"Thanks," he said. Voice about a thousand times deeper and more pain-filled than normal.

"I was really hoping you were getting me coffee," said Jack as I retook my seat.

"Nope," I said. "You can help yourself. Though I am a fan of your father's music."

"He's an asshole, but his music is good." Jack set his ankle on the opposite knee. "Cole said I'd like you. He was right."

And all the while, Patrick watched me with interest. In all honesty, I had no idea what the hell was going on with him. But it didn't matter. This was a business arrangement. Nothing more. So long as I kept telling myself that, everything would be fine.

While I'd been in some strange and ridiculous situations over the course of my life, standing in the middle of the pool in the water in evening wear with Patrick Walsh was a clear winner. The photographer stood at the edge, discussing lighting and whatever with his crew. And we waited. Turned out there was a lot of waiting involved with this sort of thing. Bringing an aesthetic and artistic vision to life did not happen fast. Now and then a stylist would call one of us over to touch up our hair or makeup. But that was about as exciting as it got.

"Are you okay?" asked Patrick, looking particularly dapper with his hair slicked back. That he could go from roadkill to hottie in a couple of hours was completely unfair.

"Just a little cold. And bored."

"Yeah," he said. "Over the years I've gotten used to it. Acting for the screen is one percent magic and ninety-nine percent waiting around, usually on uncomfortable sets in ridiculous costumes."

"I think this qualifies as both."

"Hopefully it won't be much longer."

I forced a smile. A positive attitude in the workplace being a good thing and all. "Is that suit ruined?"

"I'd say so. It's a wool Brioni. Probably cost about fifteen grand."

"Jesus."

"Come here," he said, floating me in his general direction with a hand on my lower back. Then my hands were on his shoulders and his arms were around me, our bodies pressed together. "You're all gooseflesh."

"The water is warm; it's just the breeze."

Movement was limited due to my Hervé Léger black column gown. Sleeveless with a square neckline, it had straps crisscrossing down my back. And the borrowed diamond necklace, earrings, and bracelet set came with its own security guard keeping watch. So much for the whole girl-next-door thing. Despite being drenched, we were high glamour.

"What message do you think they're trying to send with this picture?" I asked.

"I honestly have no idea." His expression grew thoughtful. "That we're in deep water, maybe?"

I smiled. "How's your hangover?"

His smile was sheepish. "I've been better. The Advil helped, thanks."

"Sure."

One of his hands rested low on my back above the curve of my ass while the other rubbed at my bare arm, trying to warm me up. If I had to be stuck in a pool wearing high fashion, then at least I had decent company. Now that he wasn't ignoring me.

"About last night," he started, stopping to take a breath. "There's something I need to tell you, just in case it comes up in the future."

"Okay."

"One of the dancers sat on my lap to take a selfie. I, ah . . . I moved her as soon as I realized. But I was pretty drunk. It took me a minute to figure out what was going on."

"Right," I said, keeping my voice quiet just in case.

"Are you mad?"

"About that? No."

"But if that picture gets out it could embarrass you."

"It would certainly undo our good work."

He blinked. His wet eyelashes were so dark and long. "You should be mad at me."

"Is that why you were avoiding me to the best of your abilities this morning?"

And there was that deer-caught-in-the-headlights expression again.

"You know, when you were evading all eye contact and grunting at me instead of talking half the damn time."

"I wasn't feeling the best," he said, tone distinctly disgruntled. Like a spoiled child. "Maybe you could cut me some slack."

"Try again, Paddy."

He sighed. "Shit. I was doing that, wasn't I?"

"Yeah." I nodded. "You really were. It seems to be a habit with you when things aren't going well. Which is disappointing, because I thought we were friends."

He just looked at me.

"But at the end of the day, this is a business arrangement. You didn't do anything that would constitute breaking the contract and I am just an employee. So I don't really have the right to be angry at you." Despite my fine words, I was kind of fucking furious. Just when I thought we had agreed to be friends he reverted to sullen and silent. I'd been doing my best to hide it and deny it, but oh well. These things were bound to come out in passive-aggressive rants now and then given I was only human. "Though I can't help but notice that's a thing for you, retreating back into your shell when something goes wrong. But yeah . . . you're my boss and this is none of my business. I'm going to stop talking now."

His forehead furrowed. "No, hang on."

"What?" I said, tone sharper than I'd intended.

"We *are* friends. I fucked up. Be mad at me."

"Would that make you feel better?" I asked, tipping my chin.

"I think so. Yes."

My laughter sounded brittle to my own ears. "Fine. Whatever. Mostly I'm just pissed that you avoided me instead of talking to me about it. I thought we were past that."

"I did upset you," he said, like it was a revelation. Men could be such idiots.

"Yeah. I guess you did."

His fingers moved against my skin all agitated like. As if he was worried I'd make a run for it. Or a swim. Then he made a low growling noise. "I'm sorry, Norah. You're right, I shouldn't have behaved that way this morning. Do you forgive me?"

Something in me eased at the words. "I suppose so."

"Friends?" he asked.

"Yes."

For a moment we were quiet, letting the pool water lap gentle waves at us in the wind. It was oddly peaceful.

"But you're not worried about the girl sitting on my lap?" he asked, out of nowhere.

"Wait. Are you asking if I'm jealous?" I asked, keeping my voice low so we wouldn't be overheard.

He froze. "No. No. Of course not."

"I didn't think so." I wound my arms around his neck. To help with my balance in the water. No other reason. It was nice to know I wasn't the only one who found this situation a little confusing now and then. Emotions were complicated things. But it was good and right that we were friends.

"Are you two finished fighting?" called out Mei from where

she was working on her tablet perched on a sun lounge. "Because this is getting awkward."

Sure enough, all eyes were on us. We had quite the audience, including the stylist, makeup and hair artists, and a collection of various assistants. Even the security guard seemed interested in our tiff.

"Time to kiss and make up," said Mei.

"Guess it's what a real couple would do," he whispered, staring into my eyes in a disturbingly intense fashion. Just friends. But also a very good actor. Little wonder my heart got confused from time to time.

The photographer picked up his camera and started clicking.

"We better make it look good," I whispered.

"Right." He frowned. "How good, exactly?"

I gave a little shrug. "I don't know. Surprise me. And stop frowning. What was it you said before? About kissing if the story needs it?"

His hands tightened on me, nose brushing mine all gentle like, his breath warm on my lips. This wasn't anything like our first kiss at the restaurant. It made my nerves jangle in a whole different way. As in a would-he-or-wouldn't-he type of situation. Now I knew he would, and the knowledge was one part thrilling and two parts terrifying.

First he executed another perfect stage kiss. A sweet pressing of his lips against mine. One, two, three kisses. Each being a little longer and more devastating than the last. A hand pressed against my lower spine still, the other curling around the back of my neck. All in all, there wasn't one iota of space left between us. Neither above water nor below. And the people watching, the awareness that we had an audience, disappeared the first time the tip of his tongue brushed against my lower lip. Asking a question. Delivering an invitation. That teasing tongue sent electricity straight up my spine.

He moved back an inch, gaze on my face.

I nodded. A bare tip of the chin.

Then Patrick angled his face and I opened my mouth and it was so good. All-consuming amazing. The sweep of his tongue into my mouth and the confidence of the man. He was sensual and forceful and knew exactly what he was doing. How he traced my teeth before returning to rub his tongue against my own. The way his fingers rubbed at the back of my neck, alternately holding me in place and urging me on. I'd have climbed the man if my tight dress allowed it. Mostly he tasted of coffee and man. A potent combination if ever there was one. But the best thing, the most astonishing part, was the noise of hunger and need he made in the back of his throat. A sound I'd treasure to my dying day. If I wasn't mistaken, he was also hardening against my belly. Just from a sort-of-fake kiss.

Everyone suddenly broke out into applause. Heat crept up my neck as Patrick and I broke apart. Lord only knew the state of my lipstick, because he was now wearing a not-so-small amount. Patrick and I stared at each other, panting. Talk about throwing yourself into a role; method kissing was no joke.

"There's the money," announced the photographer, clicking through the shots on the small screen of his camera. "We're done here."

Now would have been the time to make a joke. To say something to alleviate the weird sexual tension. Except all of my words were gone.

Patrick gripped my hips and gently set me aside with a wary glance. "O-okay."

Chapter Ten

BLISSFUL QUIET FILLED THE HOUSE AFTER ALL THE people coming and going all day. Mei had left, Patrick had disappeared to the gym, and our houseguest Jack was who knows where. After a long hot shower and donning a woolen hoodie and designer sweatpants (bet they were called loungewear) I found in my wardrobe, I'd finally managed to warm up. And get over that kiss. We'd pretended to kiss before, so it was really no big deal. It just felt like it was, for some damn reason.

"Hi," said the stranger standing in the living room, holding a butcher's knife.

I stopped dead.

"Is Patrick around?" she asked, all casual like.

"Ah, no."

"Oh." Her shoulders drooped in disappointment. "He's hardly ever here."

"He gets busy," I mumbled, gaze glued to the knife.

"I know. I've written to him so many times. Sent him messages. But his career has to come first."

I nodded as my whole body started trembling.

"You might as well take a seat." She gestured to the couch with the weapon. "We'll wait for him."

"Sure." And no fucking way was I getting any closer to her and that blade. "W-what's your name?"

The woman was in her early twenties, I'd guess. Dressed in yoga pants, a tank top, and denim jacket. Her dark hair had been cut short and her tennis shoes were dirty. Nothing out of the ordinary. Just someone you'd pass in the street, give or take the knife.

"Beth," she said. "I'm surprised he hasn't told you about me."

"He probably did and I forgot." I'd left my cell in my room. My brain scrambled for something to say, the right thing to say. But panic held me in a tight grip. "I, ah . . ."

"Sit, Norah," she said, tone impatient this time. "We should talk this out. I mean, you're going to have to leave. I can't have you staying here with him, getting in the way."

"Okay, I see that. I see that now."

Her tight expression relaxed into a small smile. "It's good that you understand. There's no need for this to get ugly. But Patrick and I will need to be alone. We're meant to be together, you know?"

"Absolutely."

"I feel kind of bad that he used you like this. You seem nice," she said. "But you know what men are like . . ."

Teeth clenched tight, I nodded.

"Now that Patrick and I are together, he won't need to go looking elsewhere. I'll take care of everything he needs." Her jaw firmed. "Why aren't you sitting? I told you to sit."

"Right. Sorry," I said. Then I bolted.

Her pounding footsteps were right behind me. I raced for my bedroom and reached for the door, throwing my whole body against the hard wood. Her fingers curled around the edge, trying to stop it from closing. But fuck her. Her enraged scream of pain filled the house as I slammed the door shut, again and again, until she let go. I flicked the lock closed, but who knew if it would hold. I had to be fast. Had to take the chance and grab my cell. Blood pounded behind my ears as I ran for the bedside table, grabbed my cell, and ran back to the door. The door shook with the force of her banging. A red mess was splattered around one section of the door. Some scrapings of skin. Holy hell. I kind of wanted to scream back at her, but couldn't find the air. Every ounce of strength went into bolstering up the door. Because if she got in here, I'm pretty sure I was dead.

"You cunt!" she yelled. "You fucked up my fingers. Patrick is going to be furious at you for hurting me. Get out here!"

Hand shaking, body propped against the door to help keep it closed, I dialed nine-one-one.

"Apparently she climbed the fence and gained access through an open door," said the police detective.

"We keep the doors open to let the air in." I sat huddled on the couch, a glass of whiskey in my hands.

While his eyes said "you rich idiots," the detective just nodded. At least another six officers were hanging around. No idea who they were or what they were doing.

What a fucking day.

"Norah!" yelled Patrick, coming through the front door.

And while it would have been neither cool nor brave, I almost fell off the couch at the sound of his voice. Relief poured through me from head to toe. Then his arms were around me good and tight and I'd never been so grateful for a damp and smelly sweat-covered hug in my entire life. Which would explain why I promptly burst into tears.

"Do all these people need to be here?" asked another voice. Jack, as far as I could tell.

The detective umm'd and ahh'd before ordering some of the people out. Thank goodness for that. All of the staring and snooping just made things a hundred times worse.

"Are you hurt?" Patrick's hands ran over me. I flinched when he pressed on my upper arm and he frowned. "You need a doctor."

"It's just bruising."

"Norah—"

"I'm fine."

He swore and growled, but I remained unmoved. Right up until he picked me up and moved me onto his lap. He was so warm and solid. All of the comfort I needed.

"Where were you?" I ever so slightly whined.

"We went for a jog up in the canyon and my cell was on silent. I'm sorry. It took me a while to see your messages."

And while this was a plausible and even reasonable excuse, now that he was here, I had officially removed my big-girl panties for the rest of the day. Let him deal with this mess. And by this mess, I meant me.

When I blew my nose on his tee he did one better, taking it off and handing it to me. There I sat in his lap, clutching his gross, sweaty item of clothing and hiding my face in his neck. All the while, the crazy woman's screams echoed inside my brain. Because she had not shut up for a minute. Not even when the police arrived. Patrick loved her. I was trying to come between them. She was going to cut out my heart Snow White style. On and on it went. And the scent of blood from her battered fingers and the scratching of the knife against the bedroom door wouldn't get out of my head.

Jack fetched Patrick a fresh tee and me a box of Kleenex

and bottle of water. The detective questioned Patrick about his fan mail and messages and so on. A quick search of his email revealed that Beth Whitmore had been obsessed with him for at least the last eighteen months. Believed him to be in love with her. A disorder known as erotomania was briefly mentioned. Since Patrick had been busy and out of the country for the bulk of the time, this was one of the first opportunities she'd had to stalk him face to face. The woman had not hesitated.

Next, Patrick made a quick call to a security firm. Still with one strong arm wrapped around me. Photos were taken and the knife was bagged and carried away. I have no idea what else the police did before they left. They talked about the gathering flock of paparazzi at the gate, but I didn't have the energy to follow along. Angie called, and she and Patrick came up with a short statement to release to the press, and that was that.

When my brain finally calmed down and my heart rate seemed mostly back to normal, I finished off the last of my scotch and slowly pulled myself together. Being scared in the place that was supposed to be my home for the next while annoyed the absolute crap out of me. How dare this woman mess with my peace of mind? My sense of security. But she hadn't gotten her hands on me. I was alright. Therefore, as a grown and capable adult, I should probably stop clinging to Patrick like he was my safety blanket.

"Hey," he said, voice gentle. Though there was an odd note of tension in it. Guess he'd gotten a shock from all of this too.

"Hey."

"What do you need? What can I do for you?"

I sighed and climbed off his lap, sliding onto the couch beside him. "I'm okay, Patrick."

Jack sat down on the far end of the couch with his own drink in hand. He seemed a little shaken too, actually.

"Can we please revisit the doctor idea?" asked Patrick.

I pulled off my hoodie to reveal the tank top beneath and inspected my arm. Black and blue blossomed beneath the skin. "Just bruised from holding the door closed."

Jack swore and reached for his cell. "The cops will want pictures."

I held still as he snapped a series of photos.

"Are you hurt anywhere else?" he asked.

"No."

"The alarm wasn't on because people had been coming and going all day with the photo shoot," said Patrick. "We need to be more careful. This cannot happen again. You cannot be in danger because of me."

I just nodded.

"Norah, are you hungry or thirsty or anything?" asked Jack.

"No, thanks." I slowly got to my feet. While no longer shaking, everything still felt off. Weak in a way. Guess it was all of the adrenaline now dissipating. "Think I'll go to bed. I want to lie down for a bit."

"Good idea," said Patrick, picking me up. And hell, he could cart me around like a baby if it made him happy. Today at least. Down the hallway we went, straight past my room and into his. There he deposited me carefully on the bed.

"I can stay in my own room."

"Do you really want to?" he asked.

The same room where she'd cornered me and promised to carve out my heart. Maybe not. I settled in, stuffing a pillow under my head, crawling beneath the blankets. Half hidden beneath good-quality linens was a wonderful place to be when things got rough.

"That's what I thought."

"Jack's still here," I said. "He thinks we're together. I should probably sleep in here anyway."

"Actually, he knows." Patrick stood at the end of the big bed with his arms crossed. "So does Cole. I told them when we were out last night."

"You did?"

"Yeah. I don't know, I just . . . lying to them didn't sit right with me." He stared off at nothing for a moment. "Cole asked me again to pass on his number."

"Oh, really?"

"Yeah. He wouldn't shut up about you. I tried to hit him, but I was drunk so I missed."

"Probably for the best." I smiled. "He only does it to annoy you."

"Hmm."

I yawned, my jaw cracking. It was barely dark outside. "What a day."

"I'm so fucking sorry, Norah." His forehead furrowed. "This should never have happened."

"Who could have imagined being your girlfriend would be quite this exciting?" The push and pull of fear and exhaustion sucked. I didn't know which way was up and which was down. "I need to call Gran. God only knows what the new reports are saying."

"I'll do it. You rest."

What a good idea. "I'm just going to close my eyes for a minute."

"Okay," said Patrick softly.

"You'll be here, right?"

"I'm not going anywhere." To further demonstrate the point, he took a seat on one of the couches in his bedroom's sitting area and pulled out his cell.

And that was the last thing I knew for hours.

"Hey, Norah. It's okay."

But it wasn't okay. That much I definitely knew. So I kicked and struggled against the hands trying to hold me. Someone grunted in pain and a low light suddenly flooded the room.

I pushed my hair out of my eyes and blinked repeatedly against the brightness.

Patrick's face was turning the most interesting shade of pink.

"What happened?" I asked.

"You were having a nightmare," he answered in a tight voice.

"Oh." I watched as he grimaced and clutched at some part of his lower extremities under the blankets. The man seemed to be in serious pain. Meanwhile, my brain was doing a fine job of catching up as slowly as possible. "Someone was chasing me and their hands were sharp as knives. Kind of like Freddy Krueger."

"Right," he said, pulling a pained face.

"What's wrong?"

"Well, Precious." He took a breath. "When you were fighting it out with Freddy you accidentally nailed me in the balls with your knee."

I winced. "Sorry."

He just nodded.

"And Precious is a no."

His lips were pressed so tightly together they started to turn white.

"Would you like an ice pack for your family jewels?" I asked.

"That might be a good idea, actually."

I climbed off the bed and carefully stretched my arm. It ached like holy heck. To be expected, I guess. It was only when I opened the bedroom door and faced the dark hallway that things went south. My mouth dried and my body stopped.

"You okay?" asked Patrick from the bed.

"Yeah." And I was. I totally was. I just couldn't get my damn feet to move.

All stayed silent behind me for a while. Then the bedsheets rustled and he limped to my side. Poor wounded warrior. He was wearing another pair of those soft sleep pants. But I was in too much of a state to admire his half-naked body. Objectifying him at the best of times was wrong. Right after I'd abused his balls just seemed plain rude.

"How about we go get it together?" he suggested.

"It's okay. I can do this. I need to do this."

He flicked on the hallway light. No boogeymen waiting to jump out at me. No stalkers hidden in the shadows with weapons in their hands. Just the gloss of the polished concrete floor and the clean white walls. The stark modern paintings. Everything was fine.

"There's two security personnel outside keeping an eye on things," he said. "You'll have around-the-clock protection from now on."

I swallowed hard.

"I want you to know, Norah, I am so fucking sorry about today. Nothing like that will ever happen again if I can help it."

I nodded and forced my foot forward. One step at a time. Past the office, gym, and home theater. Next came the guest bedroom where Jack slept. Opposite which sat my room with its carved-up door. There were some impressive gouges in the wood, care of Beth's knife. One lone dark spot of blood lingered on the floor, though the rest was gone.

And still Patrick watched in silence.

I headed on into the living room, turning on a light. The wall of glass doors leading outside showed only black emptiness and my own reflection. Perfect for making the most of the view, but damn creepy when you stopped and considered if anyone might be watching out there. My mind was wide awake. My whole body over aware. I didn't know how else to describe it. And all the while, my heart hammered inside my chest.

I made a rush for the kitchen and the freezer, grabbing a bag of frozen vegetables. Victory. Male voices speaking softly came from behind me. Jack and Patrick now waited in the living room, both wearing identical expressions of concern. Like I might burst into tears or have a meltdown at any moment. Jack still wore jeans and a tee. Guess he hadn't made it to bed yet. Unless musicians went to bed in their Levi's. Who knows?

"I hear you struck a blow for all of womankind," said Jack, fetching his acoustic guitar from the corner of the room.

"As my grandmother says, treat 'em mean, keep 'em keen."

Patrick took the bag of frozen goodies with a pained smile. His manspread was mighty as he placed the mixed peas, carrots, and beans in his lap. Then he looked to me and patted the empty space on the couch by his side. Of course he wanted to keep me close so he could keep an eye on things. He felt guilty about today. It made sense.

"What time is it?" I asked, getting comfortable.

"Just after midnight," said Jack, taking a seat on the couch. He started plucking at the strings, playing a beautiful melody without even looking. "How are you feeling?"

I gave him the best smile I could manage. It was pretty average. "I'm okay."

"Dad had a stalker for years. Sent him all these deranged messages," said Jack. "He kept turning up at the house, trying to get in. It was scary as all hell when I was a kid."

"I bet."

"Finally, they put his ass in jail."

"Are you going to see your dad while you're in town?" asked Patrick.

Jack pursed his lips and shook his head. "Nope."

"It's been a while."

"It has," he agreed. "Years, in fact."

Patrick scratched at the stubble on his chin and said no more.

I didn't know much about Angus Gilmour. Just the basics. One of the early greats of the grunge rock movement, he'd married and had a child, Jack, while young. When grunge faded, he'd moved into alt rock. The marriage had been turbulent, as detailed in many of his songs, and the couple eventually wound up divorcing. It must have been wild, growing up in that scene, in that sort of household. Being born a second-generation celebrity with money, privilege, and recognition. But I kept those thoughts to myself.

Distraction really was key. If I kept my mind on other things, then the darkness and the memories of today didn't press in on me so much.

Jack started playing an old Crowded House song.

Which was about when I noticed the flowers on the side table. A large white hat box holding what must be dozens of roses, a glass dish with a large arrangement of wildflowers, a bouquet of bright colors in an ornate vase, and a display of four white orchids in a rustic wooden box. The air did smell sweet.

My brain had to be more befuddled than I'd realized not to have noticed them earlier.

"What's all that?" I asked, nodding in their direction.

"They're for you," said Patrick. "Started arriving after you went to bed. They're from my agent, the studio I did my last film with, and the photographer from today."

"Wow." My smile came easier this time. "And I'm keeping these flowers. You can work out what you're going to tell Mei."

"Your allergies mysteriously disappeared. No one can explain it. Probably some post-traumatic shock reaction."

"I can't even remember the last time I got flowers."

"You really wanted them?" he asked, a little confused if anything.

"Of course she did, you dickhead," mumbled Jack.

Patrick frowned. "The roses are from Cole. He wanted to stop by and check on you, but I said you were sleeping."

"Don't feel bad, buddy." Jack smiled. "I'd be insecure too if Landry was after my girl."

"I thought Patrick told you we were less than authentic," I said.

"What's that got to do with anything?" Jack raised a brow. "We males love our pissing competitions."

"Great."

"Once you've finished hauling his ass out of the mire you can come rescue me. I could use a reputation revival," said Jack. "The last marriage did not go over so well. For some reason people expect you to stay together for more than two months."

"Huh," I said.

"Only took me that long to figure out she loved the money and fame a whole lot more than me."

"Ouch."

"Yeah," said Jack. "Thank fuck for pre-nups."

Despite being wide awake a minute ago, I was starting to get drowsy again. However, returning to the bedroom at the other end of the house on my own did not appeal. I grabbed a cushion and lay down, letting their low voices soothe me. Not being alone was nice. For a long time at my apartment, it had mostly just been me. I had friends that I met up with from time to time, but I don't know ... life got busy and I was lazy and before I knew it, months and then years went by.

At some stage during the drowsing, I'd stretched out, and my feet now sat on Patrick's thigh. The fingers of one hand rubbing and flexing my toes while his other thumb rubbed deep circles into the sole of my foot. Not one iota of tension remained. If being an actor didn't work out, the man had serious foot masseur skills to fall back on.

"Are you acting right now?" asked Jack out of nowhere.

"Hmm?"

"Just that you and Norah sure look cozy."

"She's had a shit day," said Patrick.

"Sure, sure," agreed Jack. "Just remind me ... when was the last time you actually lasted more than the prerequisite couple of dates with a woman you were into?"

"Never said I was into her."

"Because you rub the feet of every woman that walks in the door?"

A dismissive grunt from Patrick.

"If you're not into her, then why don't you let Cole shoot his shot?" asked Jack.

"I love him like a brother," said Patrick. "But Cole is a womanizing asshole."

"And you're not?"

Patrick's hands stilled.

The guitar fell silent. "Time for me to be off to bed."

"That's a very fucking good idea," groused Patrick.

Soon after, he set my feet aside and stood. Guess his groin was doing better. Because he oh so carefully lifted me into his arms and carried me off to bed. And I pretended I was fast asleep the entire time.

Chapter Eleven

BRIGHT SUNLIGHT SHONE AROUND THE EDGES OF THE bedroom curtains. Patrick's side of the bed was vacant, the sheets cool to the touch. Which was sad. Guess I liked waking up with someone. Or, to be honest, him in particular. It was late, though. Later than I'd anticipated. Thanks to my alarm not waking me—because my cell no longer sat where I'd left it on the bedside table. What a fucking disaster, given our big interview today. I climbed out of bed and got moving. Never in the history of hygiene has someone showered and brushed their teeth as fast as I did. I still had on last night's sweatpants and tank top, so I headed out. My upper arm still ached like a bitch and the bruising had turned the most colorful shades overnight. Without a doubt, the sleeveless dress the stylist had planned for today would be out.

Mei and Patrick were in the living room, busy talking to a man of average height in a plain black suit. A weird anxiety eased at the sight of other people. The knowledge that I wasn't in the house alone mattered more than it should.

"We're late," I said, not hesitating to interrupt their conversation.

"No we're not," Patrick said. "The interview's been delayed a few days. Some hiccup on their end."

Mei shot him a look before coming toward me with her arms wide open. "We're hugging, Norah. Brace yourself for impact."

"Okay." I smiled.

"Watch out for her arm," said Patrick, hovering protectively.

"That scared the crap out of me last night when I heard. I was going to come and check on you, then Paddy said you were resting and everything was under control and to leave it until today." She stopped to take a breath, arms wrapped tight around me. "I'm so glad you're okay."

"Thank you." I squeezed her right back.

"It must have been terrifying, having some lunatic come at you with a knife."

"Yeah." And the less said about it, the better.

Patrick watched on with his frown back in fine form. Granted shit had happened over the last twenty-four hours, but still. Seeing him upset sucked. Someday someone would make this man happy. Teach him it was okay to face life with optimism. I couldn't help but be a little jealous of that someone.

"Your cell is on the coffee table," said Patrick before I could ask. "Thought you could benefit from sleeping in."

"Thank you. Who are all those people playing in the garden?" I asked, spying activity outside.

"They're putting in extra security," said Patrick. "Cameras, motion sensors, there'll be panic buttons for inside, the works."

"We'll be out by the cars when you're ready, Mr. Walsh." The man in the black suit gave us a short, sharp nod before striding out. Talk about the ultimate blank face. Bet he always won at poker.

"Let me guess, bodyguard?" I asked, moving toward the kitchen, because, coffee.

"One of them," said Patrick. "Use a travel cup."

"Where are we going?"

He stretched his neck, frowning even harder. "Malibu. Thought we might stay up there for a night while everything's getting sorted here. Mei already packed you a bag."

She gave me two thumbs up. "I got you covered."

"Thanks," I said. "I get that today's interview has been moved. But what about tomorrow's appearance at that party?"

Patrick opened his mouth to speak, but Mei was already there. "Angie's worried you two are getting saturated. Given the events of last night, she decided it would be best to slow down for a while. Give your adoring public a chance to catch their breath."

"Okay." I nodded. "As long as it's not about me being unfit for duty. Because I'm fine and dandy."

"Of course you're fine," said Mei. I chose to ignore the doubt in her eyes. "But, Norah, wouldn't it be great to have a couple of days at the beach with your hot fiancé?"

Patrick leaned against the kitchen island with his arms crossed, continuing to say a whole lot of nothing. Though the way the muscles in his arms oh so subtly bulged in his current position did a lot of talking for him. So hot. And yet very much just my friend.

"I mean, look at him, girl." Mei gave me the most dubious wink in all of time and space. "Imagine how he looks in a swimsuit."

"Can't believe I'm getting objectified in my own house," grumbled Patrick.

"It's for a good purpose," she said. "Look, your beautiful fiancée is smiling."

"Mei, you are too good for this world." I bit my lip to stop from laughing. But there was something about this that wasn't funny in the slightest. I turned to him and said, "I feel like an asshole. Please tell her."

He didn't even hesitate, bless him. "Norah and I are fake."

"Are you though?" She cocked her head. "I mean, really?"

"Yes." I nodded. "It's all a publicity stunt."

"Hmm. If you say so. Anyway, I've got things to do and places to be. Have a nice time at the beach." And she was gone.

"That did not go how I expected," I said, bemused.

Patrick just shrugged.

"What about if you get a follow-up audition, though? Don't you need to be in town for that?"

"Malibu isn't far if they call," he said.

"You want to go."

"I do," he agreed. "And I want you to come with me."

Something inside of me liked the sound of that a little too much. The idea of him wanting me with him away from all of this. And after yesterday, I could certainly use the break. I put the lid on the cup with a smile. "Alright then."

The teak and glass house sat above a bluff. It was all rocks, gnarled trees, and sea spray. An endless expanse of blue both above and below with the ocean and the sky. Being there was like standing on the edge of the world. The city lights and everything we'd left behind seemed a dark and distant memory when faced with the salt air.

"You own this place?" I asked, more than a little in awe as I climbed out of the Range Rover. "This was a really good idea, by the way."

"No," said Patrick. "We're just borrowing it."

"It's magnificent."

One of the bodyguards who'd followed us had already entered the house while the second waited nearby. Being shadowed was weird. I kept feeling like someone was watching me. Might have something to do with the fact that someone was indeed watching me. They both had military bearing, their spines rigid and gazes alert. And they never, ever smiled.

We retrieved our bags from the back of the car and waited for the house to be declared safe. Then they'd settle into the guardhouse up at the gate and patrol the property. Sometimes it seemed like overkill, having them with us. All it took was a flashback to the woman and her knife, however, to accept that bodyguards were an unfortunate new part of this reality.

With every mile we put between us and West Hollywood, Patrick's shoulders had eased a little more. The frown had faded too. Worried glances were replaced with a smile as he watched me enjoying the trip up the coastline and its magnificent view. It had been years since I'd taken a vacation. And Patrick was no better, with his oversized work ethic. But there we were, racing up the highway, heading to the beach all happy like. It felt like a bonding moment. I'd had the strangest urge to touch him. To reach out and . . . I don't know, just make contact. But unless a photographer was around, that wasn't something we did. So I kept my hands to myself.

"There's no need to be nervous," said Patrick. "You're safe. I promise."

"I'm not nervous."

He nodded toward where I was busy picking at the seam of my flowy white blouse. I'd changed out of the sweats and tank top and tied my hair back in a neat ponytail before we left. No way would I be caught looking like a broken-down mess. Quite a few of the paparazzi followed us through the city, though most

KYLIE SCOTT

lost interest the farther north we traveled. Only a couple of in-
trepid assholes tailed us the whole way here. But this place had
been built for privacy, with high fences blocking any and all views
of the house from the street.

"Maybe I'm a little nervous," I allowed. "But it's not that I
don't feel safe. Getting away for a few days was a good idea. And
with our two new stern-faced friends, I doubt we could be better protected."

"What, then?"

"It's just . . ." I hesitated and then some. Because telling him
I was nervous about spending vast amounts of unscripted time
alone with him did not appeal. We had, however, promised not
to lie. So I settled for giving him some of the truth. "What are
we going to do here, just you and me?"

He blew out a breath. "I honestly have no idea. Why don't
we figure it out as we go?"

It sounded reasonable in theory. But a diary of events pre-
approved by Angie would have been safer. Left less room for in-
convenient feelings.

"Miss Peers, Mr. Walsh, you're welcome to go inside," said
the first bodyguard.

"Thanks, Tim." Patrick picked the two overnight bags back
up and nodded for me to go first.

Inside was even more spectacular than outside. Floor-to-
ceiling glass walls, decorative antiques, and comfy plush white
furniture in a large open-plan living space. If a romantic French
farmhouse and a modern contemporary had a baby, that's what
this place would be. God only knew what it all cost.

A dapper middle-aged man with an impressive mustache
came forward. "Hello. I'm Felix, the housekeeper."

"Hi," I said.

"I live on the property, so anytime you need anything, just let me know."

Patrick gave him a brisk nod before heading up the stairs. Because of course he was used to people popping up out of nowhere to wait on him hand and foot. Spoiled brat.

"Would you like a tour of the house?" asked Felix.

"That's okay." I smiled. "Thank you."

"I've prepared a lunch of spicy shrimp noodle salad. But I can fix something else if you'd prefer."

"The salad sounds wonderful."

"Would you like me to serve it on the patio, perhaps?" he asked. "It's a lovely day."

What with Patrick having disappeared upstairs, I put myself in charge. "That would be great."

Felix smiled and headed back into the kitchen.

I headed up the floating wooden stairs to the second level. The hallway ran in both directions, with lots of open doorways lining the way. This place was not small. "Sprawling" was a good work. "Magnificent" worked too.

"Paddy?"

"Turn right," he answered from the far room. When I entered, I found him staring out the window at the sea. "I put your bag in the first wardrobe."

"There are two?"

"Apparently." Meanwhile, his bag sat at his feet. "It's up to you where I sleep."

And because my mind went straight to sex, I just gaped at him. Way to be an adult.

"You can see how you feel about being on your own," he continued, oblivious. "If you get worried, I can always come in."

"Right." My cheeks burned. Dammit. "I sound like a little kid afraid of the dark."

"But you look like a grown woman who's coming to grips with having been through a traumatic event."

"Is that your way of saying I'm having a bad hair day?"

"I'm not joking. You know what I mean." He licked his lips. "If you'd ever like to talk to someone—"

"What, like a therapist?"

"Yeah," he said. "No pressure. Mei's got a list of recommended people and can make you an appointment. I'd cover any costs, of course."

"Thank you. I'll keep it in mind."

He turned back to face the view. "Why don't I take the room next door?"

"Are you sure you don't want this one?" I wandered into the en suite with its massive shower and immense bathtub. You could swim laps in the thing. Windows looked out at the water while small silver glass tiles covered the wall. Plush white towels sat neatly folded on the long counter and all of the floors were a warm shiny wood. This bathroom was bigger than my old apartment. Talk about fancy. "There's even a sauna in here."

"It's all yours." He stood in the bathroom doorway, watching me intensely. "Do you like it, Norah?"

"Yes. Very much."

"Good," he murmured and was gone.

Lunch on the patio was quiet. Apart from the crash of the surf and the cry of the local birdlife. I kept looking at him and he kept looking at me, but neither of us had much to say. Angie and Mei should have prepped us for being alone together. That would have been useful. While we'd managed okay up until now, things had taken a turn for the weird.

Were we still boss and employee when away from home? If no one was watching us, how were we supposed to behave? And where do all of the lost socks go?

I sipped my glass of Pinot Gris and thought deep thoughts.

"Do you like seafood?" he asked, looking at my half-finished salad.

"Yes. It's delicious. I'm just not that hungry right now."

He set his napkin on the table. "How about a walk on the beach, then?"

"Excellent idea." I smiled and rose. This was good, moving around, checking things out. Perhaps I just wasn't in the mood to sit still. Like I had the jitters for some reason.

Halfway down the wooden steps, he said, "If you'd like a massage or anything, we can arrange for someone to come to the house. You don't have to go out if you don't want to."

"Thanks, but I'm not sure about the idea of a stranger touching me right now."

He just nodded.

We left our shoes at the bottom, the sand cool and soft beneath our feet. This was nice. Very picturesque. And it should have been relaxing, but I couldn't quite get there. People were sunning themselves farther down the beach. Some swam in the surf. Far enough away to not be of any real concern. Odds were, anyone who could afford to be here wanted their privacy just as much as we did.

Together, we headed for the shoreline, edging closer and closer to the waves. The sun beat down and the water was warm, lapping at our toes. With Patrick beside me and the bodyguards no doubt nearby, I was safe as could be. But the more I tried not to think about last night, the more it intruded on my mind. Bad memories had a habit of doing that.

And all the while, Patrick keep sneaking glances at me, his frown back in place.

"I'm okay," I said.

Nothing from him.

"Just a little restless."

"You want to run?" he asked.

"No." I laughed. Then I frowned. "Actually, I want to scream."

His eyes widened for a moment. "If you want to scream, then you should."

"Really?" I smiled. The more I thought about it, the better the idea seemed. "That wouldn't bother you?"

"No." The man was serious. He stuffed his hands in his jeans pockets and stared out at the water, all serene. "Go for it."

The more I thought about it, the more I realized it was true. A knot of tension had taken up residence inside my chest. This big, dark mass. I clenched my fists, took a deep breath, opened my mouth wide, and let it out. All of the terror and rage. I screamed "fuck" with my whole heart until my throat started to hurt. Then I screamed it some more just because. Talk about being rowdy neighbors.

Patrick turned and waved at the people down the other end of the beach, letting them know everything was okay. Because we sure had their attention now.

When I finally stopped, it was with a grin on my face.

"Feel better?" he asked.

"Yes."

He smiled cautiously back at me.

"I'm not broken. This didn't break me, Paddy," I said. "You don't have to worry."

"I know. You're strong." He sighed. "I think I'm more afraid you're going to decide you're sick of my shit, of the shit that happens around me, and leave."

Huh.

"Which is selfish of me." His jaw shifted. "If you want out, then all of the money is yours. You have to know that. What you've done is . . . you've been great. What I'm trying to say is, it's your choice what happens next."

"Did you actually just admit to liking having me around?" I asked.

"Thought you figured that out days ago." He turned back to the water. "Truth is, you'd be better off without me."

"I disagree," I said. "Not saying life as your significant other hasn't had its challenges. Many of them unexpected. But, Paddy, I'm happy where I am."

The frown intensified.

"Time to cool off," I said, giving his flat stomach a light push. "What?"

"We're going in." I pushed him again and he stumbled back a step. Waves rushed in, drenching the bottom of our jeans. It was cold, but not unpleasant given the heat of the day. Seagulls cried overhead and the water and sky shone a perfect blue. Feeling the warmth of the sun on my skin was like waking from a bad dream. He raised his chin, looking down the length of his aristocratic nose at me. "You know how to swim, right?"

"Of course I know how to swim." He placed his hands over mine, anchoring them to his chest, walking backward into the water the whole time. That he went where I led, or pushed to be exact, was an utter delight. How he was willing to go with my crazy and just wander into the ocean with me. There hadn't been a lot of room for silly harmless fun like this in my life. Not for a long time. The water was a long way from summer warm, yet neither of us seemed to care. "But are you forgetting the part where we're fully dressed here, Norah?"

"Like that stopped us yesterday."

He gave me a reluctant smile. One of my favorites.

"I see this as like a spiritual cleansing," I informed him.

"That so?"

The water now came up to my thighs. My pants were soaked, with the white shirt soon to follow. Lucky I was wearing a simple cotton bra and not one of the lacy things. "A symbolic turning of our backs on the plastic and insincere aspects of society. We're embracing nature in all its glory."

He laughed all soft and low.

A sound guaranteed to make my knees weak. "You mock the depth and gravity of this moment. But you'll feel rejuvenated afterwards. Wait and see, Paddy. Total saltwater immersion therapy. Better than any Beverly Hills spa can deliver."

He picked me up in his strong arms and waded us out into deeper waters. Right before he dunked us, he said, "Whatever you say."

Grown-ass women could sleep on their own. It was a well-known fact. Which went nowhere toward explaining why I was wide awake and staring at the ceiling in the small hours of the morning.

Dinner had been yogurt-marinated chicken with garlic rice and a Greek salad. Felix was amazing in the kitchen, and I'd have asked him for his hand in marriage if I thought he'd accept. He paired the dish with a Cabernet Sauvignon and followed it up with baklava for dessert. Therefore, neither hunger nor thirst was the problem.

Since this house didn't have the recent bad memories of the other, I also wasn't afraid. Scream therapy had exorcised a whole lot of bad vibes. No longer did I seem to be stuck on the edge of a fight-or-flight panic response. Thank goodness. Hence, my restlessness came from other causes.

I could sleep on my own. It was a definite. The only problem being, I didn't want to. Having Patrick's big, warm body taking up half of the mattress was better on so many levels. Hearing him breathe, smelling his warm male scent. There was a certain simplicity in turning your back on sex. On denying the age-old call to reproduce for the good of all people. It made life easier in a lot of ways. And yet here we were. Did I really want to give up my peace of mind for this man? Was he worth that? And could I trust myself to make the right decision this time when it came to a male of the species?

Boss. Friends. These were the important things to remember. Sadly for everyone, I was apparently the forgetful type. The sad truth was, I missed him as much as I wanted him. So much for keeping an appropriate emotional distance. The memory of his arms around me today only made things worse. How good his warm, hard chest had felt against me in the cold water. Maybe I should go throw myself in the ocean again. Something in my nether regions definitely seemed to be on fire. But it was just a sex thing. A physical yearning for a one-on-one meeting with his private parts. It didn't need to mean anything more.

"Paddy? Paddy?" I tiptoed into his bedroom. A stupid thing to do since I was actively attempting to rouse the man. "Hey. Are you awake?"

Nothing from the lumpy shadow on the bed.

My heart tripped about inside my chest as I stood by him. Up close, I could see him much better in the low light. The line of his neck and curve of his shoulder against the white pillow and sheets. All of that masculine beauty sleeping so peacefully. I was a terrible person. He needed his rest. Also, maybe me making a pass at him would be just plain wrong.

Ever so carefully, I tiptoed back toward the door. A bedside lamp clicked on, illuminating the space. *Busted.*

"Norah?" He rubbed at his eyes. "What's wrong?"

"Nothing. Go back to sleep."

He sat up, the sheet slipping to his waist. While it wasn't a cold night, a sleep shirt would have been a good idea. For the sake of my raging libido if nothing else.

"I was just doing the camp counselor thing, checking you weren't getting into any mischief in here. Eating candy and watching porn after lights out. But you're all good." I gave him a finger wave. "Night."

"Hold on." He yawned. "Why are you awake?"

"I don't know. I couldn't sleep and I thought . . . actually, I didn't think. Not really. And this situation requires a lot of thought." I took a breath. "Okay. This was a mistake. I'm going to cease and desist with the word vomit and return to my room now."

He canted his head. "What are you wearing?"

"Oh." I gave my blue silk chemise a grimace. "Everything else Mei packed was sheer or had feathers. While this barely covers my boobs and ass, at least the matching panties are comfortable."

"I've got to give her a raise," he mumbled.

"She's great. You should." I took a step back toward the door. "I'll let you get back to sleep."

Instead of doing as told, he threw back the bedsheet and rose to his feet. Disheveled never looked so good. His sleepy gaze and ruffled hair. And he was wearing those saucy sleep pants that left nothing to the imagination. How was a God-fearing woman supposed to keep her thoughts chaste and pure in the face of such a garment? It was nigh impossible, not that I hadn't been in a state of high horniness already.

"C'mon," he said, ushering me out of the room with a hand on my lower back. But when we reached the doorway, he stopped.

"What's wrong?" I asked, turning to find his gaze on my ass. "Paddy?"

"Shit," he said, bracing his hands on the doorway and hanging his head. "I'm sorry. I shouldn't be—"

"It's okay."

"No. It's not." His shoulders flexed, fingers tightening on the door frame. Like he was holding himself back. "Listen ... there's something I need to tell you. The thing is, this is complicated."

"Because you're my boss?"

"Yeah." The angles of his face seemed so much sharper in the low lighting. The skin tighter somehow. "I'm more than happy to come sleep with you if that'll help you feel safe. If you want me to sit in a chair in the corner and keep watch over you all night, I'll do it."

"Thank you."

He just nodded.

"Total honesty, right?"

"Right," he said.

Was I really this brave? That was the question. I rubbed my damp palms against my bare thighs. "I didn't wake you because I'm afraid, though."

"Okay."

And that's where I stalled. Completely and utterly.

For a moment he just looked at me, then he said, "You can have whatever you want from me."

"I can?"

"Yes," he said, tone definite. "You should know that."

"No one's ever said that to me before."

Lips in a firm line, he stood there, braced in the doorway. Waiting on my decision. I took a tentative step forward, reaching up to place my hand where his heart beat strong and true. A dusting of chest hair, warm smooth skin, and the swell of his pecs. He held perfectly still, gazing down at me with more heat in his eyes than I'd ever seen. And I wanted it all. I stepped closer, close enough to rub my cheek against his chest. His grip on the door frame tightened to such a degree that some of the woodwork creaked in protest.

"This is a very nice house." I rested my chin against him so I could see his face. To be this close to him for no other reason than I wanted to felt sublime. "It would be a pity to break it."

"I just need you to make the first move," he said, voice guttural.

"Pay attention, Paddy." I smiled. "I already did."

Chapter Twelve

MY WORDS UNLEASHED HIM. THERE COULD BE NO other description for it. He rushed me, one hand gripping the back of my neck while the other grabbed at my ass. The next thing I knew, my spine was against the hallway wall and he was lifting me via the hand beneath my butt. My legs wrapped around his waist and oh yes, this was perfect. We should never not be in this position.

Our mouths met in a hot, wet kiss. All firm lips and sleek tongue, the crash of his teeth against mine. It was like we couldn't get close enough, like we wanted to crawl inside each other. Our mouths battled it out and I didn't mind if I lost in the least. Between my legs, he was long and thick and felt divine. His hand tightened on my ass cheeks, urging me to grind against him. Best idea ever.

With my arms wrapped around him, I didn't know what to paw at first. The smooth strands of his hair or the hot skin of his back. The thickness of his shoulders or the strong column of his neck. In the end, I just settled for hanging on tight. Not that he was trying to get away from me. Quite the opposite, in fact. But this whole scene felt like a fever dream. Us all over each other. Him wanting me as much as I did him. And his need was all right there, in each sure touch and the brand of his mouth on mine.

When he broke the kiss, I could have cried.

"Bed?" he asked, panting.

I nodded.

"Yours is bigger."

Down the hallway to my room, he carried me. Not wasting a moment. My back hit the mattress and he turned on the bedside light before crawling on after me, dragging me into the center of the bed. When he rested his weight on top of me, my legs wound back around him and everything was great. The way he used his strength and size thrilled me to no end. That edge of dominance he displayed.

Fingers slipped beneath the hem of my chemise, sliding up and over my rib cage. Not stopping until he could cup my breast in his big hand. His thumb stroked over my hard nipple, back and forth and around and around, before giving it a sharp pinch. A nerve sparked in my breast, sending flames licking through me headed straight for my sex. Every inch of me seemed hypersensitized. Hot and needy.

His mouth trailed a blaze of its own, over my jawline and down to my neck. He licked and sucked and didn't stop. Not until the neckline of my chemise had been tugged down sufficiently to bare my breasts. The sight of him suckling my breast almost undid me. To witness the sheer hunger of the man. The knot between my hips tightened, my sex swelling and growing wetter by the minute.

It had been a while since I'd done this, but I'm not sure sex had ever been this wild. Our desperate need to get at each other bordered on manic.

When he slid a hand between us, down over my belly then up and under the hem of my nightie, I almost came on the spot. How he slid his hand inside my panties and cupped my mound like his ownership had long since been decreed. The possessiveness in his touch and gaze. He pressed his palm against me, giving me just a little pressure and friction. But not quite enough. Next, a fingertip traced back and forth along the lips of my labia, making me squirm.

"Stay still," he ordered, shifting onto the mattress at my side.

"I can't."

"You want me to stop?"

My eyes widened at the threat. "And you seem like such a nice man when you have your pants on."

"My pants are still on, but we'll fix that in a minute," he said. "One small problem. I don't have any condoms. Didn't bring them on purpose because I was trying to avoid exactly this."

"Wait. You don't want this?"

"Norah, I want to be here with you more than I want my next damn breath."

"Oh." I licked my lips, tasting him. The hint of mint from his toothpaste and that something else that was all him. Yummy. "I didn't pack any either."

His jaw tensed and he nodded. Then he slid one finger inside me, pumping it gently. The pad of his thumb circled the hard nub of my clit, and all of those delicate muscles inside of me clenched at him. It all felt so good. Too good. While I could please myself, having Patrick touch me made it about a million times better.

"We'll have to find other ways to amuse ourselves, then," he said. "Whatever will we do?"

"It's incredibly hard to think straight when you're finger-fucking me."

"Is it?"

My smile wavered. "Paddy, I'm on the pill and I'm healthy. If you want to—"

"Yes." He took my mouth in a long, heated kiss. That talented hand of his working me higher and higher the whole time. When he stopped to rest his forehead against mine, we were both breathing heavily. "I'm healthy too. Get tested regularly."

"Okay then."

He slid a second finger into me, working me hard and watching my face the whole time. And still his thumb played with my clit, edging ever closer. Such a damn tease. His gaze roamed my bared breasts with their hard nipples. And the sight of his hand in my panties seemed to please him to no end. Lord knows it worked for me.

"You have the prettiest flush working up your body," he mumbled. "I think you're close."

I, however, wasn't thinking at all. Every muscle in me drew tight, sensation racing through me. It was too good, almost too much, and I couldn't help but want more. More of the way he looked at me, more of his touch. My breasts felt heavy and my head felt light. The ache low in my belly just grew and grew. When he started strumming my clit, my mouth opened on a gasp and it was all over. Waves of pleasure washed through me. The muscles in my thighs shook and I dug my heels into the mattress to try and ground myself. It seemed like everything in me coalesced into one perfect moment. A moment he'd given me.

Patrick's touch eased until his fingers stilled. His nose brushed my cheek, lips planting gentle kisses along my jaw. And he didn't say a word.

I wasn't actually sure what to say either. So I pushed my face against his neck and very bravely hid. Something about coming in front of him had shaken me. Like I'd just exposed some core element of myself. Not that I didn't mostly trust him, but . . .

Carefully, he slipped his fingers out of me, out of my panties.

Next came sucking sounds because of course. Waste not, want not.

"You taste good," he said. "Smell good, too."

"Thanks."

"Salty sweet woman. I like it."

I laughed softly. "I'm so glad."

"If you want to stop there, it's okay."

I eased back so I could see his face. While his hard-on pressed into my hip, his expression was a study in restraint and something more. Gentleness. Kindness. Friendship, even. Those sorts of things that had been missing with any and all of my previous bed partners. His skin seemed to have tightened across his face with his need and his pupils were so dilated they swallowed the blue. But he meant every word.

"It's up to you," he said.

"I don't want to stop."

Slowly, he nodded, letting out a breath. He slid his palm over the silk of my nightie, taking in the delicate embroidery along the lowered neckline. "As pretty as this is, it needs to come off."

Together we worked the chemise off over my head and the panties down my legs. Not stopping until I lay naked against the sheets and the lingerie was gone. Tossed over his shoulder and onto the floor. Guess he'd paid for them; he could do what he liked. And it was such an act of trust, having sex with someone. Letting them see everything. I'd forgotten how intimate taking someone to bed actually was.

Patrick wasted no time dealing with his pants. His dick pointed upward with a graceful curve, thick ridges of veins wending their way up toward the wide crown. The man was hung. And it was perfect and intimidating, like every other inch of him. No wonder he had a website solely devoted to crotch shots of him named Appreciation for Patrick's Trouser Snake. Not that I'd looked. At the site, that is. I stared at his dick to my heart's content. By the cocky smile on his face, he had no problem with my perusal. Then I held a hand out to him and he climbed between my thighs. His big body was fever hot and blocked out the rest of the world.

The blunt head of his cock lined up with my opening and in he pushed. Inch by inch my body slowly gave to him, opening for him, taking him deep. His tortured groan against my neck was music to my ears. Every muscle in him tensed as he eased out before sliding back in nice and easy. Once, twice, he took his time.

"Alright?" he asked.

I nodded. "More."

"Harder?"

"Yes."

This time he slammed into me. No hesitations or holding back. And holy shit, electricity raced up my spine. I wrapped my legs around him, anchoring him to me. It took him no time at all to set up a punishing pace. Whatever this thing was between us, it didn't do sedate. At least, not for long. The damp sheen of sweat covered both our bodies. Fingers dug into my ass cheek, angling my hips high, all the better to take him. The force of his gaze seemed absolute. Red spots marked his cheeks and he'd never been more beautiful than in this moment.

Skin slapped against skin and every single cell in me screamed for more. More of him and this friction. The feeling of too much yet not enough. I didn't think I could come again. But I should have known better than to think at all. The way Patrick fucked me into the mattress was pure animal instinct. We were rough and raw. Me with my hands grabbing at him and him with all of the superb strength in his body.

Fake

His hand fisted in my hair, pulling hard, as he stared at my face. My whole body shook and I shouted, holding onto him tight. I came again, taking him with me. It just wouldn't stop. An endless surge spreading out through my body. Nothing else existed. Nothing was left. I really was done this time. I was a light and floaty remnant of the woman I'd been before. A devastated mess left on the bedsheets. Though actually one pertinent thing remained. The knowledge that if sex had been this good previously, there's no way I would have given it up.

Meanwhile, Patrick was still bracing himself above me. His breath came in frantic movements, his face buried in my neck. I rubbed at his scalp, giving him a gentle massage. The man had worked hard. He deserved good things. Ever so slowly, he lowered himself on top of me and I wrapped my arms around him. Not to get clingy, but having him close was lovely.

Everything gradually calmed. The night silent and still once more.

Mornings after are always a bit weird. The sudden awareness of a new level of intimacy having been reached. Or the rejection of same. Usually, a swift departure follows that scenario. While I didn't believe that putting penis in vagina a relationship made, there was a definite argument to be made for the new familiarity having some sort of meaning. Not everything, but something.

Patrick seemed content, spread out on his back with my head on his shoulder and an arm curled around me. It was official. Not only was he a cuddler, but I was now a star fucker. Though maybe it took more than bedding one star to reach that status. I don't know. What concerned me were the usual things. How did this affect our friendship? And how long until we could do it again?

"Hey," he mumbled, eyes narrowed against the glare of morning light. "You're frowning."

"Am I?"

In a swift move, he rolled us so that he was on top. We were a tangle of sheets and body parts. Then he set about nuzzling my neck. "You have a little bit of stubble rash here."

"I can't imagine how that happened."

"Tell me what's wrong," he said.

"Just your usual morning-after jitters."

His semi-hard cock stiffened further against my stomach. Next, his big hand cupped my breast, skilled fingers playing with my nipple and making me gasp. Which answered the question about how soon we could do it again, at least.

"Elaborate, please."

"What, you want a list of issues?" I asked somewhat saucily.

"Yes."

I squirmed beneath him, seeking more contact. Like having the big, burly animal on top of me wasn't enough already. "What happens next? Are we still friends? Was this a one-off thing or ongoing? What's the weather going to be like today? And do you think Felix would make us Eggs Benedict for breakfast if we asked nicely?"

"That it?" he asked.

I nodded and gasped as he pinched my nipple.

"In all honesty, as to the first, I don't know. But yes, we're still friends." He notched the head of his cock against me and slowly pushed in. "Definitely ongoing."

"Huh," I said in a breathy voice.

When our hips rested against each other, he happy sighed. "Where was I?"

"Um, the weather?"

162

"Right. Sun seems to be out, so okay I guess. And I'm sure Felix would be delighted to cook you breakfast. If not, we can always head for a café in town." His licked up my neck, pausing to nibble on my earlobe. "Are you good? Can we focus on fucking now?"

"Are you always this amorous in the morning?"

"When I wake up with you, apparently."

"Is that so?" I smiled, wrapping my legs around him. "Fuck away, my friend."

He grinned and got busy.

"Surprise!"

Light flooded the living room, revealing people. A lot of them. I grabbed at Patrick's arm, more than a little startled. But then I guess that was the point of a surprise party. A surprise engagement party, at that. Silver signs, wedding bells, and a disco ball hung from the ceiling. The dining room table was covered in charcuterie and a full bar had been set up in the corner of the living room. There had been a lot of cars out in the street, along with a fresh influx of fans and paparazzi out front. I'd ignored it all due to being agitated over returning to the city lights. We'd had our own little bubble of sexy-times happiness in Malibu and leaving it sucked. One night had not been nearly enough. Especially not since we'd discovered sex and spent the day indulging in same. The drive back through the city at night hadn't been too bad and now here we were, back at work.

Paddy muttered something truly foul under his breath and pasted on a smile. To be honest, I kind of felt the same way. I definitely looked it, with my nose pink from the sun and messy hair tied back in a bun. At least my clothes were okay due to my constant fear of being photographed. My black sleeveless jersey jumpsuit and Prada ballerina flats were acceptable party wear once I dumped my comfortable baggy cardigan.

"It's a surprise engagement party!" Mei attempted to give us a group hug. "Isn't that great?"

"Do you want an honest answer?" asked Patrick.

"Shut it, Paddy. It's awesome."

"Absolutely it is," I said. "I've never heard of a surprise engagement party before."

"Oh, it's totally a thing." Mei took a sip from her coupe glass of champagne. "And it's only a hundred or so of your closest friends. No biggie."

"I don't even have that many friends." He frowned. "Who's paying for this?"

"You are, of course." Mei laughed. "You're so funny, Paddy."

"Oh, relax, you cheap bastard," said Cole, looking especially debonair in black trousers with a matching button-down shirt. "She's just joking. The wait staff, food, and drink are all from my club. Consider it my present to you both."

"That's very kind of you," I said.

He gave me a wink. Lord, but the man was handsome.

Patrick slipped an arm around me and drew me in closer. I went, happily.

"After everything that happened, Angie and I decided you needed to celebrate something good in your lives," explained Mei. "And to give your friends a chance to show their support. This is what we came up with."

A reluctant smile stole across his face. "Thank you."

"Besides which, you should see all the cool stuff you've been given," said Mei. "So many gifts. The spare room is already full.

More flowers arrived too, but we were running out of room, so I sent them on to your Gran's nursing home."

"Wow."

"I invited her and offered to send a car, but she said she had cards tonight and couldn't make it," continued Mei.

"Fair enough."

"I promised to give her more notification for the bachelorette party. She's pretty fired up for that. Suggested we all hop a private jet for Vegas." Mei obviously still had her own opinions regarding the legitimacy of my and Patrick's relationship. Or she just really liked to organize parties. "Your friend Zena, who also couldn't make it tonight due to a thing with her boyfriend's parents, seconded that idea. I guess Vegas it is!"

"When are you going to come work for me, Mei?" asked Cole, taking a sip of his vodka on the rocks. Such a serious drinker.

Patrick returned to frowning.

Mei just shook her head. "Not a chance, Mr. Landry. You'd have me following you around nightclubs until all hours of the morning, asking pretty women for their phone numbers, and keeping your weird sex secrets. I almost have a private life, right now. It's so close. My cell only rings at four in the morning once or twice a week. I haven't had to live out of a suitcase for over a month. I mean, the worst, most awkward thing I've had to do lately for Paddy apart from folding his underwear is paying a sushi restaurant to open and make dinner for him after hours. That and fly out some peonies from Paris for his fiancée's grandma and macarons for his mom. And organize this whole party in under twenty-four hours, meaning I only got three hours' sleep last night. You have no idea how good I've got it!"

"We're talking six figures here, Mei," said Cole.

"Like I'm not already getting that." Mei laughed. "Try harder, Mr. Landry."

"Don't try harder," grumbled Patrick. "I need Mei to run my new production company."

"Oh do you now?" Mei rubbed her hands together. "How exciting. Have your people call my people, Paddy."

"You are my people."

"About time," said Cole. "I've been telling you to start one for years and get in on that side of things."

"Hold up. You flew flowers over from France?" I asked.

Patrick winced. "Not a big deal."

"It sort of is. Thank you. That was very kind of you."

He just looked away all embarrassed.

"But you really should fold your own underwear," I said, giving him a nudge with my elbow.

"Please." Mei laughed. "Like me or the housekeeper doesn't deal with both of your intimate apparel."

"You have to answer calls at four in the morning?" I asked.

"Oh, that's nothing," said Mei. "There's a reason why the money for this sort of position can be high. I used to work for a director who had me carry around three cell phones at all times. Two of which had to be answered whenever they rung, day or night. It's not unusual in the industry. I was required to be present from when he woke up in the morning until he went to bed at night. Just in case he needed something."

"Hollywood can be a lot of things," said Cole. "But kind is rarely one of them."

Patrick snorted. "True."

"Yeah. He was an ass. The first time he yelled abuse at me was the last time he yelled abuse at me," she continued. "I'd already met Paddy and knew he needed someone to sort him out.

Fake

We settled on a figure and some boundaries. And now here we are in a happy place where I'm remunerated appropriately and eighteen hour days are the rare exception and not the rule. Yay!"

"Hell of a job, Mei," I said.

"You have no idea, Norah."

Over in the corner, Angie stood talking to Jack. He actually seemed to be dancing on her last damn nerve, as per normal. Her dramatic hand movements when she spoke almost smacked him in the face a time or two. And they were about the only ones I'd met before. Many more people stood nearby, waiting to say hello to us. Or they were just watching us out of interest. I don't know. As usual, everyone was very glamorous and many were vaguely familiar. No doubt from the silver screen.

Patrick leaned down and whispered in my ear. "Norah, you okay with all this?"

"What would you do if I said I wasn't?"

"I don't know. Guess we could make a run for it."

I smiled. "It's all good, Paddy."

We hadn't actually discussed what level of togetherness we were now displaying in public. And this definitely qualified as public. Damn near every eye in the room seemed to be on us. Which made sense, seeing as it was supposed to be our party. Just because we were now having sex didn't mean everything had to change. Or anything. I should probably stop overthinking things sometime soon. That would be wise.

"I just need a minute to go put on some makeup," I said.

He nodded. "I think you're beautiful as you are. But whatever you want."

And my heart basically just rolled over and offered up its belly at his words. Nothing I could do.

"C'mere," he demanded.

"You know, you seem all cool and aloof. But you're quite the carnal bossy boots once you get going."

"Boo."

"No," I said.

"Bae?"

"Hell no."

He smiled. "Give me those lips."

I did as asked.

"You make him happy, you know?" said Jack, sidling up alongside me.

While I hadn't been hiding exactly, I was kind of taking a moment to catch my breath. Patrick stood around the corner talking to a producer. And I hung out in the darkened hallway leading to the bedrooms. After hours of meeting people and making conversation, I deserved a break.

"Hey," I said. "Was wondering when I'd run into you."

"I've been around."

"How are things?"

He took a long pull on his beer. "Good. Looked at a couple of condos nearby. Got offered another gig touring with a band I like. Big name, nice money. And they're fun to hang out with."

"That's great."

"Are we just going to ignore what I said?"

I smiled. "I'm glad Patrick's happy. He makes me happy too. We're good friends."

"Friends . . . sure."

"So you'll be buying somewhere and moving out soon?"

"Eh. I need somewhere to put my stuff." He shrugged. "The

latest ex might get my place in Santa Monica in the settlement. Easiest way to make it all go away, by the look of things."

"For two months of marriage?"

"Love hurts, Norah."

"This is true." I took another sip of my drink. The rare sound of Patrick's laughter drifted down to us and I smiled. My stomach got all fluttery. This was crazy. We hadn't even been sleeping together for twenty-four hours. I needed to calm down and stop writing happy endings for us. Think with my brain instead of my vagina.

"As for Paddy's ex, Liv's a nice girl, but I think her heart is being pulled in two directions. Makes for a shitty situation."

I raised my brows. "I didn't realize you knew her."

"It's a small and sparkly town."

"Right."

"She starred in her first movie at around thirteen or so. We'd all wind up running around together at parties and events," he said. "Both the kids that were in the industry and the children of the stars, movie moguls, music industry bigwigs, and other assorted rich pricks. They were the only ones who had the money to keep up, but they could also be trusted to keep their mouths shut. If they were over your house and saw your dad on a bender, they knew better than to talk about it. Next week, it might be their parent doing something dumb like hanging from a sex swing in the kitchen. They also know what it's like to be a kid and have the papers calling you on your cell phone to ask for a comment on your parents' divorce. To get recognized on the street. To have your first after-school job be sorting your parent's fan mail."

"Huh."

"If I ever have children, not that I'm planning on having any, but if I do," his mouth flattened, "they will sure as hell not be running around doing whatever they want and getting into trouble. My first car was a custom-built Lamborghini. It's not normal."

I said nothing.

"But back to you and Paddy," he said, taking another mouthful of beer. "Do you realize you get all mushy-eyed when you look at him?"

I shrugged. "He's really pretty to look at."

"He also seems to have a problem letting you out of his sight, which is not normal behavior for him." Jack nodded at the man who was indeed peeking around the corner to check on us. "Pathetic."

"I think it's nice that he cares."

"You two could have kids. I think you'd make good parents. I know I'd make a wonderful uncle."

"You are well and truly getting ahead of yourself there, good sir," I said. "You know that's not the situation."

"Isn't it?" He scratched at his stubble. "Don't get me wrong, Paddy's a good actor. But he's not that good. And you're definitely not, no insult intended."

I laughed. "Thanks, Jack. Maybe I'm not exactly sure what the situation is between us. But let's just take things easy."

He leaned against the wall with his feet crossed at the ankles. The picture of a rock star in repose with his tattoos, ripped jeans, and big black boots. "It's a timing thing often with relationships, isn't it? I mean, it had only just occurred to the ugly-as-sin fool that he might want to be in a relationship. That it was something he could fit into his life. Then things went south with Liv. Then you appeared."

"Are you saying I'm convenient?" I asked.

"Would that be such a bad thing?"

"I'm beginning to see why you get divorced so often."

He grinned. "I'm a romantic. And there's nothing as exciting as that initial rush when you meet someone and it's all going great and the sex is amazing. Well, almost nothing as exciting. It's only after the first couple of dates when everything they do stops being quite so cute and you start to wonder if they're actually an asshole. Or maybe you are. One of those things. Or possibly a mix of both."

"Right," I deadpanned.

"I actually think that's why you and Paddy are doing so well together," he said thoughtfully. "Mei and I smoked a joint last night and talked about it."

"Oh, really?"

"Yeah." Muscular arms crossed over his broad chest. "For as long as I've known him, he's never actually managed to last past the second or third date. Just has nil interest in taking anything further. In actually getting to know someone. But with you, he has no choice. He has to be there. If he wants this whole reputation reversal to work, then he has to stick it out."

I just blinked.

"What?"

"So I'm inescapable and convenient?"

"Exactly!"

Not saying he was necessarily completely wrong, but his summation of the situation did not please me. Patrick and I might be new and untested, we might even just be friends who fuck, but we had the possibility of a future. Maybe.

"Is this idiot bothering you?" asked Patrick, slinging an arm around my neck.

Cole joined us with another drink in hand. "His mouth was moving. That's usually the sign."

Jack flipped them the bird. "You know, we should all fuck

off for a few days. Dad's got a private island in the Bahamas we could use."

"No can do, sadly," said Cole. "I'm due back on set tomorrow, then there's the awards ceremony tomorrow night."

Patrick wound a strand of my hair around his finger, giving it a gentle tug. "Also, you haven't talked to your dad in years, remember?"

Jack snorted. "The man took a lot of drugs in the nineties. He wouldn't even notice if we visited. It's not a place he goes often."

"Ready for your first red-carpet event tomorrow night, Norah?" asked Cole.

"Sure," I lied.

"You'll be great." Patrick placed a kiss on top of my head. "Just wait and see."

Chapter Thirteen

TURNS OUT THAT WALKING A RED CARPET IS HALF FUN/ half bitch. The Actors Foundation Awards were televised and huge as heck. I might only be the fiancée, but the preparation was intense. First came waxing, followed by a facial; my hair color was touched up and a light spray tan applied. Some of these things had been planned for a day or two before, but we'd been in Malibu. It made things busy. Angie tried to force a last-minute juice cleanse on me. However, Mei saved the day with a soda and burger. Love that woman.

My nails were done, hair styled into a textured loose bun that sat on the back of my neck, and about a gallon of makeup applied. Which was good and right given our late night. Times like these were why Baby Jesus invented concealer. Given the weather had warmed up, the underarm sweat patches seemed like a great idea. But the really fun part was squeezing my ass into not one, but two pairs of Spanx. Who even needed to breathe or bend at the waist?

Then, at long last, it was down to the Dolce & Gabbana black heavy lace cocktail dress, a pair of Jimmy Choo pumps, and dangly teardrop diamond earrings on loan from Chopard. The assistant stylist smiled, showed me a couple of ready poses for the red carpet, took a photo to send to his boss, and dashed off to dress another client.

"What do you think?" asked Mei.

I stared at the glamorous stranger in the mirror. "I don't know. You think he'll like it?"

"Paddy," Mei hollered.

"Patrick's opinion is irrelevant," said Angie, handing me my clutch. "This is all about what works on camera and gets us the likes. We were looking at a red Carolina Herrera gown, but given recent events we thought this would send a better message. More refined and dignified. Not quite as sexy. Now, the rules of the red carpet are as follows . . ."

Patrick emerged from the hallway. One of the first times he'd dared venture into the chaos of the living room today. Men had it so much easier than women. He'd hid out at the gym before being groomed. I'd never seen him in a tuxedo before. Not in person. Talk about needing to gird your loins.

Angie snapped her fingers in front of my face. "Norah, stop making heart eyes and pay attention."

I gave her a look of displeasure.

"Give us a minute, please," said Patrick.

Mei smiled and Angie grumbled, but they did as told, disappearing into the office.

"You look beautiful." He took my hand, straightening the rock on my ring finger before placing a kiss on my knuckles. "How do you feel?"

I sighed. "Nervous. How about you?"

He shrugged. It was just another day in Hollywood for him.

"Car's here!" said Mei.

"We could always stay home and have sex," he said, leaning

in to place a kiss on my neck. Such a romantic. "That's always an option."

"Aren't you up for an award?" I asked.

"Yeah. But I'm not going to win. It's a popularity contest as much as anything and I'm still catching up on that front."

"But you never know. You might win."

"Are you sure you're good with doing this?" he asked.

"I didn't spend all day getting ready just to miss the party."

He smiled and offered me his arm. "Okay then. Let's go."

"I just need a moment to powder my nose," I said. Because needing to pee the minute we hit the red carpet did not sound like a good time.

We took the prerequisite at-home picture for social media, then got moving. Angie wasted no time laying down the law as soon as we were in the limousine. "We're not giving interviews. Don't answer questions. Don't even talk to the photographers. Let them take their shots, then get out of there."

"Got it," I said. "Is that normal?"

"It is this year." And that was all she said about that. "When they ask for a fashion shot, that's the polite way of telling you to get out of the way so they can take a picture of Patrick on his own."

I nodded.

"And remember, you two are in love," she said. "Only just got engaged. That means PDA."

Patrick frowned, but didn't comment.

Outside, Los Angeles passed by in a rush. It was only late afternoon, sunset still a good hour away. Patrick poured two glasses of champagne and handed them to Angie and me. Mei had stayed back at the house to tidy things up and one of the bodyguards rode up front with the driver. That this was my life right now still boggled my mind.

When I talked to Gran earlier, she asked me what being famous was like. Having people want a piece of you was both strange and tenuous. My adoring public might lose interest at any moment and I could be back to schlepping drinks in some bar.

"We'll be met with a minder when we get there who will see you all the way to your seats," said Angie, continuing with her lecture.

I sipped my champagne and tried to keep my shit together. My stomach had long since dropped to around ground level. Millions would be watching this event. Crazy town.

We joined a long line of limousines, but it moved quite quickly. When we drew to a stop and the car door opened, the first thing that hit me was the noise. So much screaming and shouting. There were people everywhere and many of them were very excited. Security guards and police officers monitored the fans and onlookers gathered behind the fences.

Patrick helped me from the car, Angie got busy on her cell, and we were off. Our minder was a woman about my own age with burnished skin and Pacific Islander heritage. Her name was Leilani, and she wore a headset and seemed to have a talent for looking everywhere all the time. Nothing got by her.

Ahead of us on the red carpet was a big-name actor with his entourage, and ahead of him appeared to be the reigning queen of pop. I have to admit, my knees went a little weak at the sight of her. So cool. The famous director we'd seen out at dinner was nearby too. Reporters with camera crews stood at intervals, ready to get the gossip. A woman in a sleek white dress stood about midway, holding a tray of bottled water. The whole thing looked to be run with military precision.

Patrick waved to the fans screaming his name. An easy smile sat on his lips. Even my name was getting called out, which was wild. He tucked my hand into his elbow and on we walked.

Oh, God. So many people. So much noise. In the face of it all, my limbs went weak and I wobbled on my high heels. Deep, even breaths were the key. I could do this. Though I probably should have stolen the bottle of vodka out of the limo and swilled my way down the carpet. That might have been a smart move.

"Smile," hissed Angie.

I pasted a somewhat demented grin on my face. I could feel it. It was all types of wrong.

Angie made a noise of despair. "That does not look natural."

"She's fine." Patrick leaned down to whisper in my ear. "I'm right here. We're doing this together. Everything is going to be okay, Pookie."

"Pookie?"

Smile lines appeared beside his beautiful blue eyes. "Don't like that one? How about Cutie Patootie?"

"Wow. No." I laughed. "Where do you come up with these? Are you outsourcing to five-year-olds?"

His gaze filled with amusement.

"That's better, Norah." Angie sighed. "Keep that look on your face."

Our minder moved us along as more people disembarked from their fancy rides behind us. The paparazzi seemed to have all been corralled into one large box beside the carpet. We stopped in front of a backdrop advertising the Actors Foundation Awards. Patrick slipped his arm around me, his hand resting lightly on my hip. Okay. All good. With Patrick at my side, things didn't seem so bad. I stood tall, shoulders back, one hand atop his and the other holding my clutch.

Making sure my ring was visible, of course. Photographers yelled out our names and instructions to look at them. Like I could see anything with all of the flashes. Then they started calling for a fashion shot and I moved well out of the way. Patrick gave them his devil-may-care grin and whoa.

"Gonna ride that man like a pony when we get home," I murmured.

"What?" asked Angie.

"Nice weather we're having."

She narrowed her eyes and took a step closer. "Normally I would take this opportunity to lecture you on the wisdom of getting involved. Don't bother to deny it. It's beyond obvious."

I kept my mouth shut. To my mind, this fell under the heading of none of her business. Patrick and I were consenting adults. Her opinion was not required. But here we go.

Someone in the crowd yelled out a question about Liv and we all ignored the idiot.

"But, Norah, we're currently standing on a red carpet, one I didn't think until recently I'd be able to convince him to walk. We're waiting to hear if he's gotten a role in a big-budget movie being made by one of the most promising up-and-coming directors of our time," she said. "And Patrick is actually honestly smiling. So I'm going to keep any disparaging comments I might have to myself."

"I appreciate that, Angie."

She sniffed. Then she straightened. "Liv and Grant have arrived. Let's move along."

I caught Patrick's eye and tipped my chin. And he came straight to me, all long, sexy strides in his black tuxedo, his gaze locked on mine. This time I trembled for all the right reasons. It was a little scary to feel this much this soon. To realize how in over my head I was when it came to him. Of course, I might just be sex addled. That made sense and was bound to wear off sometime soon. No one's dick was *that* good.

I swallowed hard. "Time to go."

"One thing first." He cupped my face with one hand, pressing his mouth to mine in a gentle kiss. So tender it made my heart stutter. Nope. Not sex addled. More like besotted. Dammit. The photographers went crazy and the fans cheered.

With a satisfied smile, he took my hand and led me on.

The awards were held in the grand ballroom of a big fancy hotel. No less than nine after-parties were taking place on site afterward. Patrick steered us toward the one for the biggest streaming service in town. He'd been in a popular series of theirs a few years back. Though the best thing about the party was the lack of photographers inside. For four hours while the cameras rolled, my expressions had ranged from engrossed to delighted, stoic at Patrick's loss, and back again. My face needed a break.

"I still think you should have won," I whispered for not the first time.

"I know you do, Norah. That's why you're my favorite person here." He grabbed two drinks off a passing waiter's tray and handed me one.

"Why, thank you."

I downed half of it. Four hours really was a long time and it's not like the bar had been readily accessible. Nor did I want to run to the bathroom too often. The first filler who'd taken my seat during a bathroom break looked like a supermodel and had been a bit too into my fake fiancé. No idea if Patrick liked males, but still. Then there'd been the starlet who'd looked at him with ovaries in her eyes and done her best to throw herself at him on the way out. Lucky the man knew how to deflect. Guess for some people, the presence of a significant other standing beside the object of their lust was an unfortunate thing best overlooked. I hope she got to be on the receiving end of such behavior someday.

Karma and all that.

Ugh. When had I become such a jealous shrew? I should be nothing but happy hormones; however, being smitten for the first time in a long time seemed to be messing with both my head and my heart. Single really did have so many overlooked benefits. And on the off-chance that the family curse was real, I was prepared for life on my own. But no, here I was freaking out over a man. This was not the time for me to revert to being the queen of questionable choices. I would enjoy my time with Patrick for however long it lasted, then move on with my life.

Some of the party's attendees had swapped out their glamorous gowns for everything from more extravagant dresses to designer tracksuits. What a winner that last idea was. Seriously. Though the Jimmy Choos were mighty pretty, I'm reasonably certain I stood in a pool of blood. My ears ached from the heavy earrings, too. Such was the price of wearing weighty diamonds and not breaking in your shoes. On the plus side, Liv and Grant didn't appear to be at this party. Insert sigh of relief here.

"What are you thinking about?" Patrick asked, leaning in.

"Should we be schmoozing?"

For a moment, he just looked at me. Then he smiled.

"Sure. Let's do that. Right after you tell me what you're thinking that's got you looking so serious."

A Hollywood heavyweight walked past and my mouth fell open. "Oh my God. I worshipped her as a child. And that person has sushi. I wonder where they got it from."

"I'll be happy to help you track down some food as soon as you answer my question."

I sighed. "Do you want my current real concern or just a list of general discomforts?"

"Let's start with the first and take it from there."

"Okay." I took a breath. "I get jealous sometimes when it comes to you. I don't like that. I don't want to be that person."

He nodded.

"And I know you're not doing anything to encourage them, it's just . . . I don't know." I downed the other half of my drink.

Patrick took my empty glass and handed me his full one without comment.

"You're beautiful and famous—of course people are going to want to look at you and hit on you and be in your general vicinity. It's the nature of being successful at your job," I said. "I just need to get over it."

He licked his lips. "Norah, my looks are useful. But they're not helpful when it comes to making real connections with people. Do you understand?"

"Yeah."

"Here's the thing. If I got into a terrible accident tomorrow and scarred my face, would you walk away?"

I shook my head. "No."

"Would you wear a sexy nurse's costume and bend over inappropriately in front of my hospital bed?"

"Yes."

"Well," he said. "That's all that really matters then, isn't it?"

I grinned. Ah, yes. There was the rush of oxytocin, serotonin, and dopamine I was after. This somewhat perverted man made me so stupid. And happy. "Let's go forth and socialize and find food."

"You got it."

One in the morning had come and gone by the time we got home. Parties were still in full swing when we left. Lord knows what time they'd be winding up. Given our surprise engagement party the night before, however, we'd had enough.

"Don't get me wrong," I said, continuing our conversation, "some of them were raging assholes only interested in what you could do for them. Then there were the narcissists who didn't even recognize that other real live people with wants and needs shared their world. But some of them were remarkably normal and nice."

"Guess you get a mix of people everywhere."

"Even in Hollywood."

Patrick followed me into the quiet of the bedroom, discarding his bowtie and jacket. With a universe worth of relief, I toed off my shoes and placed the earrings back into the waiting velvet box.

"Can you get the zip for me?" I asked.

I showed him the back of my dress and careful as can be, he lowered the zipper. Then I began the not-so-elegant process of wriggling out of said dress, discarding the underarm sweat patches, and peeling off my pantyhose, all before starting in on the double Spanx and the underwear waiting beneath. The things women did in the name of fashion and beauty. Talk about sexy.

"Turn your back," I ordered. "You don't need to see this."

"I already know you didn't wake up looking like that."

"Well, that's harsh."

"You woke up with my face planted in your bed hair and my morning wood pressed against your ass," he said, sounding perfectly pleased with the situation.

"As is good and right."

"And you were gorgeous."

"Thank you," I said, my heart feeling too big for my chest again.

"I thought you were remarkably cool in the face of your childhood heartthrob," he said. "You only stared at him dumbstruck for a full minute."

"Hey, at least I didn't drool."

"This is true."

"Makes me nostalgic for my teenage years. Would you mind if I put up a few posters in here?" I asked with a teasing grin.

"That would be amazing, Norah."

"Right?"

"Why don't we stick them on the ceiling? I know I paid thousands to an interior designer, but a few pretty boy posters here and there is bound to add to the aesthetic." He smacked me on the behind. "Smart-ass."

"Ow."

He chuckled and headed for the shower. "You coming?"

"Yes."

Patrick's en suite had a soaking tub and a generous-sized rainfall shower. A truly amazing invention. He stripped off his clothes, tossing them over a wooden chair in the corner. The man had the most amazing ass. All toned, with just the right amount of roundness. Made my hands get all grabby.

"What are you looking at?" he asked.

"You."

He held out a hand and drew me underneath the warm water with him. Ah. So good on my back.

"Had you met the woman who was with Cole before?" I asked.

"No. She's new."

"The way he was watching her was . . . interesting."

A grunt from him.

Without being asked, he started plucking hairpins out of my fancy do and placing them on the built-in bench running along one of the gray marble walls. Washing off my makeup took no less than three rounds with the foaming face-wash stuff. Next, he poured shampoo into his hand. Strong fingers massaged it into my scalp, washing all of the styling gunk out of my hair. I closed my eyelids and enjoyed it. What a day.

Soapy hands cupped my breasts, clever fingers tweaking my nipples, and hello.

"Cleanliness is next to godliness," he said at my look.

"Sure."

When I soaped up my own hands and reached for his hard-on, however, he lightly pushed me away. "No. Hop on the bench for me. Sit near the edge."

"So bossy."

The surface was cool beneath my bare wet butt. I pushed the collection of hairpins aside as he knelt before me. He spread my legs assertively and I gripped the edge. An awareness swept through me. My nipples hardened and my pussy ached. Though some of that had been happening for a while. Being naked with

Patrick tended to cause such things. Though, so did being around him dressed.

One hand slicked his hair back off his perfect face, while he guided my leg over his shoulder with the other. This put his perfect face in just the right place to eat me.

"Okay?" he asked.

I just nodded.

First he kissed my belly, tonguing my belly button. Which tickled.

"Stay still," he muttered.

"I'm trying."

He placed a line of kisses down to my mound, then his thumbs held me open. "Such a pretty pink cunt."

A wave of warmth swept up me at his words. The tip of his tongue traced delicate circles around the nub of my clit. He teased me until I was panting. And he'd just gotten started. With the flat of his tongue, he lapped at me from rear to near. The muscles in my legs tightened, my shoulders inching up. It was so good. Though my insides clenched on nothing, which was sad. Like the sex god he was, Patrick read my mind and started fucking me with his sleek tongue. All of those tongue twisters actors perform to warm up came in use for other things too, apparently.

One of my hands found his hair, fisting the wet strands. Whether to force him closer or away, I couldn't have said. It was a lot. From the thumb pressing gently but insistently against my asshole to his talented tongue making merry with my pussy, the man gave oral sex his all. I shook and strained and climbed higher and higher. While he might have missed out on winning the award earlier tonight, he sure as hell deserved one for this.

"Fuck," I gasped. "Paddy."

"Yeah?"

And he called *me* a smart-ass. Like either of us was interested in conversation right then.

He fastened his lips to my clitoris and started sucking. That he took turns doing this while flicking it with his tongue and sliding two fingers into me from the hand not busy threatening my rear messed me right up. My whole body seized. Light and sensation rushed through me. A sea of stars shone behind my closed eyelids. I hoped he could breathe okay with my thighs clamped to his head, holding his face pressed against my sex. Unless the humming noise he was making was a death rattle or plea for air. Either way, it set off a whole new wave of aftershocks. I was helpless to do anything but ride them out. His welfare would have to wait.

"Shit. Paddy. Oh."

Bit by bit, my body started to ease. My brain took a little longer to come back to earth. The orgasm had definitely been heavenly. "Satiated" was the word of the day. Or night. Whatever. He eased my limp legs off his shoulders and stood, washing off his face and hands with soap beneath the water. With the head of his hard cock flushed a dark red, the man not only deserved but needed immediate attention.

I licked my lips and sat up. "Come closer."

"No." He shook his head, grabbing my hands and drawing me to my feet. "You're going to ride me, Norah."

"Am I now?"

"Oh, yeah."

He took my place on the bench with a charmingly lecherous smile. They should really put that one on billboards. Women would flock to his films by the billions. At least, I would. Hands gripped my hips, urging me onto his lap, holding me steady. I rested one hand on his shoulder, the other lining his cock up with my entrance. Talk about a great idea. With the water raining down and the steam filling up the space, it was glorious.

The thrilling slide of his dick going deep into me had me catching my breath all over again. How thick and good he felt. Not to mention his mouth was right there, ready and waiting. Mouth damp and swollen from going down on me. Like a hero. The dark need of his gaze as he watched me was exhilarating. His fingers dug into my ass cheeks, helping me work myself on him. We should never not end the day this way. Loving Patrick was perfection.

And that's what it felt like. Love. A little foolish and a lot fast, I know. Though I didn't have it in me to deny it right then. Later I'd be sensible and put some much needed distance between us. When I wasn't busy losing myself in him. Sex didn't have to mean anything, but this did and I couldn't fake it. Not in the moment.

So I claimed his lips in a hot opened-mouth kiss. Our tongues entwining. The perfect distraction. All the while, I rode him faster and harder as his hands demanded. Nothing but friction mattered. The way it lit me back up inside. Coming is an excellent antidote for unwanted feelings. Everyone knows that. My nails dug into his back and the man all but snarled at me.

I wanted to watch him come. I wanted his come in me. Because getting messy with this man had become my everything.

With a muttered curse, he slipped a hand between us. Him and his tricky fingers. In no time at all, my insides were clenching at his cock, my whole body overrun with the need to reach that height again. I sobbed and clung to him, fucking myself onto him. No hesitation. Nothing else mattered. He clasped my hips tight again, urging me on, using my body to get himself off. I gasped and he groaned and we both won that one. Together.

Chapter Fourteen

I WOKE UP TO THE USUAL ASSORTMENT OF NICE TO CRAZY messages. This included an urgent one from Angie sent at five a.m. Not good. But I couldn't face it until I was fully awake. I wouldn't. Drama would not rule my life. So I dressed and headed out to the kitchen for coffee before reading it. Fortification via caffeine was required before I faced the day. After all, if it had waited this long, then a bit longer wouldn't hurt.

Patrick had been insistent about us having some downtime. Taking it easy. Something told me this was him still protecting me after the home invasion. Given how huge yesterday had been, this wasn't a bad thing. And quiet time with my man sounded awesome.

Note: Referring to him as my man within the privacy of my own skull was okay. But problematic if I let it out of my mouth. We hadn't even had the are-we-exclusive talk yet. Any and all claims made by me on his person would have to wait.

And none of this mattered when I found Mei standing in the entry talking to Liv Anders. Yes, Liv. In the flesh. Her eyes were red, though her makeup remained perfect. Not only was she gorgeous, she was also half my size, which was just plain rude. If this was the competition, I didn't stand a chance. There could be only one reason why she'd be here in this state after everything that happened. She wanted Patrick back. And who could blame her?

Too bad I didn't know to dress for the occasion. Armor would have been better than my slim jeans and white tank. Because even if her life was falling apart, the woman was going down in couture. We're talking immaculate black pantsuit and stiletto heels. I'd never felt so insignificant and average. Not that I'd ever admit to it. At least if my life was about to be ruined, it would be by someone in Prada. A much higher class of destruction.

"Oh," said Liv, staring at me. Like she hadn't expected me to be here.

Mei pressed her lips together. "Norah, this is Liv."

I nodded.

"I was just explaining to her that Paddy is out jogging," continued Mei. "So it might be best if she called him and came back later."

"He doesn't answer my calls." Liv clung to the handle of her Hermès bag. "I've been trying for days and he hasn't answered one."

Kind of wanted to high-five the man for that particular life choice.

"Can we talk?"

"You want to talk to me?" I asked, surprised.

"Please," said Liv.

"I don't know . . ."

She frowned (this was also done in a ridiculously pretty fashion). Her gaze turned confused and oh boy. Perhaps no one had ever dared to deny her. People loved to please the beautiful, rich, and famous. And she was the ultimate triple threat. Meanwhile, Mei gave me a surreptitious shake of the head. She was probably right. There were lots of good reasons to say no. But a big fat tear chose that exact moment to roll down Liv's cheek and dammit all to hell. It couldn't have been more perfect if it had been scripted. And I've been in her shoes . . . messed up by love. I knew what that was like all too well.

"Would you like a coffee?" I asked.

"Yes."

Mei shrugged and went about her business. Washed her hands of both of us. Who could blame her?

Once I'd filled two cups with brew, I asked, "Creamer or sugar?"

"No. Thank you."

I passed her one of the cups before adding sugar to mine. Today would be a two-sugar day on account of it needing all the sweetener it could get. She stood on the other side of the kitchen island. Best for us to have our space.

"What do you want, Liv?" I asked, my voice mostly steady.

"I guess I was curious about you." While she played with the handle of her coffee cup, she never actually put it near her lips. "You've gotten so popular all of a sudden. Seems like I can't escape you online. Anything mentioning Patrick and there you are. You're not his normal type. No insult intended."

"None taken," I lied.

She looked up at me from beneath her long, dark lashes. "It wasn't easy, seeing him move on. No doubt you know what happened between us. Everyone knows what happened. And even when it doesn't quite work out with someone, it's hard to see them with someone else."

I just waited.

"But then I heard a rumor . . ." Her shoulders straightened and her chin jutted out. So much self-righteousness. "I'm here because I want to know the truth."

The woman could only be talking about one damn thing. *Shit.*

"No," she said, voice firming. "I *need* to know the truth."

"About what, Liv?"

She blinked. "About you and Patrick, of course."

"Huh."

"What does that mean?" she asked, tone snappy.

I set down the cup. "It's means you're a stranger to me and I don't owe you a damn thing. Now Jack swears you're one of the good ones, but right now, I am not seeing it."

She opened her mouth to speak, but I got there first.

"No. You had your turn. Now it's time for you to listen," I said. "Whatever went down between you and Patrick has nothing to do with me. In the same way that my relationship with Patrick has nothing to do with you."

"Your *relationship?*"

"Yes."

She snorted. Even that was oddly attractive. Bitch.

"Did you really think you could just come in here and make demands and I'd just roll over and play dead?"

A flash of guilt crossed her face.

Patrick strode in and his jaw shifted at the sight of Liv Anders. Though Mei must have alerted him to her presence, he still seemed thrown. Guess this was the first time they'd really been together since it all happened. His forehead furrowed and his lips were pressed tight. Not angry exactly. But not happy, either. I'm not sure what I expected; however, him immediately throwing her ass out into the street would have been grand. Because this whole damn scene hurt my heart and it was only going to get worse. I could just feel it, dammit.

"What are you doing here, Liv?" he asked, sweat still dripping off him. A damp tee hung over one shoulder and his shorts sat low on his hips.

I grabbed a bottle of water from the fridge and handed it to him. His answering smile was weak, making my spirits sink straight through the floor. Liv had most certainly come to get her man. Stupid of me to try to stand in the way. Yet I couldn't bring myself to leave. Not until he came out and asked me to. I took a couple of steps sideways instead, putting some much needed distance between us. Then I crossed my arms and rested my butt against the kitchen counter, propping myself up and giving myself as much protection as possible. Just what the situation required.

"I called," she said. "You didn't answer."

Before responding, he downed half of the water. "I've been busy. You shouldn't have come here. What if you'd been followed? You're just lucky there aren't any photographers out front today. The last damn thing I need is a repeat of what happened in front of your place."

"I know you two are fake," she blurted.

He just blinked.

"It makes perfect sense, really. The way it all happened so fast." Her chin rose all defiant like. "A nice, normal girl to save your reputation after you'd rolled in the muck with me. I'm sure Angie was delighted with herself when she came up with the idea."

My breath caught in my throat. Whatever he said next, however he handled this, would tell me what I needed to know. If we had a future or if we were just fucking around. Finding out it was the latter would hurt like hell. But better to know now and get my heart broken a little before things got more serious, and a little turned into a lot.

Patrick said nothing.

Liv's chin dimpled and her eyes turned glassy once again.

"We need to . . . can I talk to you alone? If we could just sort this out. There's so much I need to tell you."

His gaze moved between the two of us, all befuddled. The big idiot.

"Grant and I are over. I swear it's true this time; I'm filing for divorce later today. We can be together," she said, her voice breaking. "Just like you said you wanted. I panicked last time. Grant got all upset and I just . . . I gave in and said we could try again. But I know better now."

My throat hurt. But I sure as hell wouldn't be bursting into tears. This scene had enough drama in it already. Besides which, I didn't cry nearly as attractively as Liv Anders. I was more of a bright-pink-nose-and-splotchy-skin mess. Not something anybody needed to see.

Another tear slid down her face. "Please can we talk? Alone?"

Patrick turned toward me and he was actually going to do it. He was going to ask me to leave so they could be alone. At such times, I found it was best to channel Gran. My heart was in splinters and my pride was shaken, but I knew exactly what she'd have to say about the matter and none of it was nice or polite. Because I'd been raised to speak my truth. It was about time I started doing just that when it came to men and relationships.

"You have a choice to make, Paddy," I announced, hands on hips. "Right here and now, her or me. If I walk out of this room and you and her have your chat—then that's it. As far as I'm concerned, you've made your decision."

His brows descended. "You're giving me an ultimatum?"

"You're damn right I am."

He rubbed at the stubble on his jaw, watching me warily. So he damn well should. While I might not be a Hollywood princess, I still knew my worth.

"I know you and her have been friends for a long time and that your relationship is complicated. I'm not asking you to explain any of that to me. That's between you and her. But Liv asked you a question," I said. "Though I guess it was more of an accusation, wasn't it? What do you say, are we fake?"

"Norah . . ."

"I know that you are," inserted Liv snootily.

"You shut the fuck up," I said.

Her mouth fell open. "Patrick! Are you going to let her talk to me like that?"

Give me strength.

His gaze jumped from me to her and back again. And still not a word was said.

"Paddy, is it her or me?" I took a deep breath and let it out slowly. This was it. "I need to know. Guess we both do."

For a moment, he stood frozen, staring at me. Long enough for the last vestiges of hope in me to shrivel up and die. I was such a fool to think we had a chance. Me and a Hollywood heart-throb. What a joke.

Then his lips finally opened and he said, "No, Norah, we are not fake."

Liv squeaked. "What? But . . ."

"Okay." My shoulders descended on a sigh of relief. "Alright."

His smile was small, a bare trace of a curve. But it was the best one I'd ever seen.

Liv's beautiful face, however, was set in stark lines. "You're . . . you want her?"

"Yes," said Patrick, tone final.

"I'm too late."

His gaze saddened, but he didn't disagree.

She scowled at the countertop. "I, um, I owe you an apology, Norah."

I had nothing.

"This won't happen again." Then she grabbed her expensive handbag and fled. Thank fuck for that.

And there was too much going on inside of me. A giant upswell of emotion I didn't know how to handle. It was good and bad and everything in-between. Maybe I was having an anxiety attack. I don't know. I kind of wanted to try some more scream therapy, to just get it all out, but our neighbors would probably call the cops. So I did the next best thing. I seized an oven mitt off the counter and threw it at his head. Given it was soft and I'd never been much of an athlete, the man wasn't in any real danger.

In fact, he snatched it out of the air easily. "What was that for?"

"You hesitated. You hesitated so much."

"Were you really going to leave?" he asked. "Tell the truth."

"You bet your ass I was."

His brows rose in surprise. "Huh."

"We've been all over each other the past couple of days and you're stunned that I wouldn't just step aside and let another woman move on in?" I screwed up my face. "I am neither that nice nor that understanding, Paddy. Or maybe I'm just not that much of a schmuck."

Nothing from him.

"Feelings are a real thing."

"Right."

"And you need to respect mine."

"Got it," he said with all due seriousness. Just as well.

"Oh my God," said Mei, appearing behind Patrick with her

cell in hand. "You're right, Angie. He's a freaking mess. It's like he's been mauled by a tiger."

Patrick's gaze turned questioning.

I grabbed his upper arm to turn him so I could see. Oh, wow. Two distinct sets of bright red grazes ran on either side of his spine. One line embedded in his skin for each of my nails. Holy shit.

"I don't even remember doing that," I said, sort of numb.

"You're a wildwoman, Norah." Mei smiled and snapped a photo.

When Patrick saw it, his eyes went gratifyingly wide.

"Your horniness and territorial markings have actually saved the day," she continued. "Turns out an assistant left Angie on less-than-stellar terms and took to the internet early this morning to get his own back. This was done by blabbing to anyone who would listen about you and Paddy being less than genuine. However, a fan followed Paddy on his jog and when he took his shirt off . . . internet gold was made. The photos are going viral as we speak. You are officially the kinky celebrity couple of the week. Not only did you stop the photographer from seeing Liv arrive here, but you validated your sexual relationship in the eyes of the world."

"By mauling him?" I asked.

"Yes," said Mei.

"I wonder how many people are slut-shaming me."

"Not nearly as many as are saluting you for your healthy and indeed natural carnal appetites." Mei grinned. "Okay, you crazy kids. Keep up the good work."

I winced. "How mad are you on a scale of one to ten?"

"Why would I be mad?" asked Patrick with a smirk.

"I've probably scarred you."

"You haven't scarred me. Relax." He reached out, fingers digging into the stiff and sore muscles in the back of my neck. What a man. "Now everyone knows I give you good dick."

Heat rushed to my face and I laughed.

He drew me in closer, wrapping his arms around me while maintaining the massage. Which was right and good and very necessary. "I'm sorry I hesitated. Guess it was just a surprise, her being here and everything."

"Hmm."

"Are you sniffing me?"

I happy sighed. "Yes."

"Right. Like I was saying, we might have started out questionably, but we're not fake now," he said. "Okay?"

I nodded and slipped my arms around his middle.

"No idea where we're headed, but I'm a hundred percent along for the ride."

"Thank you," I said, sniffing some more. "Me too."

"Are you crying or still smelling me?"

I pressed my cheek against his chest and took a deep breath. "A bit of both."

"Why are you crying?" he asked, holding me tighter.

"You chose me. I wasn't sure you would. Also, that was a very stressful situation to find myself in before finishing a first cup of coffee."

"Why wouldn't I choose you?" he asked, voice bewildered. Which I kind of adored him for.

"Because she's Liv Anders and I'm not."

"You think I'm still hung up on her?"

I thought it over. "I honestly wasn't sure. But I guess you're not."

"What I felt for Liv . . ."

"Go on," I said.

He groaned. "Let's just say that what I felt for Liv was a lot less than I feel for you. She was a maybe. Someone I used to think a lot about and wondered if we'd be any good together. But all of that is past tense. You're a definite. You have my back. Literally."

"Ha."

"You're funny and you're sexy and you don't take any shit. I like that. I'm not going anywhere, okay?"

"Okay."

He rested his head on top of mine.

"I like you an awful lot, Patrick Walsh."

"Mm."

"You listen to me and you make me feel safe. Apart from just now . . . but we're moving on from that."

"That would be good," he mumbled.

"Guess we're exclusive."

"You're damn right we are. You thought we weren't?"

"Well, we hadn't discussed it . . ."

He just shook his head. Like it was all so obvious. Jerk. "Want to go dirty up the shower again with me?"

"I thought you'd never ask."

Chapter Fifteen

I F ZENA FLIPPED HER HAIR ONE MORE TIME THE WOMAN was going to hurt her neck. But there she sat on the couch, laughing throatily, flirting for all she was worth. Like she wasn't engaged to a hot high school teacher. For shame. Not that I could blame her. Jack was turning it on and then some. With her dark skin and wide smile, she was certainly a beauty. I loved her because she was hilarious, loyal, and damn smart. It was great to see her. I hadn't realized how much I missed my friends. Not that I had a whole lot.

Patrick had suggested I invite someone over and start behaving more like the house was my home. A big step. But then today seemed to be all about the big steps in our relationship. After Liv's visit, he stayed by my side, but retreated into himself. Either due to guilt over his friend's marriage being on the rocks and the part he'd played in that or concern over possible repercussions from Liv filing. The media was bound to want to link him to the latest developments. That story sold so well last time, after all.

To everyone's surprise, however, there'd been no announcement. All was quiet in West Hollywood. Maybe Liv would rather be unhappy than alone. Who knows? Gran always said the only people who really understood a relationship were the people in it. Not that it ever stopped her from giving her opinion.

"She got my order wrong," said Zena, dragging me out of my thoughts.

I snorted into my martini. "I did not. You were drunk and changed your mind like five times."

Zena giggled. "I remember, that fool had just left me. What was his name?"

"We dare not speak it. He does not deserve to be named."

"Amen." She held her hands up in prayer. "But you did get my order wrong and you forgot my guacamole."

"It was like my first week waitressing. I was an idiot baby who had no idea what I was doing. Stop picking on me, lady."

Patrick watched us, bemused.

"I hope you didn't tip her," said Jack, stretched out in the corner with a beer.

"She snuck me a free margarita, so I took pity on her. We've been friends ever since." Zena gave me a wink.

"How's the shop going?" I asked.

"Ugh. When are you coming back? I cannot be left alone with the accounts—you know this. A shipment of new-season stock arrived just yesterday and I would kiss your feet if you'd come help me process it," she said, giving me a come-hither look, batting her eyelashes and everything.

"Would you, now?"

"You'd have to demonstrate you'd properly washed them first, though. I have high standards."

I laughed.

"Mine are diligently and thoroughly washed on a daily basis," said Jack, raising one of his big black boots.

Zena looked down her nose. "I bend at the waist for no man."

"Hear, hear." I raised my drink in toast to her. Seriously.

The woman was my second favorite vagina-wielding person after Gran.

"Are you thinking of getting more help?" asked Patrick, taking hold of my hand.

Zena raised a brow. "You're not going to let Norah come back?"

"Norah does what she wants."

"Good answer," said Zena. "But yes, I have been giving serious thought to expanding the boutique for a while. What I'd really like to do is move to a bigger location."

I smiled. "That's a great idea."

"I think so. But while things are going well, I don't see me having the funds for another year or two. Especially with the wedding coming up," she said. "A pity, because the perfect space has opened up down the street."

"What about an investor?" asked Patrick.

"There is someone who's interested but . . . they'd need to be silent," said Zena. "I can count the people I'd trust to actually be actively involved on one hand. And the bulk of those people are busy with their own thing. Such as your fiancée, here."

I cocked my head. "But I don't have a thing."

Patrick just looked at me.

"I mean, I had jobs that I liked. But I wouldn't exactly call that me doing my thing, you know?" I asked. "I've been thinking about getting a thing, now that I've got the time and money."

Zena raised a brow again.

"What would you like to do?" asked Patrick, giving my hand a squeeze. "I mean, if money were no object?"

"I don't know."

"You were talking about online courses."

I shrugged. "I think I'd rather do than learn right now. Or

do and learn at the same time. Cole has kind of inspired me with this entrepreneur business. Maybe I should talk to him."

"Nah," said Jack. "Don't get me wrong, he's a good-looking guy. But dumb as a box of hammers."

Patrick bit back a smile and nodded in agreement. "Sad but true. You could talk to me, though."

"Sure he is," I said drily. "And I *am* talking to you."

"You know the boutique just about as well as I do," said Zena thoughtfully. "Just putting that out there. Though if you were serious about it, you'd need to make your mind up fast. That investor I told you about is pressuring me for answer. I also don't know how long that other shop will be available, which is my main reason for considering doing this right now."

"Investing in a business you have intimate knowledge of sounds sensible." Patrick ran his thumb back and forth over my knuckles. "You know I'd be happy to help, Norah."

"I know, thank you. But I'd rather do this on my own."

"Okay," he said.

"I'd want to be a part of sales and ordering. Not straight away, obviously. But moving in that direction."

Zena nodded. "Of course. So you're serious about this?"

"Yeah." I smiled. "I am. And depending on what amount you have in mind, this is something I'm able to do. So long as you're sure?"

She took a sip of her martini, watching me over the rim of her glass. "Excuse me while I get nosy for a moment, but it's required. How is this going to work with your new fancy lifestyle? If Patrick disappears for months on end to make a movie are you planning on following him?"

My mouth opened and nothing came out. Because that was an excellent question. We hadn't talked about the future in the two or so seconds we'd been together. The present seemed precarious enough. Patrick watched me carefully. No doubt waiting to hear what I'd say. Talk about pressure. But while he meant a lot to me, I needed to have my own life. A purpose beyond wearing nice clothes and getting my hair and nails done. Otherwise, how long would it be before we both grew bored? Before he saw me as being no better than any of the other fame and money vultures who hung around town?

"No," I said, finally. "It's been a long time since I had the opportunity to do something more. I won't throw that away."

Zena nodded.

"Though I wouldn't mind visiting you on set now and then, if you'll have me."

Patrick's smile didn't reach his eyes. "Definitely."

"You're mad at me."

"What?" Patrick threw back the blanket and pushed the pillows up against the padded headboard. "What are you talking about?"

Zena left half an hour ago and Jack had disappeared off to wherever Jack usually disappeared to. Probably off visiting Cole at his club.

I stood at the foot of the bed, battling with my belt buckle. A certain number of martinis apparently messed with my fingers. Oops. "When Zena asked if I planned to follow you around and I said no. But then I said I would very much like to visit you on set."

"And?"

"Your smile was fake, Paddy."

"No, it wasn't."

"Oh my God. You just lied to me again."

"Allow me, drunky girl." He pushed my hands aside and made short work of the belt and the stud and zipper beneath. Then he dragged the jeans down my legs.

I set a hand on his shoulder so I didn't lose my balance and land on my ass during the de-pantsing. How embarrassing. "Tell me what you were really thinking."

"I was thinking that partnering with Zena sounded like a good opportunity," he said.

"Tell me what you were thinking about you and me."

He stood tall, gazing down at me. "Norah."

"Paddy."

"I'll tell you what I'm thinking now." He filled his hands with a butt cheek each. The butt being mine. Then he squeezed. "How do you feel about doing it doggy style?"

"Are you suggesting it because you don't want to have to look me in the face and talk to me?"

"No. I'm suggesting it because I like your ass. A lot."

"That's sweet. Get on the bed." I set my hands against his bare chest and pushed until he gave in and flopped back onto the mattress. Such a beautiful sight. I crawled on after him, sitting astride his hips. One of my personal favorite places to be. "We never discussed the inevitable likelihood of this, at times, being a long-distance relationship. Of course, we never even discussed us having a future before today."

"Things are moving fast," he said, and he didn't appear happy about it.

"Yes, they are."

With his hands fastened to my thighs, he sighed. "Guess I just figured we'd be together. Whatever that involved. But I understand that you don't want to be my shadow."

"To the contrary, I would love to be your shadow. I can think of nothing better than following you around all day."

"But you're not going to."

"No," I said. "I'm not. And I'll miss you like crazy. But even though I'd rather cling to you like a limpet, I believe we need to be fully functioning adults independent of each other for this to work."

"That's very mature of you," he said with a frown.

"Is that really all you're going to say?"

"What do you want me to say?"

Males. Seriously. Maybe I hadn't consumed enough alcohol for this conversation after all. "I want you to be brave and open up to me a little."

Next his hands grabbed the hem of my shirt, working it up and over my head, before starting in on my bra. And he grumbled all the while. "How is this even relevant when I don't have any jobs lined up?"

"But you will. You're still getting offers, aren't you?"

"Nothing I want to do."

"Yet."

"Yet," he agreed.

"It'll happen, Paddy," I said. "The right script will come along and you'll be in New Zealand or Czechoslovakia or who knows where for half a year. This is something we ought to be prepared for."

"Relationships are hard," he said crankily.

"This is true."

"Come here."

I snuggled down against his chest with his arms wrapped around me. Nothing like a hug to make everything better. In his arms, I was safe. Bigger and braver and capable of anything. Like

I could take on the whole damn world, or at least one small corner of it, that's how he made me feel.

"Okay. Here's the truth, then. I fucking hate the thought of being away from you." His fingers tightened their hold. "But acting is my job, the only thing I ever wanted to do. And you deserve to have something like that for yourself."

"Yeah."

"Lots of long-distance relationships in this industry, but I've got to say, not many of them work out."

My turn to sigh. "No. I haven't seen a lot of them work out either."

We were both silent for a minute.

"Why do you still have panties on?" he asked.

"Focus, Paddy. We're talking about us."

"I am focusing. I just think you'd be more comfortable sprawled all over me bare-ass naked."

I laughed.

"You're my kitty cat."

"I am not your kitty cat."

"Some days I wonder if we'll ever settle on a pet name for you," he said. "You're being so difficult about it."

"I'm the worst, it's true."

"Yeah, well . . ." He sighed. "I'd rather your worst than anyone else's best."

My heart stuttered. "That was a pretty great thing to say."

"I got something right?"

"You get a lot of things right. Give yourself some credit. You're better at this relationship stuff than you think."

His lips curved up in a gentle smile.

"In fact, you're a good man who deserves good things," I said, sitting up. "Scoot up the bed a little."

With a curious glance, he did as told. Not stopping until his head hit the pillows and the hard-on I'd been ignoring sat about level with my face. Half-naked hugs definitely did things to him. The crown poked out from atop his pajama pants, swollen and proud. Skin like velvet stretched over the thickness. I slipped my hand beneath the material and wrapped my fingers around him in a firm grip. "I do like your dick."

"I am very glad to hear that."

"The rest of you isn't bad either." I bent down, taking his broad head into my mouth and swirling my tongue around it. The way his stomach muscles flexed was gratifying. He smelled of musk and salt, his body deliciously warm to the touch. The man was temptation itself. I doubt I could ever get close enough to him, spend enough time touching and tasting him. Not if I tried for a hundred years. "I appreciate you opening up and sharing your thoughts and feelings with me."

He grunted.

Nice and easy, I pumped his cock, throwing in a slight twist of the wrist just for fun. Friction really was everything. He hardened further, pre-cum beading at the top. I trailed the tip of my tongue up the length of him, tracing the veins. The heat and intensity in his gaze as he watched me . . . he didn't even blink. I could have been a mighty goddess kneeling there playing with his private parts. Or I could have been just me. Either was fine.

When I took him in my mouth again, sucking hard, he gasped. Such a thrilling sound. My tongue lashed him before digging in, working the sweet spot at the indent beneath the rim. And all the while I stroked him, working him higher. My grip on him tightened and his hips shifted on the bed. Something about the softness of the skin versus the hardness beneath worked for me. A visceral thing making my breasts ache and my sex wet. The scents and sounds and just everything. Doing this to him, for him, was truly a pleasure.

With a soft growl he raised his upper body, reaching out to gather up my hair. All the better for him to see. "The way you use that pretty mouth on me, Norah. Fuck."

I hummed in agreement and he growled some more. Then I took as much of him as I could deep into my mouth, tightening my lips. How the muscles in his thighs and belly flexed. All of his strength contained and at my mercy. My hand pumped faster and he swore some more.

"Fuck yes," he said, voice guttural. "That's it, my beautiful girl."

His grip on my hair tightened, making my scalp sing. Not something I was usually into in bed. Goes to show how much farther you could go with someone you trusted. A thought to ponder when I wasn't otherwise occupied. And he was so damn close. All panting breath and frantic movements. I drew hard on him, sucking and pumping and getting him off. The thick shaft spasmed in my hand and he came with a shout. Lost in the pleasure, he rutted my mouth like an animal. Hips bucking and the hand in my hair holding me in place. Damn hot.

I eased him down with soft touches. He collapsed back onto the mattress and lay there spent. I'd never seen a lovelier sight in my life. The sweat glistening on his skin and relaxed lines of his face. Only I got to see him like this now. To watch him come undone in all of his savage male beauty. Sad to note that love was quite possibly making a bad poet out of me. But oh well.

One blue eye opened and spied me sitting there staring at him. Without a word, he grabbed my arms and dragged me up his body. Not stopping until I was lying on top of him. Strong arms anchored me to him. The thud of his heartbeat constant and steady beneath my ear. Patrick Walsh was a cuddler. It was official.

His hands slid down my bare back, slipping beneath the elastic of my panties to grip my butt cheeks once more. Such an ass man. Honestly. He gripped and squeezed and massaged while I tried not to squirm. And I needed to come too. The sooner the better. If only there was a set etiquette about when it was acceptable to ask a man if you could sit on his face. And it was such a nice face, too.

We were still new and hadn't done it before. Maybe he had claustrophobic tendencies. Or it might just not be something he liked. Then there was the small yet stupid fear associated with this act. What if I accidentally smothered him? I'd go down in history as the woman who killed a Hollywood heartthrob with her thighs. The shame of it all.

"If that's your method of rewarding me," he said, "then I'm honestly happy to talk whenever you want. Thoughts, feelings, whatever. I am at your disposal."

"I'll keep that in mind."

"Lady's choice. What would you like?"

"I, um . . ." And all the words up and left me. Ugh.

"What does it mean when you look like that?" he asked. "The tips of your ears are turning pink, Norah."

"Huh."

"What's going on inside that head of yours?"

"Funny you should say the word 'head.'"

He smiled. "Oral it is. Then I think we should fuck a time or two. Just because."

Before he could flip me onto the mattress, I scrambled

back. I don't know what was stopping me from just asking. This was stupid. Like it would be impolite to grace his gorgeous face with my thighs. I was a grown woman, dammit. And allowed to want what I wanted. "Wait."

"What?"

"I want to, um . . ." I gifted him my most salacious grin. "Why don't you lie back and get comfortable there and I'll just show you?"

Chapter Sixteen

"**H**OW ARE YOU DOING?" ASKED PATRICK, appearing behind my chair.

Kelly, my makeup artist, gave him a brief smile before returning to contouring. Total lack of bedazzlement on her part. Guess seeing stars would get old fast when working on a major talk show.

"Good," I said, hardly shaking at all.

"Everything's going to be fine."

I nodded. Sometimes you just got to fake it until you make it. And appearing on daytime TV in front of an audience of millions definitely qualified as one of those times. Perhaps everyone would be busy or watch something else today. You never know. Margarita Ramirez had been one of the reigning talk show queens for over two decades. Which was why Angie chose her as our sole big interview together as a couple. On school holidays Gran and I used to watch her show together. Now I was going to be on it. Whoa.

My outfit had been carefully chosen. A black crepe belted midi dress by Valentino with short sleeves that hid the worst of the bruising and low-heeled suede boots. Patrick complemented me perfectly in a dark suit with no tie. We looked like total couple goals if I said so myself. Let's hope everyone else thought so too.

It had been a rushed morning, but I'd managed to sneak in some calls. First to the lawyer who would represent me and the second to a real estate agent regarding the shop Zena wanted. Tomorrow, Zena and I would do a walk-through of the space and then have a long talk about what being partners would entail. It was really happening and I couldn't be more excited.

But back to the here and now.

Kelly gave me the okay and I said my thanks. This was it. A sound assistant wired us up. Then I held my hand out to Patrick and an assistant led us onto the soundstage to wait in the wings. A full audience packed the back of the room and a myriad of camera people and other types filled the floor between them and the set. A collection of cream armchairs and a comfy-looking couch along with a dark wooden coffee table. Big vibrant flower arrangements sat on pedestals farther back, in front of a screen currently displaying Margarita's name.

"You're going to be great," whispered Patrick in my ear.

"I haven't been on TV before."

"The awards were televised. People saw you on that and you were wonderful."

"This is different," I said.

"I know, but you're a natural."

I frowned. "What if they think I smell funny or something?"

"Fortunately for us, not even digital television has mastered the art of scent yet. No one outside of this room will ever know."

"That's still a fair amount of people."

Patrick bent down and sniffed at my neck. "Nothing funny smelling about you. Try not to worry. We're going to do this together, okay?"

"It's live to air. Live, Paddy."

"I think there's like a five-second delay, but yeah."

Fake

"What if I mess up and people think you're an idiot for dating me?" I asked.

"Fuck 'em."

The intro music started and the audience clapped and cheered and, oh shit. There was a good chance I was about to pee myself. This is exactly why stars and average people shouldn't date. It was much too dangerous. I could have been hiding from the world, highly dissatisfied with my life, and polishing silverware right now. Yet here I was, dressed in designer gear and holding his hand. Despite my palm being slick with sweat, he didn't let go.

From the other side of the set, Margarita walked onstage in a cool pale blue pantsuit, waving all the while. Her unbound hair bounced with each step while her smile grew and grew. She took a seat and started to talk, welcoming everyone to the show. Her voice was even warmer in person, her gaze sharper. Talk about competence porn. I wanted to be her when I grew up. Then she started talking about Patrick. About his early beginnings in Arizona and his career up until now. About his past dating history and our recent engagement. There were photos of him in character for various movies, walking into clubs with this supermodel or that, and then him and me being chased by the paparazzi outside the grocery store. His arm around me at the awards. And finally, there was us making out in the pool dressed in diamonds and formal wear. It was all there, both the lust and the bond between us, in the grasping hands and the hungry mouths. Talk about not being fit for public consumption. I hoped Gran wasn't watching. Someone needed to slap an R rating on the damn thing.

Margarita made a show of fanning her face as the audience went wild.

"Just in case this all goes to hell and I say the wrong thing and you never want to talk to me again," I said, "I enjoyed every moment with you."

For a long moment, Patrick just stared at me. Then he opened his mouth and said, "Norah, they're going to love you just like I do."

I froze. "Wait. What did you say?"

But there was no time. Our names were announced and we were walking onstage while the world watched. I slapped a smile on my face and straightened my shoulders. So many people staring at us, and that was just the studio audience. Given that I lacked the space and time to properly overthink what Patrick had said, I put it to the side for now. After all, he was probably just being nice and supportive. Things like that. While he might have thrown the L word out there, he couldn't possibly mean it *that* way.

We settled into the sofa and Margarita went straight into it with, "Patrick, you're notorious for being tight-lipped about your private life. What's changed?"

"In a word, Norah," he said. "There's been a lot of interest in me over the last few months and I wanted to set the record straight. I'm with this beautiful woman and everything is great."

Margarita grinned. "Oh, my."

I clung to his hand for all I was worth.

"What do you say, Norah?" asked Margarita.

"What can I say?" I grinned. "I'm a very lucky woman."

"And he's a very lucky man."

"I am," agreed Patrick.

The audience went wild at our lovefest.

Margarita sat forward in her chair, inviting confidences. "How did you two meet?"

Fake

"Where I used to work, at a wonderful restaurant called Little Italy," I said. "Patrick would come in every few weeks or so when he was in LA."

"They had good food?" asked Margarita. "I love pasta."

"They have great pasta. Best in the city. You should try it sometime." Patrick gave her his devil-may-care grin. Oh my God. That smile slipped off your panties while it slapped you on the ass. No wonder he earned the big bucks. "But I went there because of her. Every time I was back in LA, I couldn't resist sticking my head in and seeing if she'd finally talk to me."

Margarita raised a brow. "She made you work for it?"

"She did. She'd take my order and be perfectly polite, but she wouldn't talk to me otherwise. Never asked me anything. Never asked me for anything either."

"You liked that I gave you your space," I said, not sure where he was going with this. Or how real we were being. That was the problem with fake. After a while it got hard to tell fact from fiction. And I sure as hell wasn't going to start asking him personal questions on prime-time TV.

"Yeah, I did," he agreed. "But that's not why I kept going back. I did that because I wanted to get to know you. So I'd sit near the back of the restaurant where you tended to hang out doing things and I'd just kind of see if today was the day."

My smile didn't fit quite right. It felt off center or something. "Never really told you that before, did I?"

"No," I said, "you didn't."

His smile turned into something more genuine. Something just for me.

"You never talked about this?" asked Margarita. "Why didn't you tell her, Patrick?"

He licked his lips. "Guess I figured she knew. I didn't want

215

to be the creep that kept turning up at her job, you know? I was trying to play it cool." He turned to Margarita before looking back at me. "I really thought you knew, Norah."

"I didn't," I said, laughing. How awkward. "I thought you liked the food. Are you being serious right now?"

"Absolutely." And his gaze gave away nothing. Or possibly everything. It was really hard to tell which.

"You kept coming into the restaurant because of me?"

"Of course I did," he said, tone definite.

My smile stayed weird and hesitant. Angie would probably smack me upside the head and tell me to get with the program. He was just saying what everyone wanted to hear. Selling the grand romance of the century, a Hollywood heartthrob and the fan girl. I just wish I hadn't wanted to hear it so damn much. That maybe he'd been choosing me all along and not the Penne Ragu and Meatballs with Parmesan. Not the quick fix to his damaged reputation. Just me. Was it even possible?

But this was work and we were playing our roles. Now was no time to get carried away and start questioning everything. Later maybe.

"How does that make you feel, Norah?" asked Margarita, her voice low.

He watched me like nothing else mattered. Like everything I said and did was important. And I couldn't have looked away from him if I tried.

"Special," I said after swallowing hard. "But he makes me feel special all the time. Between you and me, that's why I keep him around."

The audience laughed, delighted.

"Oh, I like you. And the bond between you two is beautiful," said Margarita with a smile. "I'm so glad you came on the show today."

"So am I," I said, relaxing a little. As much as I could, given the situation. "So am I."

You can tell when everything is exceeding expectations. When life is so damn close to perfect you can taste it. It's when things are inevitably turned upside down again. Because we'd not only survived the TV interview, but it kind of felt like we'd worked wonders. We'd won them over. Patrick and I had charmed the studio audience and our interviewer, it seemed. We'd been funny and authentic in a way I hadn't expected, especially since so much of us and our relationship wasn't real. So of course, when everything was great, we hit a wall. *The* wall.

His cell rang as we arrived home and were walking in the door. When he looked at the screen, his whole body seemed to switch from relaxed to alert in an instant. "Janisha. Hey."

Janisha was his agent's name. I hadn't met her, but apparently she was fearsome, charming, and generally not to be messed with. Which is about what you'd want in a Hollywood agent.

"Of course the answer is yes." His gaze jumped to me before his jaw tensed and he turned away. "That soon? Shit." Next, he shoved a hand through his hair, all agitated. "If that's what they want. Okay. 'Bye." And he disconnected the call. There was something in his eyes, a mixture of sadness and resignation.

"You got the job."

"Yeah," he said.

"Congratulations." Of all the fake smiles I'd flashed over the course of my life, this one would go down as the hardest. My cheek twitched violently and I kind of wanted to cry. But I wouldn't. It felt a little like what I'd imagined getting punched in the chest would be like. My heart might never be the same. "That's great, Paddy."

"They want me on a flight to Hungary tonight, if possible."

"Hungary?"

"I'll be there for a bit over three months."

"Wow." And despite knowing this was bound to happen sometime, it just seemed so soon. Too soon. Though I didn't let any of that out of my mouth.

"We did it," he said, slipping his cell into his back pocket with a smile on his lips. And he was so happy now, his big body all but radiating joy. "Or *you* did it. That's the truth—you rescued me. I'm officially no longer persona non grata."

"There are plenty of raging assholes out there deserving of being publicly shamed; you're just not one of them," I said, and smiled back at him.

"Either way, I learned my lesson."

My smile wavered.

He stepped closer and drew me in against him. I don't know why it felt awkward. As if everything had suddenly changed. This moment had always been coming and now here it was. I slipped my arms around his waist and held on tight.

"I want you to stay in the house," he mumbled against my head. "Will you, Norah? I know you've got things you want to do and you're not coming with me. But just because I'll be gone for a while doesn't mean this can't still be a home for you."

"It would look pretty dubious if I moved out—public relations and our relationship and the whole contract thing."

"I honestly don't give a fuck about any of that right now. I just want to know you're going to be okay while I'm away."

I snorted. "I'm a big girl. Of course I'll be fine, Paddy."

"You're getting paid the rest of the money tomorrow and the contract is getting ripped up. Should have done that days ago. Don't know where my head was at."

"We've been pretty busy, what with the sexing and everything."

"You know you can come with me," he said. "You have to know that. But I get that you have your walk through with the real estate agent and Zena tomorrow and how that's all time sensitive."

"Maybe once I've got that sorted . . ."

"Take care of your business here then we'll talk."

"Yeah."

He rubbed a soothing hand up and down my spine. But this time, it just didn't work. He was leaving and I had to stay here. While I had been used to being alone, after getting to be with him as a couple, this was going to suck. Even if it was temporary. I actually felt a little sympathy for Liv. Being pulled in two different directions at the same time really did suck.

"We'll be okay," I said, willing it to be true. "We can text and chatk and internet sex over Skype. It'll be fun and educational."

"My hours will probably be a bit crazy. But we'll work it out."

Mei wandered around the corner with her cell in hand. "Janisha is blowing up my phone, demanding I get you packed and on a flight."

Patrick grinned. "I got the role."

"That's great!" She beamed. "So you're flying out tonight?"

He nodded.

"Looks like the weather in Budapest is mild, heading into hot and wet in a month or two. I'll sort out what you'll need. We should have a quick chat, too."

"Sure," he said. "Norah—"

"I'm fine. We're fine." I gave him another of those smiles. "Go do what you need to do, Paddy. This is the win. This is what we've been working toward. It's a good thing."

His jaw shifted. Seemed his fake smile was no better than mine. It was a compliment, really. That he didn't try to act in front of me. That we could read each other this well. Then he grabbed my face and pressed his mouth against mine. And I grabbed him right back. There we stood, clutching at each other again, holding on for all we were worth. It was a positive sign. It had to be.

The time flew. After he and Mei had had their meeting, we got busy. With Patrick grabbing clothes, and me folding and packing them into suitcases, while Mei sorted out everything else required for a swift exit. Three months was a long time. Over a quarter of a year. I might have been kind of shell-shocked by the suddenness of it all. It's one thing to know something is bound to happen eventually and another to have it smack you upside the head.

"Do you have enough socks?" I asked, stuffing one more pair in for good luck.

"You made me grab a dozen pairs. That's a lot. Pretty sure they also have socks in Budapest." Patrick dumped a bunch of toiletries on the bed. "I can always buy some. How soon do you think you can come out and visit?"

"I don't know."

"We can wait and find out when I've got a few days off to play tourist with you. That'd be fun."

"Yes."

"Looking forward to doing some of the car chase stunts in the film," he said. Like it was nothing. "There's one they've got planned involving the vehicle being suspended off a cliff."

"I would take it as a personal favor if you refrained from hanging off cliffs."

He laughed. God, he was so happy. How could I not be happy for him? His hand slipped around the back of my neck and he leaned in close. "Norah, you're killing me. You look like you're about to cry."

"I'm not about to cry, you're about to cry," I joked. Worst joke ever. He was so not about to cry. Not even a little.

In fact, he just blinked. "Right. Let me get the rest of this shoved in there; then we're going to talk."

"Car is arriving in five, Paddy," yelled Mei. "Oh, forget that, it's here!"

"There's no time to talk. You have a plane to catch." I took a deep breath. "Call me later."

"Yeah. Okay." He frowned. "Wish this wasn't so rushed."

"I know."

"We're going to be okay," he said, like it needed confirmation.

"Of course we are."

"Bags ready?" asked Mei, charging into the bedroom. "Kiss the girl, Paddy. Time to go."

He did as told. A soft, gentle kiss I wanted to hold onto forever. A sweet thing full of adoration and regret. When he rested his forehead against mine, we stared into each other's eyes for a long moment. Total love-struck stuff. But I needed it. Maybe it would always be like this. Him running off to the far corners of the world for work and me being left behind. Maybe one day I'd be used to it and send him off with a real smile. I looked forward to that day. Given there was no time and nothing to say that would change things, neither of us spoke. We just took that moment together, breathing in each other's air, memorizing each other's faces. Then we ran out of time. He was in a car on his way to the airport. He was gone.

"Your face right now is the reason I haven't missed dating since my divorce." Mei sipped her beer beside me on the couch. That we were pairing it with a selection of ice creams was kind of gross, but oh well. "You're all forlorn looking, Norah. I hate to see it."

"I didn't know you were divorced," I said, digging through the chocolate chip cookie dough ice cream for the good stuff. Only fats and sugars could save the day. Or night, as it were. Lovesick and heartsore, I sat there in a kind of a daze.

"Happened a few years back. He inherited a house in Toronto and we hadn't been doing so well. I didn't feel like moving countries was the right thing for me." She sighed. "So he left and I stayed."

"Did you try doing it long distance?"

"No. In all honesty, it was already over." She took another pull on her beer. "You either grow together or fall apart, I guess."

"I'm sorry that happened to you."

She shrugged. "Eh. We got together when we were young and it just didn't last. You change so much in your twenties and then heading into your thirties. Priorities, wants and needs, they're all up in the air."

"True."

"I think you and Paddy have pretty good odds of making it," she said.

I perked up. "You think so?"

"I mean, you either put the effort in or you don't. But I think you two could make it."

"We've only been together for like five seconds. That's what worries me the most. That there isn't this great big well-established foundation for us to build on."

"Yeah," she said. "Relationships are tricky. It's not just how into each other you are, it's how you fit into each other's worlds. How badly you want it and what you're willing to sacrifice."

I slumped back against the couch, abandoning my pint of ice cream on the coffee table. "Do you think I should have gone with him?"

"I can't make that decision for you." She tapped her nails against the bottle of beer. "It was hard enough for me deciding to let him go alone and have a new assistant assigned to him over on set. But I want to get the production company rolling. I want to start moving forward, you know?"

"I hear you. It seemed so straightforward in theory," I said. "Of course I wasn't going to be his shadow. But now that he's gone . . ."

"You're all sad face."

"Yeah."

"Poor Paddy. He's been abandoned by both of us."

"He's a big boy. He'll manage."

She smiled. "He's come a long way since you walked in the door. I think Paddy's one of those nothing-or-everything types. And no one else made him want to make the leap before."

I made a humming noise. "Tell me about your plans for the production company."

"Ah, I have two books I'm hoping he'll be interested in getting options on. One is a romance and the other is more of an action-adventure thing," she said. "I'll leave you a copy of the romance. See what you think. It's an angsty story."

"That would be great. Paddy is an exceptional brooder."

"Right?" she asked. "I think he'd be amazing as the lead. I

figure we start out looking for a few vehicles for him. Then maybe expand and see about establishing new actors and directors and so on. It'll be hard work getting everything together, but we've got the right connections to make it happen."

"You're going to be great, Mei."

"Damn right I am."

"Thank you for staying and keeping my mopey ass company tonight," I said. "And for ordering all the ice cream."

"Anytime, Norah."

I couldn't bring myself to go to sleep in his room. The scent of him lingered on the pillows and it made me miss him too much. In fact, I couldn't bring myself to go to sleep at all for the longest time. Instead, I stared at the shadows on the ceiling and second-guessed just about every choice I'd made since birth. As you do.

But mostly I revisited the things I'd said and done since stepping foot inside this house. I couldn't say I'd have done anything differently. My brain, however, regurgitated it all for my overthinking pleasure anyway.

For all of my good intentions to remain single and get my shit sorted, I'd ended up in a relationship. A bit of a failure on my part, though I'd been wildly attracted to him from the start. There was no way I wouldn't have found myself in bed with the man having been given half the chance. Patrick Walsh naked and willing was always bound to blow my mind. How we'd wound up having a relationship above and beyond the contractual obligations and attempt at friendship was a doozy. I really hadn't seen that coming. Yet now we were together even though he was on the other side of the world (or halfway there) and I had no idea what the future held. Or if we had a future at all.

This was the problem with me and relationships. I always fell too far, too fast. Long before I knew what I was doing, it was already too late and I was in over my head. At least I'd had the sense to pick someone who wanted me back this time. Thank goodness for that. And I wanted all of Paddy. Fake had been fine for a while, but real was light-years better. Being with him couldn't come at the cost of me building a career for myself, however.

Sensible Norah would not allow it. Love-struck Norah might wail and gnash her teeth, but too bad. I could not afford to revert to thinking with my vagina and my heart alone. My brain must be allowed to have a say. The fact was, relationships weren't always forever. I'd learned that from my earlier epic dating misadventures. I couldn't exist solely for the benefit of a man. As tempting as that might be. It was time to seize the fucking day and get a life.

I would totally do that right after I cried myself to sleep.

My first morning without Patrick went like this: No messages from Angie for the first time in forever. No Patrick-centric timetable to be managed. My life was once more my own and I had all this time on my hands. Which was a slightly strange feeling after the past couple of weeks. There'd always been something nerve-inducing coming up on the schedule. Some huge public spectacle. But no more. Now that he was gone, there probably weren't even any paparazzi up at the gate. I might be able to dump the bodyguard soon and be a free woman. How extraordinary to go back to blending in with the general public.

I washed my face, brushed my teeth, and applied approximately three tubes of concealer to cover the dark patches beneath my eyes. My teary pink-tinged eyeballs required eye drops, which I didn't have. Maybe I could hide them behind big dark sunglasses in the meantime. I refused to be the sad lonely girl. I was a fully grown and capable woman. So even if I was dragging my somewhat despondent ass around town, I'd do it in style. I tied my hair back in a ponytail and donned a Carolina Herrera blue gingham summer dress. Made me kind of look like a quaint country picnic come to life, but it was cheerful, dammit.

This was the first day of the rest of my life. I could do this. I could be someone besides Patrick Walsh's fiancée. It had only taken thirty years, but I would always be a work in progress, on the way to being the best possible version of me. Hell yes.

And I believed that right up until I walked into the kitchen to find Mei and Paddy sitting at the table drinking coffee. He was rumpled, his tee all creased and hair in disarray. The way it got when he'd been all restless and shoving his fingers through it over a prolonged period. Stubble lined his jaw and the bruising under his eyes was even more pronounced than mine. An impressive feat.

"What are you doing here?" Oh, dear. That was me screeching. Never a good look. "Paddy?"

Mei stood. "I'll leave you to it."

"Thanks," he said.

She just nodded, giving me a quick smile.

My knees were shaking for some reason. That my back rested against the wall was about the only thing holding me up.

"Why don't you sit down?" he asked.

"Why don't you answer the question?" My hand flew to my mouth and my voice went deathly quiet. "Shit. Did something happen? Did they take back the job offer? Was it something I did?"

He frowned. "Why would it be something you did?"

"I don't know. I'm having a panic attack," I grumbled. "You're supposed to be on a flight landing in Hungary in a few hours and instead you're here, and it's really thrown me because it was everything you've been working toward and wanted since the moment I met you."

"Yeah." He winced. "It's sort of a long story. First the flight got delayed. After all of that rushing. Some sort of last-minute mechanical failure that dragged on and on. And I was sitting there the whole time in the lounge just thinking about everything. Just going over and over it inside my head. And when we finally got told to board . . . I couldn't get on the plane."

"What?"

"I know. I just couldn't do it."

"Why not?"

"You," he said.

"Me?"

"Yeah. You."

My butt hit the floor. Which kind of hurt. But never mind.

Patrick rose so fast his chair scooted across the floor. "Are you alright?"

"I think so."

He knelt in front of me. "I couldn't get on the plane, Norah. The thought of leaving you so soon . . . it just didn't feel right. Maybe if we'd been together for a while it would have been okay. But not right now. Since you couldn't come with me, I'll just have to stay here with you. At least for the next little while."

"Wow."

He shrugged. "Anyway, my career isn't in such bad shape. And it's not like there won't be things getting filmed here in LA. In the meantime, I can work with Mei on setting up the production company. Won't hurt me to take a break. I've been working pretty much nonstop since I was twenty-one."

"You're serious about this?"

"Absolutely. This way, I'll be here to support you with whatever you're doing for the next few months or so. Much better than screwing around on Skype and trying to figure out time zones."

I collapsed back against the wall. "Paddy, you're being pretty much perfect right now."

"Don't get too used to it. I'm bound to fuck up sooner or later."

"I don't believe it." I sighed. "Though I had pretty much already decided to get the shop sorted and fly out and spend at least a couple of days with you before I started working with Zena full-time. You'd only been gone a few hours, but I missed you like crazy."

"Baby," he said with a gentle smile that made my heart swoon. I'd seen its facsimile in films, but this was about a billion times better. It was all true and it was all mine.

"You said I wasn't a baby. That was like the first pet name you tried."

"I lied. It just felt too personal or something. But now it fits you perfectly." He grabbed me around the waist, lifting my ass off the floor. Then he deposited us both on a seat, with me on his lap. Of course I wrapped my arms around his neck and got as close as I could. I wasn't a complete idiot. He looked me over with raised brows. "Not to be critical. But why are you dressed like Pollyanna?"

"You left. My heart was broken. I was trying to be cheerful."

"Right," he said. "Why weren't you sleeping in our room?"

"It made me too sad."

"It's nice to know that being apart doesn't work for either of us."

"Not even a little."

I lifted my chin and he met me halfway, pressing his lips against mine. The kiss stayed chaste for approximate half a second. Which was good and right. Then his sleek tongue slid against mine and we were devouring each other to the best of our abilities. Hot, wet kisses really were their own reward. I hoped we'd always be clutching hands and eager mouths. The familiar taste of him was delicious. The faint scent of his sweat mixing with his cologne a dream. Our teeth knocked against each other, our making-out getting frenzied. Because the feel of him hardening against my rear was nothing less than divine. We needed to get somewhere private and do away with our clothes as soon as possible.

But first, he'd made a huge concession by not getting on that plane. He'd put me first when no adult male had chosen to do that for me. I needed to put myself out there too. Take a chance.

"I love you, Paddy," I said, my voice about as firm as possible, given the situation.

"You do, huh?"

"Yes." I happy sighed. "You don't have to say it back or anything. I know it's early days. Though you did sort of say it before the TV interview. We never did get around to discussing that, did we? But I want you to know—"

"I love you, too."

I paused. He was so beautiful inside and out. All I could do was stare. "You do?"

"Why do you think I didn't get on that plane?"

"Huh."

"You can have anything and everything you want from me, Norah. I've told you before. Maybe this time you'll believe it."

"I believe it." I smiled, heart full to bursting. Which would be messy, but oh well. I was starting to realize that love was like that. Messy and magical and everything in between. And hands down, living this reality with him beat anything up for offer on the silver screen.

The End

Continue reading for a sneak peek of

Pause

Prologue

"WHAT'S WRONG?" I ASK. OR TRY TO ASK. ONLY my throat is sore and dry, so my voice barely rises above a whisper. Not even swallowing seems to help. "Mom?"

She wipes away the tears in a rush. "Sweetheart."

Everything in the strange white room seems hazy and insubstantial. I blink repeatedly, trying to clear my view. There's a vase of fading pink roses sitting on a small side table and I'm hooked up to a drip along with an array of machines. My body is one long, dull, horrible ache. What the hell happened?

"You were in an accident," says Dad, answering the question I hadn't yet asked. He rises from a chair in the corner of the room. "Do you remember?"

Before I can answer, Mom's there with her tremulous smile. "You've woken up before, but never for long. You keep going back to sleep."

None of this makes sense. "What . . ."

"The doctor told us that we have to ask you how you're feeling and what you can remember," she says.

"W-wait," I stutter. "Where's Ryan?"

They share a worried glance.

"What's going on?" I ask.

"What do you remember?" Mom perches on the edge of the bed. "How do you feel?"

"Can you move your fingers and toes?" asks Dad.

"I feel confused and frustrated." I stop to swallow again. Still not helping. "But yes, my fingers and toes are fine."

Mom rushes to fetch a plastic cup full of water with a straw sticking out for me. I try to take it slow, try to just sip it, but it tastes so good.

"I don't remember an accident," I admit once I'm finished.

"Another car hit you and you lost control."

They both wait for me to react. For recognition to strike. But I've got nothing. "When?"

"Let's wait for the doctor," says Mom, wringing her hands.

"Just tell me. Please."

"It's the fourteenth of February." Dad straightens his tie in a rare show of nerves. "That's the date today."

I frown. "No. No, that can't be."

Mom nods, adamant.

"What?" I ask, incredulous.

"Seven Months. Yes," says Dad.

"It's a long time to be in a coma. No one thought you'd wake up." Mom balls up a Kleenex in her hands. "The doctors said . . . it doesn't matter what they said now. You're a medical miracle. I knew you'd be okay. My daughter's a fighter."

Holy shit.

While none of this makes sense, it's all too real to be a joke. Not that my parents have much of a sense of humor. But there's nothing false in my mother's pained eyes. The last thing I can remember was it being July and we were at home planning a barbeque. Only a summer storm hit on my way to the store, the first rain in over a month. Then nothing.

Seven months of my life just gone. Halloween, Thanksgiving, Christmas, and New Year's. Summer, autumn, and winter. A whole half a year. It can't be. It isn't possible.

My brain won't cooperate and even attempting to lift my hand is a strain. It doesn't look any different, but I'm so damn weak and locked up. And where's my engagement ring, my wedding band? Guess they took them off me for security reasons, but still. I don't like it.

"Where's Ryan?" I ask again.

Dad flinches.

Mom turns away.

"Where is my husband?" This time my voice is trembling. There was no one else in the car with me. Ryan stayed home to sweep the deck and clean the grill. To get everything ready. I don't remember anyone being in the passenger seat. But then I don't remember an accident either, just some vague shadowy dreams. This is hell.

"Oh, sweetheart," says Mom, eyes glossy with unshed tears.

"He isn't . . ." I can't say the word *dead*. I don't want to even think it. "What happened?"

"He's on his way." Dad slips his cell phone back into his pants pocket, all while avoiding my eyes. "Just try and stay calm, Anna. Getting all upset about the situation won't help anything."

Despite my father's words, my breath comes faster. A full-on panic attack all of about two seconds away. Not easy to do from a prone position, but I'm giving it my best damn shot. "What the hell is going on?"

Chapter One

THREE MONTHS LATER . . .

L EIF LARSEN LIVES IN A BIG OLD BROWN BRICK BUILDING with a sprawling dogwood out front in a cool urban neighborhood. No one answers when I press the buzzer. But according to the details on the scrap of paper the nurse gave me, I've got the right place.

What to do?

The rational response would be to give up and go home. Because hiding out in my childhood bedroom has worked out great so far (and this would be sarcasm). It's been months since I left the house for anything other than a medical appointment. Weeks since I've heard from any friends. Right on cue, my cell buzzes inside my tan Coach purse. I don't bother to look. Mom requests proof of life every hour on the hour. Not even dinner at the country club can distract her, apparently. Her parental concern for me is well past claustrophobic.

My hand clenches the iron railing against a gust of unseasonably warm evening wind. It's been a while since I stopped using a mobility aid, but things can still feel tricky. The whole damn world does, if I'm being honest. So many things I took for granted have now been turned upside down.

This is the problem with living the supposed dream. With having an airtight plan for your life. Meet Prince Charming and marry him. Find the perfect job. Only problem is, if something goes wrong, when reality smacks you upside the head and sends you reeling, then there's no system for putting the pieces back together. There's no Plan B because it never occurred to you that you'd need one. A lack of imagination on my part, perhaps.

A motorcycle pulls up to the curb and it's like everything happens in slow motion. Something about this long, lean man just makes time want to stand still. A denim-clad leg is swung over the back of the iron beast. A helmet is removed and shoulder-length hair tumbles free. High cheekbones and perfect lips are framed by stubble and all I can do is stare.

I don't know if I'm intimidated or turned on or what.

"Can I help y . . ." he begins. There's the faintest spark of recognition in his eyes.

I continue to stand there frozen.

"Fuck me," he mutters, stalking closer. His gaze slides over me from top to toe, lingering on the small scars on my left cheek from the glass. There's no attempt made to hide his curiosity. "It's really you."

Nichelle the nurse described him as being a nice young man. Nothing more. Certainly nothing that would prepare me for this. And I dispute "nice." Ripped denim, battered leather, and a Harley-Davidson motorbike are not *nice*.

"Never seen you conscious before," he says, getting even closer.

I just blink.

From beneath the collar and cuffs of his leather jacket emerge colorful tattoos. Lots of them. Blue waves and black letters. Red flames and white flowers. The man is a walking, talking piece of art. My parents would be horrified. Ryan too, for that matter. Not that any of their opinions matter. I need to forge my own path. Go my own way.

"How did you find me?" he asks with a faint frown.

"Oh. Ah." I smooth down the front of my pale blue midi-length linen summer dress. My dark hair is slicked back in a low ponytail and my makeup is simple but perfect. It's nice having some things I can control. "One of the nurses from the ICU told me about you and I wanted to come say thank you. But maybe an apology would be more in order?"

For a moment he pauses, then he asks, "Do you want to come in?"

Good question. The fact is, I don't know. Nor do I know how to do this. Something made obvious when my mouth opens, but nothing comes out. So much nothing for such a length of time that it's beyond embarrassing. Dammit. Whatever it is I came here looking for, it wasn't this. Him. Whatever.

"We've never properly met, have we?" He holds out his big hand. "Hi, I'm Leif."

"Anna."

While I'm tentative, he shows no such reserve. Strong, warm fingers enfold my own stiff and cold ones. There's no attempt at a dominating handshake or groping. He gives my hand a squeeze, just the one gentle squeeze, before setting me free.

"I'd say it's nice to meet you, but that would be weird." He grins conspiratorially and oh my God. Everything low in my stomach wakes up and takes notice. Shame on my lady parts, but the chemical pull of the man is ridiculous. It takes me a minute to remember that I'm a married woman. Mostly. Well, somewhat anyway. I certainly have no business smiling at him like I am. My life is messed up enough without adding a crush. Perhaps it's in reaction to me, I don't know, but the mirth disappears and his gaze becomes serious. A little bleak even. "I still have nightmares about that day, you know?"

"I'm sorry."

"Not your fault."

"I shouldn't have come."

"Don't, Anna. Don't look like that. I didn't tell you to hurt you or make you uncomfortable. I was just ... sharing." His expression changes again, a more subdued smile taking the place of the brief hint of trauma. Then he suddenly winks at me all flirty like. I don't know how to react. I can barely keep up. The man is a whirlwind. "Want to come in and have a beer with me?"

"Are you sure?"

"Yes."

"I just ... I don't want to remind you of things you'd rather—"

"I want you to come inside. I wouldn't have asked otherwise."

A drink with a pretty wild man that I have a strange sort of history with or a swift return to safety and boredom? I don't overthink it. I don't even hesitate. "Then yes, Leif. I'd love to."

The police report states that when I lost control of my car, a man on a motorcycle was forced off the road to avoid impact. This was after I was hit by the other vehicle, but before I hit the tree. While the other driver fled the scene, the man on the motorcycle sustained a compound fracture to his right arm and was transported to the same hospital as me for treatment. The man who sat by my hospital bed every night reading to me. Until he stopped showing up.

None of this explains, however, why he doesn't own a single piece of furniture in his condo, besides a king-size mattress. Not a single thing hangs on the blank white walls. And the mattress is just lying there, in the center of the open kitchen/dining/living space. There are two small bedrooms, but he's not bothering to use either one of them. The mattress is covered with rumpled sheets and discarded pillows. My brain is far too happy to imagine all the obscene acts he might have participated in on that bed. It's disturbing to say the least. Porn thoughts aren't my usual go-to.

"You're probably more of a white wine drinker, huh?" He pops the top on a can of Swish Bissell Brothers beer and passes it to me.

"This is fine. Thank you."

After downing a mouthful of his own IPA, he gives the mostly empty room a glance. "Only got the place a couple of months back. Still working on furniture and stuff."

I nod in acknowledgment, my grip on my purse strap tightening. It's kind of my safety blanket. But he's had months to get organized. Good Lord. Medical bills would have done their damage, but still. The place is all but empty. A hollow shell. Not a home.

"Maybe we should have gone out," he says.

"It's fine."

He lifts himself up onto the kitchen counter and looks down at me, swinging his legs like a child. "You know, you keep saying the word 'fine.' But I can basically see the tic in your eye from my lack of a sofa and ottoman."

I am not amused.

"An armoire and a side table too, maybe. A couple of lamps for some mood lighting." He shrugs off his leather jacket. The short sleeves of his gray tee reveal even more ink along with the ripple of a whole lot of lean muscles. I don't let my gaze linger on the gnarled and jagged pink scar on his upper arm. And meanwhile there's a gleam in Leif's amber eyes, one that suggests he's enjoying himself way too much. "Don't even get me started on the lack of suitable glassware and drinks coasters. Probably for the best that I don't have any furniture or we'd be leaving water marks everywhere. I don't even have a linen napkin to my name. I'm really not prepared for guests at all, am I?"

"You're teasing me."

"You're judging me."

Shit. "I don't mean to," I say, subdued. Horrified at being called out.

Coming here was such a bad idea. He's a veritable stranger and we have nothing in common. Nothing good, at any rate. Then there's the part where I've been standing for too long. I hate the lingering weakness. My therapist says feelings of frustration and anger are to be expected. The accident has changed me. But mostly I'd just like to stop falling on my ass sometime soon.

"Come here," he says, jumping down with ease.

"What?"

"I'm going to lift you up onto the counter so you can get off your feet."

I just look at him.

"You need to sit, don't you? That's what the panicky face and the shakes mean. Believe me, I know it all too well, having recently spent some time in rehab myself with the arm."

"Yes," I reluctantly admit.

He makes a come-hither motion with his hands. "It's okay, Anna. I'm actually sorry I don't have a sofa for you to sit on. May I help you?"

My options aren't great. The floor, the mattress, or this counter. And there's no way I can get up there on my own. "Thank you. Yes."

He's standing so close. The man must be a bit over six feet

tall because I barely come up to his nose. Strong hands grip my waist and my breasts brush against his chest on the way up. Accidental, as evidenced by the slight widening of his eyes. As if he's never been up close to a bosom before. Please. And he smells ridiculously good. Clean, warm male sweat with a hint of spice. It verges on nirvana for a woman who hasn't had sex in almost a year. Not to mention the recognition that I am in fact a real live breathing person, with feminine wiles. The sensation that he's actually seeing me when I've felt nonexistent for so long is a heady thing. I've been a patient, a problem, everything but a strong, capable woman with a beating heart with wants and needs.

"Thanks," I say again, a little breathless this time.

"No problem." The way he stops and studies my face is weird. It's probably because I'm being weird. But finally, the odd moment ends, and he takes a step back. "Nice dress."

"Thank you."

"Tell me about yourself."

I counter with, "Nichelle said you visited me every night for a while in the hospital."

He sighs and crosses his arms. "I read to you at night for a few weeks. It's not a big deal."

"It kind of is. That was very sweet of you."

"Anna—"

"Don't," I say, harder than I mean to. "Don't diminish it. That you took the time to sit with me means a lot."

"Yeah. Well." He scratches his head. "Truth is, you were lousy company."

I bark out a surprised laugh. Then slap a hand over my mouth, because what an unholy loud noise.

Leif smiles behind his can of beer. "So come on, tell me about yourself."

"What do you want to know?"

"Start with the basics." He leans against the wall, one of his big-ass boots tapping out a beat in the silence. "Or surprise me. Whatever."

"Twenty-six. I was in hospitality, but that's all on hold." I shrug. "Grew up in Cape Elizabeth."

"Fancy neighborhood."

"If you say so. Only child. Went to college in New Hampshire." And that's basically me. "What about you?"

"Thirty-one. Local born and bred. Youngest of three sons. And I'm a tattoo artist."

I wrinkle my nose. "Wow."

"No ink for you, huh?"

"Not after all of the needles in the hospital." Not that it was a remote possibility beforehand, I mentally add. While I can appreciate how they look on him, I am nowhere near that interesting. Nor do I enjoy pain.

"Current relationship status?" he asks, gaze dropping to my bare hand. I'm sure it doesn't mean anything. Just your standard heteronormative reaction.

"Um." This question causes an even mix of awkward and painful. I should be used to it by now, but oh well. "It's complicated. Well . . . separated. Yeah."

"Right. I, um . . ." His mouth opens, then closes, as if he's thought better of whatever he was going to say. Which is curious. "I'm sorry."

I just nod. To be honest, I'm still experiencing culture shock. My marriage and my husband were huge parts of my life. As they should be. Now it's like someone hit pause on all of that and I'm not sure how to feel or what to think. With my heart and mind in a permanent state of confusion, there's not much I can do. Not yet. And it's been like this for months. Betrayal has one hell of a sting and I can't get past the pain to come even remotely close to forgiveness. Not yet. Maybe not ever. Forget about putting my wedding ring back on any time soon.

"Favorite food?" he asks, moving on, thank goodness.

"Mexican."

"Excellent choice." He pulls his cell out of his back jeans pocket. "How hungry are you?"

"I could eat."

At this, he gives me the stink eye. "You know, women always say that all casual like and then they eat half of your food."

"Order enough and I won't eat half of your food." I hold back a smile. "It's that simple."

He sighs. "I get the distinct feeling that nothing about you is simple. But I'm going to feed you anyway. How do you feel about tacos?"

"I love them."

"Carne asada?"

"Would be great."

"Queso and chips?"

"Please. And Mexican corn if they have it."

"They do. Okay," he says, busy with his cell. "We're set. You know, you're the first person I've had come visit me here outside of family."

"Really? Why?"

A shrug. "I don't know. Just busy, I guess."

I take another sip of beer. Which is when I realize I feel comfortable here, and I'm even having a good time. My first in a while. "Let me pay for half."

"No. I'm buying you dinner. It's a done deal." He tosses his cell on the counter. "Next time you can pay."

"There's going to be a next time?" I ask.

"Sure," he says, fetching himself another beer out of the fridge. "We've already had our bonding moment. I watched you get cut out of your car and everything. I was even holding your hand for a while until the paramedics arrived on the scene. So yeah, we survived a traumatic event together. More than the other guy who caused the accident and took off without helping can say."

"Am I a bad person for fervently hoping that God smites him?"

"Nope. I got a titanium plate and eight screws in my arm. Not my idea of a good time." He winces at the memory. "That compound fracture could have ended my career. Let alone what he did to you."

I raise my brows. "Subdural hematoma, hemorrhagic contusions, a dislocated shoulder, and five broken ribs."

"Exactly."

"How is your arm? Is it okay now?"

"Eh. Pretty much. I had okay insurance, so I didn't come out of it too badly. And I can tell when it's going to rain now, which is always handy," he says, his expression darkening. "That was a fucked-up thing, that accident. We're lucky to be alive."

"Very true. You didn't see the other car?"

He winces. "It was a silver sedan. Beyond that, I've got nothing. I sure as hell wish I'd seen the driver or the license plate or something useful."

I take another sip of beer, thinking it all over. My cell buzzes again inside my purse. I will not look at it. I won't.

"You need to get that?" he asks, settling himself on the floor.

I shake my head. "No. It's my mother. I appreciate her caring, but she's gotten clingy. I'm trying to deprogram her back to a manageable level."

245

"Fair enough."

"Just because I'm a little fragile doesn't mean I'm no longer an adult," I say, and boy do I sound cranky. On the verge of ranting, even. Not good.

"How are you doing with all of that, if you don't mind me asking?"

"Better than I was at first. I had to learn to walk and feed myself all over again. And there's a lot more rehabilitation in front of me."

He just nods.

"It's unlikely I'll be running anytime soon."

"Running sucks. My brother and his wife live next door and he makes me go with him all of the damn time."

"I have to be honest, I'm not really missing that part of it. Though it would be nice to have the option."

"Any white tunnel moments? Did you go toward the light and see your life flash before your eyes?" he asks.

"No." I shake my head. "Some weird dreams about spooky shadows, though. I think it was just the difference between day and night. Nothing interesting."

He leans his head back against the wall, watching me thoughtfully. "If I can say one thing on the subject of your mom . . ."

"Okay."

"I was only in the hospital for a few days. Long enough for them to operate and put some screws in to hold my arm together," he says. "But it was enough to see what was going on around you. The way your people were taking turns to stay with you. So you wouldn't wake up and have no one there, you know?"

I nod because I do know. Mom and Dad don't like to talk about it, but Ryan was only too willing to discuss all he'd done. Sharing the many and varied details in an attempt to prove himself the dutiful husband. The hours he spent by my bedside. The sacrifices he made. The long, lonely hours, et cetera. Poor Ryan.

Mind you, waking from a long vegetative state is no small feat. That the odds were against me was made abundantly clear by posts on my Facebook page. Old stories about me. Thoughts and prayers. Messages of loss like I'd already died. There was even a "rest in peace." No wonder Ryan gave up on me—just about everyone else had. Though those others hadn't stood up in front of a preacher and taken vows.

Anyway.

"Your mom took the night shifts," Leif continues. "She didn't mind me sitting with you because it meant she could go grab a coffee or go for a walk or whatever without worrying. Even though the first time we met she looked at me like I was there to steal her purse."

"I come from a judgmental family, apparently."

"You upper-middle-class suburbanites, you're all the same." He winks at me. "But, Anna, she was a wreck. It's probably not my place to say this, but that woman would do anything for you."

I sigh. "I know."

"Despite being a wreck, she was all over your treatment, grilling the doctors and nurses, getting all up in their faces if she wasn't sure something they were doing was best for her baby girl. It was a beautiful thing to see."

"You're making me feel like a bad daughter."

He downs a mouthful of beer. "No one could blame you for being pissed about the situation. It's got to be a huge adjustment."

"I had to move back in with them when I got out of the hospital for various reasons and . . . it's been an adjustment for everyone, I think."

"My mother is a wonderful woman. But she does have white

carpet and a special day of the week for doing laundry," he says. "So trust me, I understand. There's no way I could move back home."

I give him a glum smile and look around to buy myself time. To put my thoughts in order. It's really quite a nice condo. Older, with character. The kitchen could use some work and I'm guessing the bathroom is similar. But still. The high ceiling and wood-framed windows have charm.

He clears his throat. "What about your friends, they being supportive?"

"Oh. That too is complicated." And while I don't particularly want to say more, he just waits patiently for my explanation. "Most of the people I was close to . . . their lives have kind of moved on. Or I can no longer keep up. I get so easily exhausted."

"That must suck."

I nod. "Mom insists on driving me to all of my medical appointments, so we spend a lot of time together. She's had to cut back on church and her Scrabble group to fit it all in."

He says nothing.

"The truth is, I hate putting her out all of the time. I feel like an inconvenience in my own life."

His gaze is soft and sympathetic. "Anna . . ."

Oh, God. I'm the worst. The absolute ruling queen of negative losers. "And then for fun, I whine at hot guys."

At this, he immediately perks up. "You think I'm hot?"

"What? No."

"You said *hot*. I distinctly heard the word *hot*."

"I know, right? Would it kill you to turn the AC on?"

He snorts. "Very funny."

"Thanks."

Despite not having flirted in forever, it would seem I haven't lost the knack entirely. It's heartening. There's also not even one iota of guilt inside me. So there. Not that I'm interested in or looking for more. My life is confusing enough right now. Nor would someone like Leif really be interested in me. I'm okay looking, but he's on a whole other level. Though the curious glance he gives me strays into titillation.

"You don't want the AC on, do you?" He raises a brow. "You'd tell me if you did, right?"

"No, I don't want it on. And yes, I would tell you." Despite my mother's belief in suffering in polite silence, I do not like to sweat. My milkmaid complexion turns lobster red and it all goes downhill from there.

"Good," he says, relaxing back against the wall once more. "I have a feeling this is the beginning of a beautiful friendship."

I take a deep breath. "Leif. Thank you. That's very kind of you. But I don't need your pity. I—"

"It's the resting bitch face that does it for me," he carries on, as if I hadn't said a word. "And who else is going to teach me all about linen napkins and matching silverware and the various stuff I now apparently require as a new homeowner?"

"Good sir, you mistake me for Martha Stewart on a bad day."

"Nuh." He grins. "You're way hotter."

Heat rushes into my face. Despite this, it's kind of impossible not to smile back at him. Not only is he pretty, but happiness is apparently contagious around this man. And that's exactly what I need right now.

To keep reading, purchase
PAUSE
from your favorite online retailer today!

Purchase Kylie Scott's Other Books

Stage Dive Series
Lick
Play
Lead
Deep
Strong
Closer

Dive Bar Series
Dirty
Twist
Chaser

Trust

Flesh Series
Flesh
Skin
Flesh Series Shorts

It Seemed Like A Good Idea At The Time

Repeat

Lies

The Rich Boy

Novellas
Colonist's Wife
Heart's A Mess

About Kylie Scott

Kylie is a *New York Times* and *USA Today* best-selling author. She was voted Australian Romance Writer of the year, 2013, 2014, 2018 & 2019, by the Australian Romance Writer's Association and her books have been translated into twelve different languages. She is a long time fan of romance, rock music, and B-grade horror films. Based in Queensland, Australia with her two children and husband, she reads, writes and never dithers around on the Internet.

Facebook: www.facebook.com/kyliescottwriter

Instagram: www.instagram.com/authorkyliescott

Twitter: twitter.com/KylieScottbooks

Bookbub: www.bookbub.com/authors/kylie-scott

Website: www.kyliescott.com

Reader Group: www.facebook.com/
groups/599197093487040

Goodreads: www.goodreads.com/author/show/6476625.
Kylie_Scott

Bookbub: www.bookbub.com/authors/kylie-scott

Amazon: www.amazon.com/Kylie-Scott/e/B009CJ8188